jos

W9-CFW-967

---

*LADY PHILIPPA
WAS DRAWN TO
TROUBLE LIKE A BEE
TO HONEY. AND NO ONE
IN THE VILLAGE COULD
BE EXPECTED TO KNOW
THAT HER ARRIVAL
WAS THE
CATALYST THAT
WOULD UPSET THE ENTIRE
COUNTRYSIDE—AND
BRING A SHOCKING
MOMENT OF HORROR
TO THEM ALL.*

Fawcett Crest Books
by Maggie MacKeever:

LORD FAIRCHILD'S DAUGHTER

A BANBURY TALE

A NOTORIOUS LADY

A
NOTORIOUS
LADY

Maggie MacKeever

A FAWCETT CREST BOOK

Fawcett Books, Greenwich, Connecticut

A NOTORIOUS LADY

Published by Fawcett Crest Books, CBS Publications, CBS Consumer Publishing, a division of CBS, Inc.

Copyright © 1978 by Maggie MacKeever
ALL RIGHTS RESERVED

ISBN: 0-449-23491-6

Printed in the United States of America

10   9   8   7   6   5   4   3   2   1

A
NOTORIOUS
LADY

One

An elegant luggage-laden traveling carriage crawled along the Great North Road to Inverness. Pale green and heavily gilded, this whimsical equipage had often aroused amused comment in the crowded streets of London; and the less sophisticated Highlanders who were privileged to witness its passage blinked several times and stared again.

"The devil!" muttered the coach's owner and thrust her shining red-gold head through the carriage window. Lady Philippa Harte had scant interest in the reflections of legendarily dour Scotsmen; she was as little likely to wonder what the world thought of her decidedly eccentric trappings as she was to concern herself with the world's opinion of her even more outrageous conduct. "More speed, I beg you, Barnabas!"

Lady Philippa, known to her somewhat irreverent intimates as Pippin, was a striking creature with fair, flawless skin and slanting emerald eyes. Her mouth was too generous for beauty, her aristocratic nose was flawed by a small but undeniable bump half-way down its length, and there was a tiny but unmistakable gap between her dazzling front teeth; but these small imperfections were outweighed by high cheekbones, curling masses of reddish-gold hair, and those startling green eyes.

"Very good, my lady," replied the coachman, stiffly. This individual was almost as noteworthy as his mistress, and not just for his masterful handling of the reins. Barnabas Parrington, as many a serving-wench between London and Inverness could testify, was almost indecently handsome, with that sort of somber reckless looks that have, since time immemorial, played havoc with feminine hearts.

"Tiresome creature!" snapped Lady Philippa unappreciatively, and withdrew into the coach. "I do wish he'd come out of the sulks." She frowned at her companion. "Not that I can blame him! It is clearly midsummer moon with Barnabas, and you treat him abominably."

The coach's other occupant grinned. She was a pert young miss of eighteen years, sandy-haired and hazel-eyed. She was clad in the height of fashion, in a Jubilee cloak of violet velvet trimmed in swansdown, and atop her saucy curls perched a charming cottage hat. Beside her on the wide seat was a large wicker basket. "Lud!" said she. "Barney's a slow-top. But he's a top-sawyer with four-in-hand, I'll give him that. What puzzles me is why he's so close-mouthed about himself." The girl's eyes widened pleasurably. "Lady Philippa, mayhap he's been in quod!"

A more sensitive woman might have shrieked at so unservile an attitude and so improper a suggestion; Lady Philippa merely laughed. If it was highly improper to converse with one's servants in the same unreserved manner that one might adopt with a social peer, this was not the least of Lady Philippa's flights from propriety. "Mind your tongue!" she advised. "Barnabas's past is none of our concern, whether he's been in prison or no." Her expression turned severe. "Understand this, Nabby: I will not have Barnabas plagued. He is the best of my retainers, and I do not know how I would go on without him."

Nabby suffered this stern set-down with no discernible lessening of spirit. "Aye," she agreed. "I'm being cheekish. Barney's a good lad, for all he's wild to a fault." She surveyed her mistress and grinned. "But I won't be talking of that to you! Most improper it would be."

"Good God!" said Lady Philippa, but with more amusement than horror. "Do you mean to tell me that the rogue has offered *you* a slip on the shoulder?"

"No," retorted Nabby, with the outraged air of one who would have indignantly refused an improper proposal but who would have enjoyed the experience immensely. "Not me or anybody else, as far as I know." Nabby had a positive genius for ferreting out information of this sort. " 'Twas something else altogether I was referring to."

"What, you wretched creature?" It was, of course, not at all the thing for a lady to engage in a discussion, with her abigail, of her coachman's *amours,* but Lady Philippa had once been described by a sporting gentleman of her acquaintance as a filly with a queer kick in her gallop, and by another disgruntled suitor, whose hunting pursuits were conducted in a different field, as possessing the tongue of a vituperative puritan and the soul of a *fille de joie.*

Nabby's eyes twinkled mischievously. "Lady Philippa! You yourself told me we shouldn't pester poor Barney."

"The devil fly away with you, Abigail Wiggins!" retorted Lady Philippa, without malice. Nabby grinned.

Despite her apparent lack of proper respect for the lady who paid her extremely generous wage, Nabby was utterly devoted to her mistress. A discerning miss of no little wit, Nabby knew that she held her current exalted position, no small accomplishment for one of her tender years, entirely to the happy chance that Lady Philippa was fond of her. The relationship was a long-standing one, dating back to the day when Lady Philippa's mother, a philanthropic and absent-minded widow, now deceased, had introduced Nabby into her somewhat irregular household, and the young Philippa had promptly enlisted the newcomer as her personal maid. It was an act that neither of them had ever found cause to regret; and as Nabby gave thanks daily for the whim that had prompted the humanistic Lady Harte to rescue her from a dank horror-filled prison, where she had been sentenced to expiate her offence of shoplifting, so did she also offer thanksgiving to the Deity for the greater boon of granting her a mistress so unaware of her own consequence as Lady Philippa. Nabby would cheerfully have allowed herself to be boiled in oil for her mistress's sake. Fortunately, Lady Philippa had thus far demanded no such sacrifice.

Pippin, who would have been rendered acutely uncomfortable by knowledge of the exact extent of her maid's devotion, grimaced ferociously at an exquisitely hand-drawn map. It was a measure of Nabby's devotion that she had accompanied Lady Philippa on this long and arduous jaunt. They had traveled in easy stages, and the coach was unusually well-sprung, but much as Nabby might enjoy racketing around the countryside, the trek between London and the Scottish Highlands was a bit extreme. Nor was Nabby enamored of the countryside. It was wild and haunted, and the light was such as Nabby had never before seen. Constantly changing combinations of sun, cloud, and mist endowed the mountains and lochs, the glens and tarns, with an unholy eeriness. Nabby

9

would have much preferred to remain in London, skillfully preparing her mistress for appearances in Hyde Park, at Almack's, or Carlton House; but it was the time of year when the *haut ton* retired from town to country seats or watering places. Because Lady Philippa was a connoisseur of such unearthly scenes as the Highlands offered in abundance, Nabby voiced only minimal complaint. And it was best that she keep both her wayward mistress and the devastating Barnabas under her sharp eye.

A sleepy yowl issued from the wicker basket, and Nabby opened the lid to release a large and malevolent-looking brindled cat. The monstrous creature stretched and yawned, then rose on strong back legs to peer out the carriage window. Finding the passing countryside of negligible interest, he leaped to the opposite seat and deposited himself on his mistress's lap, to the detriment of the map. "Not much longer, Udolpho," murmured Lady Philippa, rescuing the chart. "If Amanda's directions are correct." Not likely, thought Nabby skeptically. Lady Amanda Viccars, her employer's dearest friend, was a frivolous flibbertigibbet whose keen eye for a comely gentleman was equaled only by her fine disregard for such unessential details as village names and inconsequential roads. It was a matter of some puzzlement to Nabby why Lady Amanda had sent them haring off to the Highlands, but she had to admit the journey was well timed. A nasty scandal was brewing in London, and Lady Philippa was best away.

Nabby regarded her mistress with a doting eye, and her mistress's cat with a trifle less opprobrium. Udolpho—being the possessor of a vast amount of mottled black and orange fur, a nose that was half black and half orange, paws and a tail tip of solid black, deep orange eyes, and a fiendish temperament—was a source of local wonder greater even than Lady Philippa's unusual coach. His fond owner had this day made an unusual concession to fashion and wore a charming dress and pelisse of a shade of green that matched her magnificent eyes. The elegant bonnet that completed the ensemble, however, had been tossed carelessly on the floor, and Lady Philippa's curls were in riotous disarray.

Nabby's lips tightened as she thought once more of their hasty departure from town. Even she lacked sufficient temerity to mention to her mistress the marquis, though she dearly longed to ask if Lady Philippa regretted the abrupt termination of that particular flirtation and her impending involve-

10

ment in an extremely unsavory divorce. Nabby surveyed her neatly gloved hands. It was her fondest wish to see her employer happily wed, but Lady Philippa proved decidedly unmanageable on that score. Countless were the opportunities that she had turned down, among them one of the wealthiest men in England, and now, at five-and-twenty, despite the countless flirtations for which she was notorious, she could well be considered at her last prayers. Even though Nabby had recently bloodied a kitchen maid's nose for referring to the mistress as an ape-leader, the little abigail privately considered it the melancholy truth. It would be miraculous indeed if Lady Philippa contracted a marriage at so advanced an age and with a reputation that was frankly scandalous. But perhaps here in the wilds of Scotland there would be a gentleman for whom Lady Philippa might develop a partiality, one who might never have heard of her various escapades. Despite the vast array of potential suitors that the headstrong lady had thus far surveyed enthusiastically, and the disaster that invariably followed in the lady's wake, Nabby had whispered a quiet little prayer into the wishing well at Culloden Moor, and tied a piece of her petticoat to a nearby tree, all the time knowing she had as little hope of seeing her mistress peacefully settled in matrimony as Bonnie Prince Charlie once had of restoring his father to the English throne. Even Nabby could not deny that Lady Philippa appeared totally heartless where the gentlemen were concerned.

In this she was mistaken: Lady Philippa indeed possessed a heart, for all she kept it securely locked away. Nor was she unaware of her maid's aspirations in her behalf though, as she scowled thoughtfully at the finely drawn map, thoughts of her own romances were the farthest thing from her mind. Lady Philippa had once, in a moment of spleen, taken up her pen and with it ripped the *ton* to shreds; and so successful was that initial effort that she had recently delivered to her discreet publisher her sixth novel. Lady Philippa scribbled romantic effusions, strongly interlaced with the supernatural, that alternately titillated and terrified her reading audience, the polite world into which she had been born. Of all her secrets, this was the best kept. It was not to be expected that the Upper Ten Thousand would equate the popular, if extremely retiring, novelist, Mrs. Watson-Wentworth, with the unconventional Lady Philippa Harte—nor did they. Unhampered, Pippin cheerfully continued to blacken the characters

11

of her peers; enchanted, they continued to clamor for further punishment.

But Lady Philippa was not totally without feeling for her fellowman, and she noticed that her abigail had not only fallen silent but looked remarkably serious. "You are unusually quiet," she said, abandoning the map. "What has cast you into gloom?" On her lap, Udolpho rumbled and vibrated like a minor earthquake.

"Not a thing in the world." Still lost in wild speculation concerning the marquis, Nabby restored Lady Philippa's neglected bonnet to a semblance of its original splendor. "It's tired I am of traveling, and I'll be glad to see it end."

"Soon," lady Philippa promised rashly and turned to gaze through the window upon purple-blue heather moors. Udolpho leaped to her shoulder and settled there, his tail draped around her neck like a magnificent boa, albeit of startling hue. The solitude of this beautiful countryside suited Pippin, particularly after that all-too-public encounter with the irate marchioness, whose voice was quite as stentorian and forceful as a cannon's boom. Here, however, one heard only the burn that gurgled down the hillside, and the far-off bleating of sheep. "Marvelous," she said aloud.

Nabby, observing the fervent gleam in her mistress's eye, remained prudently silent. Lady Philippa was a zealous sightseer, and Nabby already had a bellyful of historic sites. Lady Philippa turned away from the window and gazed upon her abigail's woebegone expression with amusement, while Udolpho teetered wildly but maintained his balance via the extension of all his claws. Lady Philippa winced, and he purred.

"Tell me again of this place we're going," Nabby said quickly, for her capricious mistress was quite capable of ordering an impromptu party on the spot, with the sorely tried Barnabas sent to harvest suitable provisions from an astonished, and not particularly hospitable, countryside. "It sounds a gruesome spot."

"Strachan is one of Scotland's less hallowed monuments." Lady Philippa removed Udolpho from his perch, stretched, then settled herself more comfortably upon the seat, an act which revealed a shapely ankle and an immodest amount of equally shapely bosom. "A tiny village, it remains much as it was during the infamous witch trials that caused its ill fame over two hundred years ago. How Amanda learned of it, I do not know, but she waxed enthusiastic over the coaching-inn and took steps to assure our welcome there."

"Witches," repeated Nabby, and twitched her cloak disdainfully. "Flapdoodle!"

"Legend claims for the village a witch's curse. Complete nonsense, of course, but interesting." Despite the grisly horrors, including headless corpses and clanking chains and haunted crypts, with which she spiced her macabre tales, Lady Philippa was of a sensible turn of mind, a fact which she secretly mourned. "But you will agree Strachan sounds an ideal place for ruralizing. We shall have peace and quiet and plenty."

"Not if I know you, Lady Philippa!" No enthusiast of bucolic settings, Nabby tweaked the brim of her mistress's bonnet rather viciously. "You'll be off on one of your queer starts in no time."

"Of all the unjust things to say!" Impervious both to pertness and censure, Lady Philippa stroked the cat on the seat beside her, and he sank his teeth into her glove. "You make me sound the greenest girl, with no notion of how to go on."

"I'll make you a wager," Nabby retorted, in a brilliant last-ditch attempt to dissuade her mistress from further ruinous shenanigans. "We shan't be there a sennight before you've fallen into a scrape."

"You may make yourself easy on that score." The fact that Lady Philippa spoke with resolution did not set Nabby's qualms to rest. "I mean to be very, very good. And if your prunish countenance suggests that you doubt I know how to go about it, I warn you I shall consider it the grossest impertinence!"

Doubtfully, Nabby met her employer's laughing gaze, and Lady Philippa's green eyes turned quickly away. "Strachan," she said, with an odd satisfaction, and Nabby dutifully peered through the window. White-washed cottages were interspersed with the thatched stone buildings that lined the narrow streets; among them was a venerable church, and above the village towered an ancient castle whose worn grandeur made all else shrink into insignificance. "How peaceful," sighed Lady Philippa, with a genteel weariness that didn't deceive her abigail for an instant. "We shall all have a delightful rest."

Deftly avoiding sharp and extended claws, Nabby lifted the protesting Udolpho from the seat and deposited him in the wicker basket. "Did I not tell you," inquired Lady Philippa of her suddenly pensive maidservant, "that we would arrive soon?"

13

But Pippin was no favorite of Fate. She had barely placed the mistreated bonnet upon her unruly curls when the coach gave a mighty lurch, several bone-jarring jolts, and came at last to rest in a shallow ditch.

Two

Racing down the road as if fleeing the hounds of hell, Janet Kirk was witness to the accident. Ah, but small Sandy was as quick as lightening! One moment he had been beside her in the church, as cherubic-looking a lad as one might hope to view; the next he had slipped from his seat and through the open door. Andrew Macgregor would not be pleased! But all thought of the minister's disapproval fled Janet's mind as Sandy, intent on the capture of some small creature, darted in front of the oncoming coach.

It was the carriage that suffered the most, and perhaps its occupants; small Sandy stood untouched in the middle of the road and shrieked like a fledgling banshee. Assured of her charge's continued good health, Janet stopped to gape at the outlandish vehicle. Even sideways in a ditch, the gold and green coach lost none of its bizarre splendor. It might have come straight out of a heathen fairy tale, as might the splendidly attired coachman, handsome as Lucifer.

And then a woman appeared in the carriage's gaping door, and the coachman rushed to assist her to the ground. Janet disliked Lady Philippa on sight, instantly recognizing that tall and striking creature as the embodiment of Andrew Macgregor's strictures against vanity and pride. True, the woman, obviously of the Quality, appeared to be careless of her appearance, for her dashing bonnet was askew and her skirt terribly wrinkled; but Janet was feminine enough to know that no woman who possessed those magnificent eyes could be free of the sin of vanity. Even small Sandy paused to stare, then erupted into renewed wails of rage.

As yet unaware of her audience, Lady Philippa gave voice to several very satisfying oaths, then turned her attention to the pink-cheeked urchin whose lusty bellows promised to rouse the entire village. Barnabas's white-faced explanations were unnecessary: Lady Philippa saw at a single glance that this was precisely the sort of lad who caused entire buildings to topple and dams to overflow. "Quiet!" she said sternly. Young Sandy was so astonished that his strong jaw fell open, and he unwittingly obeyed.

Janet Kirk suffered a similar reaction, but retained sufficient presence of mind to snap shut her mouth. She might have moved forward then, for she was jealous of her authority; but the fairy coach spewed forth additional passengers. One was a young lady dressed to the teeth and looking, to Janet's critical eye, remarkably like a tart; the other was a huge and malevolent brindled cat.

"Gawd!" said Nabby, with commendable restraint.

"It's not as bad as it looks." Barnabas frowned at the carriage. "The horses suffered little harm." Nabby appeared skeptical and moved prudently away from the nearest wild-eyed beast.

Young Sandy, not pleased to have the green-eyed lady's attention stray from him, inhaled deeply in preparation for an outburst of temper that would knock the birds senseless from the trees. "No," said Lady Philippa firmly and knelt in the dust to regard their small Nemesis. Enchanted, he returned her interested regard. "An imp of Satan!" observed Lady Philippa and pinched his dimpled cheek. "But you must not run in front of my horses again. It frightens them, you see." But Sandy had no interest in beasts of the field. One small and extremely dirty fist immediately clutched a red-gold curl and tugged. "Brat!" remarked Lady Philippa. She rose and guiltily brushed at her now dusty attire. The effort was not remarkably successful.

Janet regained the use of her wits and marched forward. "I'll thank you to unhand the lad!" she announced grimly. It was a somewhat unfair remark: young Sandy, upon observing his strict preceptress's determined approach, had taken refuge behind Lady Philippa's dust-splotched skirts.

"My dear," protested Lady Philippa, with the enchanting smile that had disarmed even disapproving dowagers, "you are welcome to him! Did you think I meant to make off with the little wretch?" She glanced down at the curly head that

16

burrowed into her arm. "It seems to be the other way around."

Perversely, this unwarranted cordiality only increased Janet's animosity. She grasped Sandy's arm in a gesture that was simultaneously protective, hostile, and painful. Squalling, Sandy tightened his grasp on Lady Philippa's waist.

"There's no need to be hard on the child," said Lady Philippa and gently loosened his fingers. Added to the dirt on her traveling-costume were grubby fingerprints. "Boys will be boys."

"Even when they creep out of church and cause dreadful accidents?" This strange woman's tolerance was incomprehensible to Janet, who had never once in her life savored the delight of rebellion. "His father will tan his hide for this, and it's no more than he deserves!"

"Nonsense!" retorted Lady Philippa, while the coachman and the younger woman exchanged a resigned glance. But Janet did not mean to stay and argue with this brazen stranger, whom she by now considered to be at the very least a painted Jezebel. She grasped her charge firmly by his ear.

Small Sandy might have allowed himself to be docilely led away, had not Udolpho, sensing hostility, then leaped from Nabby's arms. The Hallowe'en-colored cat stalked majestically across the road, and Lady Philippa bent to lift him in her arms. The cat perched upon her shoulders, knocking the doomed bonnet further awry, and gazed upon the intruders with disdainful contempt.

"Kitty," observed Sandy wisely and reached for the twitching tail. Janet gasped and dragged him back; and Lady Philippa winced as Udolpho secured his perch with needle claws.

Barnabas cleared his throat. "The carriage is beyond my repair, Lady Philippa," he said, and turned his dark eyes on Janet Kirk. "Perhaps this young lady might tell us where we can secure assistance."

Janet felt the force of that gaze like a suffocating weight and wrenched away from it. "There's a wheelwright in the village," she muttered, eyes fixed firmly on the ground. "You can't miss him." Vindictively, she failed to add that the wheelwright himself was in church, along with the rest of the villagers. Due to the length of Andrew Macgregor's sermons, there he was like to stay.

For all that she led him a merry chase, Nabby did not care to see Barnabas's hypnotic gaze fixed on any damsel but her-

17

self. "Perhaps you can also tell us," she said with fine condescension, "where we can find The Hanging Man?"

This simple request brought Janet's gaze upward again, and it was horrified. Taking advantage of his custodian's distraction, Sandy slithered eellike from her grasp and circled Udolpho warily. The cat regarded the approaching menace with one bright orange eye.

"The Hanging Man," repeated Nabby, and wondered if this odd girl was aghast at the request or at being addressed by a creature whom she obviously considered to be of ill repute. "The coaching-inn. This is Strachan, is it not?"

Janet nodded, but moved back a pace. Lady Philippa frowned. "Have we been misled?" she inquired. "Is there no inn here?"

"Aye, it's here right enough," Janet spat, "and would to heaven it were not!" She turned and pointed to a distant side street. " 'Tis there, but you'd be best advised to have your carriage fixed and go back the way you came."

Lady Philippa's brows rose. "Oh?" She was not accustomed to such blunt and belligerent advice.

"It's an evil place. Go back to where you came from. The inn's not fit for the likes of you."

"Surely you jest!" Lady Philippa protested. Janet's face darkened most alarmingly.

"Joking, am I?" she demanded. "You'll see, my lady, you'll see." Unnoticed, Sandy slid within inches of Udolpho's luxurious tail. "The powers of darkness are among us, and the time of judgment is at hand."

"That," announced Nabby wrathfully, "is the most ridiculous thing I've ever heard." Protective of her mistress's position, Nabby was quick to resent a slight.

Janet Kirk drew herself up for battle. "Leave Strachan!" she cried. "Else you come to rue this day. We don't welcome your kind here."

"That," murmured the irrepressible maidservant, "is obvious." Small Sandy's small fist reached out, and Udolpho yowled.

"Stop!" said Lady Philippa, and Sandy froze. "I do not mean to remonstrate with you again, young man. Henceforth you will behave."

To Janet's stark amazement, Sandy obeyed. Downcast, he shuffled back to her side. "I rather fear," remarked Lady Philippa, "that you don't know exactly how to deal with children of this age. One must be kind, but always firm." She

18

lifted the cat from her shoulders, and Nabby hastened to provide the wicker basket. "Now, perhaps you will be kind enough to conduct us to the inn."

"Never!" cried Janet, pale with dismay. She grasped Sandy so roughly that he wailed, bent two fingers in a stabbing gesture, and set off rapidly down the road, casting furtive glances over her shoulder as if she feared pursuit. "Cor!" breathed Nabby. "She made the sign against the evil eye!"

"I wonder," murmured Lady Philippa, "what prompted her to do so." There was a sparkle in her eye. "Perhaps she saw in me a figure of malevolence." In the wicker basket, Udolpho purred.

"Encroaching little slyboots!" snapped Nabby, forgetting that her exalted position as lady's maid didn't entitle her to such freedom of speech. Lady Philippa, with difficulty, dissuaded her loyal retainer from following their unamiable Samaritan for the purpose of engaging in physical combat. Nabby subsided into wrathful mumbling.

Barnabas, who had little time for feminine foibles, a trait that did not advance his suit with the volatile Nabby, once more carefully inspected Lady Philippa's rig. "I cannot fix it myself, my lady," he repeated.

"Tsk!" said Nabby provocatively. "A task that is beyond even our Barney's resourcefulness." He turned on her with a look that was positively satanic but Nabby only sniffed, uncowed.

Lady Philippa was inured to the constant squabbles between these two servitors. "The inn cannot be far," she said and hefted Udolpho's basket. "We will send back help." In disapproving silence, Nabby wrestled the basket from her determined mistress. Slowly they moved down the deserted street, accompanied by Udolpho's indignant and very vocal protests.

"The evil eye," mused Lady Philippa, not with as much real interest as a desire to persuade Nabby from her sullen mood. "I believe we are in a place where superstition has firm hold. I have heard such things of this country. Glamis Castle stands in a valley because the fairies would not allow it to be built on the heights above." She glanced sideways at Nabby. "You know of Glamis Castle: it's where Macbeth murdered King Duncan."

Nabby was in little mood for such tales, ordinarily the breath of life to her, partially because she was burdened with

19

an extremely heavy and restless cat. "Myself," she snapped, "I'd rather go to Gretna Green!"

It was, perhaps, as well for the continued harmony between maid and mistress that at that moment they approached Strachan's only church, for Lady Philippa was on the verge of making an unforgivable comment regarding the incomparable Barnabas. She motioned Nabby to silence, then stepped into the church's dim interior.

An old man stood behind the pitch-pine pulpit, his back to the narrow windows that adorned the small church's western facade. Box pews flanked the podium; benches were placed on both sides of the central aisle. The building's interior was devoid of ornamentation.

Andrew Macgregor practiced the religion of his forefathers, the fundamental Calvinism that had come late to Scotland and included such pessimistic doctrines as predestination, original sin, and infant damnation. His task was not an easy one. The Highlanders were too fond of referring to the Archenemy as Auld Hornie, or Clootie, with the diminutive that denoted affection; too prone to slide back into the old heathen ways. He paused for breath, so entranced by his own words, and so nearsighted, that he failed to note the stranger's entrance.

"Even if the witch has entered into her unholy alliance with the intention of doing good," he said, fixing Agnes Campbell with a speculative eye, "still shall she be damned. Even though she uses her charms and potions to cure instead of kill, her immortal soul shall suffer eternal torment. For she has bound herself to the service of the enemies of God, and God's just punishment is death. A witch shall not be allowed to live!"

Aggy was a creature of habit. She had attended church regularly all her life, but she allowed herself an old woman's luxury, that of wandering thought. Her gaze was fixed on Andrew Macgregor, her expression was rapt, and her thoughts were briskly centered on her duties at the newly reopened inn. Agnes Campbell would have been startled to learn that her knowledge of simple cures had aroused the minister's suspicions.

Andrew Macgregor leaned forward. "There are those among us," he hissed, "who have forsaken the paths of righteousness to ally themselves with evil and traffic with hell. They adore devils and do sacrifice to them; they have given themselves to the most shameful of servitudes to gain the basest of ends."

"Lud!" breathed Nabby, who had deposited her burden on the church steps and crept to Lady Philippa's side.

The minister mopped his brow. "Think!" he admonished his congregation. "Cast your minds back over these past weeks and search out signs of Satan's influence. Can you recall unnatural events or strange behavior? Have you seen indications of depravity?"

This was too much: Nabby snorted and her mistress—whose fertile mind was grappling enthusiastically with such terms as pilliwinks and turkas, Spanish boots and caspie claws—shoved her quickly outside. Behind them was a sudden silence, then a startled murmur. Lady Philippa grasped her maid with one hand and the wicker basket with the other and hauled them both firmly away.

Three

―――――――――――――――――――――――――

Not all the inhabitants of Strachan were drawn to Andrew Macgregor's brimstone services, and most notable among the exceptions were the nobility. While the villagers—among them Janet Kirk, alternately flushed and ashen from old Macgregor's evangelical fervor; Paddy Maclean, so overwhelmed by these serious matters that he only occasionally remembered to pinch his small brother Sandy into polite passivity; little wide-eyed and anxious Katy, barmaid at the inn—trembled for the well-being of their immortal souls, the laird played whist in his castle and engaged in a desultory discussion of the latest *on dits* with the inn's new owner, who had never yet set foot within the church and had been heard to remark that he'd doubtless be struck down by lightning if he dared with his presence profane such sacred premises. The statement was remembered and resented— Severin St. George, fifth Earl of Afton, was that sort of gentleman. Meanwhile, the most widely accepted of the strangers in the village and the village's most rebellious daughter were engaged in the enjoyment of a simple stroll.

Andrew Macgregor's rolling tones flowed down the street to meet them, and the girl drew closer to the man. "I despise this abominable place!" Geilleis Graham shoved her hands deep within the side sleeves of her pelisse, while her companion studied her from beneath bushy brows.

"Then why stay, acushla?" he inquired. "Shall I throw you across my saddle and carry you away?" The proposal did not amuse her; she simply glared at him. "My poor beast is lame, but surely some kind person wouldn't begrudge me the borrowing of a steed for such a romantic purpose."

"Stop your blathering, do," Gilly retorted. "Can't you ever be serious? My God, Lucius, can't you feel it? The horrid brooding atmosphere of this accursed place?" But how could she expect him to grasp instinctively what she could not explain? Andrew Macgregor had spent his life in the shadow of his ancestor William, even now revered by the villagers for his part in the brutal witch trials of two hundred years ago. Then the clergy had acted as inquisitors; now Andrew Macgregor would be pleased to act the same. The old man's belief in the justice of his God was stern and inflexible; and his thwarted ambition was both blighting and dangerous.

Lucius Cunningham chewed contemplatively on the stem of his battered pipe. He was a great bear of a man, with a wild mane of tawny hair and a beard to match. Blue eyes peered beguilingly out of his weathered face. "I don't know where you get your fantastic notions. All I feel is dejected," he mourned. "My lassie has a cruel, cold heart."

Gilly sighed, flattered by this nonsense all the same. "You know full well that I cannot leave Strachan," she said. "My mother is ill. She has lived her whole life here and anticipates that old Macgregor will personally attend to her salvation."

"A fine way to speak of the local gateway to heavenly bliss," Lucius interrupted. "Myself, I believe he suffers from the effects of a classical education."

Gilly grimaced. A frown lay heavily on her fair features. Had she been free of practical responsibility, Gilly would have been strongly tempted to forget her ladylike upbringing, flee with Lucius to Edinburgh, and the devil take the consequences; but this wasn't the matter that caused her such concern. "It's changed so much. I don't recall all this hostility."

"Children don't, you know. And you left to live with your sister before the advent of the heathenish Sassenachs."

Gilly's laugh was without humor. "You begin to sound like old Macgregor," she retorted. "Next you'll be telling me to beware lest I succumb to temptation."

"No," said Lucius, with a ferocious grin. "I wouldn't be saying that. Don't I pray daily for that very thing?"

But Gilly was of a somber frame of mind. "Have you never thought about it?" she asked, with a small shudder. "About how terrible it must have been? All those poor people murdered because Ailcie Ferguson was no better than she should have been?"

He'd been given little opportunity, mused Lucius, to think of little else. Ailcie Ferguson had brought upon Strachan its troubles, and upon William Macgregor his questionable fame. Witch or harlot? he wondered, and inclined to the latter, though it hardly mattered now. In this Lucius erred, but he could not be expected to know of Lady Philippa, or that her arrival would be the catalyst that upset Strachan's precarious peace. "They didn't call it murder then," he replied.

"And what would *you* call it?" His love, reflected Lucius, could be quite as ferocious as a gaming-cock.

"Usually," he retorted placidly, "they strangled them first." What a topic of conversation for a peaceful Sunday morn!

"Not Ailcie." Gilly was obstinate. "She was burned alive."

"Because she wouldn't confess." Lucius was too prudent to admit his admiration for Gilly's distant ancestress. "Strachan wasn't the only place where supposed witches were slaughtered out of hand, lass. It happened in England, in Germany."

"And in Aberdeen and North Berwick and Pittenween," Gilly agreed. "But it didn't happen anywhere like it happened here."

Lucius carefully avoided the stone that marked the spot where one unfortunate heretic had been rolled down from the hill above, in a barrel studded with sharp nails, and burned. He wasn't inclined to argue the point.

Their wandering brought them to a freshly painted building of vast and indeterminable age. Black beams framed the white-washed walls of the large and rambling structure, investing it with a vaguely Tudor air; overhanging gables added a hint of raffishness. At the front of the building was a remarkable window diagonally paned with green, mauve, and opaque glass. On the cliff above, the castle towered, a grim sentinel. Gilly scowled. "The man must be mad," she said. "This horrible place should have been torn down long ago."

Lucius removed his pipe. "Why?" he inquired. "It's a good sound building, a veritable antiquity, and a prosperous enterprise."

"Where they kept the accused witches awaiting trial."

"Long, long ago."

"You can still feel it." The inn's unhallowed portals were always open to its enigmatic owner's friends, among whom was Lucius. Gilly allowed herself to be led inside. Ancient timber framing curved to the roof, causing visitors to compare the dark beams with cathedral arches, a highly unmerited simile. "Andrew Macgregor would have us not go next or nigh it, and refers to Afton as Satan's spawn. I tell you, there'll be the devil to pay!" she added.

"Don't be forgetting the ghost," Lucius advised, clamping his teeth around the pipestem. It was a rare occasion when he had Gilly to himself, and it was not encouraging to discover that her thoughts were centered not on romance but on ancient atrocities.

"I'm not." Gilly looked around at the taproom thoughtfully. Dominating it was a huge fireplace that Lord Afton had discovered and resurrected from the plaster that had hidden it for centuries. The walls were lavishly adorned with articles of warfare among other things. In one corner stood a magnificent and priceless harp. "I wonder who he is."

"Who? Our local ghostie, or mine host?" Lucius was rapidly sinking into ill humor.

"I grew up on tales of the hanging man," Gilly retorted, with some acerbity. "It's Lord Afton I'm wondering about. That's a very strange man, even if you vouch for his authenticity. He has the manners of a marquis and the morals of a Methodist, as my mother would say. Why is a nobleman demeaning himself by engaging in trade?"

Lucius laughed and led her to a small table. "He inherited the place, nothing more sinister than that. And you will not persuade me that you dislike our raffish earl! I've seen you succumb to missish blushes when he smiles at you."

"Nonsense!" retorted Gilly, indignant. "I'm not so goosish as to be overset by the empty blandishments of a London gentleman. Be he never so comely, there's wild blood in Severin St. George." She lapsed into somewhat sulky silence as Lucius left her to procure for them both a glass of frothy ale. He presented Gilly's with a foolish grin and an airy flourish that slopped suds onto the tabletop.

"You should have remained in Edinburgh," she said abruptly, well aware that her conduct was hardly conducive to impassioned declarations from a devoted swain, and mopped up the mess with her handkerchief. "Strachan is far from what you have been used to."

"Whither you go, my lass, I follow," retorted Lucius, with an absurd grimace. Gilly met that comment with the silence it deserved, and he sighed mournfully. The girl turned her brooding attention to the pleasantly furnished room.

"Lord Afton is a puzzle," she repeated. "I cannot but consider that he is playing a deep game."

"What's this?" Lucius inquired, hastily removing his elbows from the still damp tabletop.

"Why is he here?" Gilly demanded irritably. "Is he reduced to such straits that he must ruralize in this godforsaken place?"

Lucius ruminated as he sipped his ale. "Afton has come to inspect his inheritance, it appears. And I wouldn't call Strachan godforsaken. It suffers from an excess of godliness, morelike."

"But why do so himself?" Gilly persisted. "He must have agents to handle his affairs. Yet here he is, for all the world as if he means to set up as an innkeeper. I cannot like it, Lucius; it argues an insensibility, or worse."

"That's a damned silly notion." Lucius was nearing the end of his patience. "A man's reasons are his own. He's entitled to his privacy, and to his secrets, if it comes to that."

"Not necessarily." Gilly was as sober as a magistrate. "Not if those secrets cause other people harm."

Lucius stared at her. "The devil! What nefarious things are you accusing Severin of? Murdering pure young girls in their beds?"

"I cannot think that Lord Afton would so exert himself for the sake of a pure young lass," Gilly retorted. "I don't really suspect the man of anything, save supreme deviousness of mind. But the villagers have always been leery of incomers, and you know things have come to a pretty pass since the earl appeared. God only knows what they think of him."

"Probably that he has windmills in his head, as you seem to do." Lucius refrained from adding that, in his opinion, his beloved was the one with an overheated mind. "But you do him a disservice, Gilly girl. The inn is a thriving business, and he does well to consider carefully its disposition. Few travelers will be put off by tales of local ghosts, not when this is the only decent accommodation for many miles around."

"I cannot like it," Gilly repeated stubbornly and with fine inconsistency. "A gentleman should not engage in trade."

"I had thought you possessed of a good understanding." Lucius wiped foam from his luxurious beard. "Are you determined to prove me wrong? The earl is merely a man of impulse, with a sufficient fortune to indulge his whims, yet you persist in crediting him with sinister motives. Dash it, Gillian, Afton is no scoundrel!"

"So this is a perfect gentleman, and I'm indulging in women's fantasies? Your attitude is not precisely loverlike."

"Don't fly into a pelter." Lucius took her hand. "I'm saying he has his own reasons, whatever they may be. Why are you so damnably out of humor? Afton will sell the place for a handsome fee, and we'll see no more of him."

"Providing he keeps his head on his shoulders long enough," Gilly retorted waspishly but did not withdraw from his grasp.

"First you accuse the man of harboring murderous intentions, then you say his head will be severed from his neck. Which is to be? You can't have it both ways."

"I wish I knew." Gilly's expression was morose. "I can't seem to decide whether he's villain or hero and cannot truthfully acquit myself of vulgar curiosity." She awarded her companion a glance from pure gray eyes. "Lucius, you don't see these things. You're either busy painting or playing the fool for me. But I know these villagers, and I tell you they're working themselves into a very nasty mood."

Lucius didn't care to hear his determined courtship referred to in such frivolous terms. "Elaborate," he said. "I am agog with curiosity."

"It was bad enough when Duncan Galbraith married an Englishwoman and brought her to the castle," Gilly explained. "The villagers were not pleased that their laird had wed a Sassenach, for all her fortune. Nor has it proved felicitous that Duncan must exercise his seignioral right with the local lasses. I will not trust myself to express an opinion of his conduct."

"Are you telling me," Lucius demanded with great interest, "that the esteemed laird is a libertine? Fancy! I thought he was disliked because he lives in great state at the expense of his people." He shook his head. "You're right. I lack perspicacity."

Gilly laughed, thus transforming her rather plain features. Lucius restrained an impulse to run his hands through her clouds of fine hair. "Don't interrupt," she said severely, when her chuckles had subsided. "I am explaining."

Chastened, Lucius bowed his head.

"At that time," Gilly continued, "the villagers might have become reconciled to Lady Cassandra, had she showed a mellowing influence on their laird, but she soon proved to have no thought for any but herself. Then what must she do but be so imprudent as to import the remainder of her family? It had the effect of uniting the people against her."

"But why?" Lucius asked. "I'll grant you that they're a worthless lot, but there's no real harm in any of them."

Gilly shrugged. "It is their behavior that causes the villagers offense. No one really minded when Lady Cassandra tried to raise spirits—at least, no one but old Macgregor."

"Oh? Was she successful?"

"I wasn't there. Pay attention. Don't you want to know what's created all this enmity?"

"I'm all ears, acushla."

"As I said, old Macgregor was aghast at Lady Cassandra's heathenish ways. It does not pay to underestimate his influence here."

Lucius stared at her, open-mouthed; then rescued his pipe before it hit the floor. "You can't be serious!" he protested. "The old man's behind all this ill will?"

"Sounds ridiculous, doesn't it?" Gilly didn't appear amused. "The villagers take their sacred cows seriously, and they were black affronted. That was only the beginning. Lady Cassandra has been unearthing all manner of charms and spells. Not discreetly, I might add. She *will* chatter indiscriminately to everyone she meets, including shopkeepers."

"Saints preserve us!" Lucius thought of the laird's lady, a vague and faded individual with wispy hair. "Everyone knows Lady Cassandra's at least half mad."

"You don't understand the villagers," Gilly replied. "They blame the Sassenachs for the loss of the old ways, and besides, witchcraft is as real to them as ever it was. Now the earl has brought the others right into Strachan with his accursed inn, and they no longer hold themselves aloof. They think the villagers are superstitious idiots and laugh at them, while Katy's behind the bar listening. You can be sure old Macgregor is told every word that's said."

"What people say doesn't mean a thing, lassie, especially when they've a few drinks in them." Abstractedly, Lucius gazed upon her gloved hand as if he might read in it the outcome of his dreams.

"Tell that to old Macgregor," the practical Gilly snapped. "He has been preaching hellfire for weeks now and saying the unrighteous should be driven out from among us. Next he'll have the villagers marching on the castle with pitchforks in hand!"

Lucius lifted his searching gaze to her face. "Why so great an animosity toward the old man?"

"He makes my skin crawl."

"Gilly, you're building mountains out of anthills! Old Macgregor may be somewhat fanatic on the subject of poor Ailcie and her ilk, but he's harmless. In truth, he's a pleasant enough old gentleman."

Gilly glared and snatched her hand away. "Pleasant!" she cried. "He's as crazy as a loon. Have you seen those horrid relics of his?"

"Well, no," Lucius admitted with appropriate chagrin. "That's a pleasure I've denied myself." He looked at her wistfully. "Here we are, at last alone, and all you talk about are ghosts and witches and things of a similarly unlovely nature. A less persevering man would be cast into the depths of despair."

"I'm sorry." Gilly reached out to touch his cheek. "It worries me, Lucius."

Lucius leaned across the table and firmly grasped her shoulders. "Then pack your portmanteau and we'll be off to Edinburgh."

Gilly disengaged herself. "You're forgetting my mother," she said quietly. "She's ill. I can't leave her alone."

"We'll take the old harridan along!" Lucius exploded. As is the way with genial men, his wrath was as startling, and effective, as a sudden lightning-storm. "Hell and the devil confound it, you've been telling me all the morning how much you dislike this place!"

"No." Gilly hugged herself but stood firm against the gale. "It would be cruel of me to make her leave."

Lucius regarded her with incensed perplexity. "Despite this danger you're so sure is coming?"

"It's coming, right enough." Somberly, she contemplated life without him and wondered if it might be possible, for his own safety, to drive him away from her. "Lucius, why don't you go back to Edinburgh without me? You'll be much more comfortable there."

"What am *I* suspected of?" he demanded indignantly. "Consorting with demons? Dancing with the fairies in the moonlight?" Had Gilly but known it, his devotion to her was complete, despite his growing conviction that she was all about in her head.

"It's enough that you're consorting with me, or trying to." Gilly's expressive face was wry. "I'm high on Macgregor's

30

list, you know. And the person who consorts with a witch is as guilty as the witch herself."

"You?" Lucius roared with laughter. "Next you'll be telling me you have the sight!"

"Sometimes," retorted Gilly sourly, "I wish I did."

Four

Mist had fallen upon the village and the travelers proceeded cautiously. Nabby, flushed and disgruntled by both her squirming burden and her mistress's lamentable tendency to explore every interesting side street and lane, fervently wished herself back in London, where her customary perambulations included no greater exertion than walking out with the second footman or the linen draper's boy. To add to her discomfort, the villagers, released from Andrew Macgregor's stern admonitions and not yet inured to the presence of the Quality, regarded them with a furtive interest that was heightened by the indignant yowls that issued from Udolpho's basket. Lady Philippa appeared sublimely oblivious to the whispered comments that followed them, but Nabby's Irish temper boiled.

Lady Philippa, lost in convoluted macabre plots, nearly collided with a newly painted sign. She gasped and started, then, head tilted to one side, studied it judiciously. A man hung by a knotted rope from a gnarled tree limb. His palms were turned outward, Christlike; eyes and blackened tongue protruded horribly from his blue-tinged face; and he was clad in long-unfashionable attire. Beneath his head was a legend: The Hanging Man.

"Gawd!" breathed Nabby, and swallowed hard.

There was no doubt that they had reached their destination; even without the sign's enlightenment, the bustling inn-yard with its typical arch proclaimed this ancient structure to be a coaching-inn. Nabby promptly pushed open the massive, carved front door and found herself in a small entryway, where she gratefully put down her burden. Her gaze fell upon an ancient narrow-necked urn that bore a triple fierce and bearded face. Nabby wrinkled her nose. In time past, the jug had held an interesting assortment of items—human hair and urine, salt, fingernail cuttings, cloth hearts pierced with pins—and a faint, unpleasant odor lingered on.

Udolpho, released from bondage, hissed and stalked away. Nabby donned her guise as the perfect maid, a paragon of efficiency and sobriety, and prepared to bully any number of underlings into treating her mistress with all due respect. She anticipated that her task might prove unusually difficult, for Lady Philippa, as a result of her adventures, resembled nothing so much as one of the Fashionably Impure.

But Lady Philippa had, as usual, scant thought to spare for her disheveled state. The inn pleased her. She followed her instincts, which unerringly led her to the inn's housekeeper and the dining room.

Agnes Campbell, the inn's unofficial ruling light and Strachan's version of a wise woman, surveyed this newest guest with a keen and not unappreciative eye and gestured brusquely toward a table. "You look worn to the bone, m'lady," she said. "Rest yourself a moment and I'll fix you a wee bite, and then I'll tell the master that you're here."

"Thank you," murmured Lady Philippa and sank down onto a chair gratefully.

So this was the creature that had interrupted old Macgregor's sermon, and sent him to ranting of prideful harlots and the wages of sin. Little wonder! thought Aggie. Andrew Macgregor had little opinion of women, considering them flighty, imaginative creatures given to heathenish notions and unguarded tongues. Aggie noted Lady Philippa's riotous red-gold curls, the slanted green eyes and luscious mouth. As well it wasn't two hundred years ago! This one would have stood trial on the basis of her appearance alone.

"Cock-a-leekie, m'lady," Aggy said, and slapped a steaming bowl into the table. Lady Philippa—who had already become acquainted with haggis made of the heart, liver, and lungs of a sheep or calf combined with onions and suet and mixed with oatmeal, then traditionally boiled in the stomach of the contributing animal—eyed the food cautiously. She then lifted her unenthusiastic gaze to its provider. A thin, wiry, old lady, Aggy possessed an abundant crop of gray bird's-nest hair. Her vaguely cronelike appearance was exaggerated by the rusty black that she habitually wore out of respect for her husband, fifteen years dead. "You must not mind the master," Aggy added abruptly. "He says mair nor he means."

Too hungry to pursue this puzzling remark, Lady Philippa turned her attention once more to her food. Under Aggy's stern eye, she tasted the mixture and found it a pleasant soup, comprised of chicken, leeks, and pepper. Only briefly did Lady Philippa allow herself a wistful thought of London's tea gardens, where one might dine upon thinly sliced ham and a superb punch. She finished her meal and rose, murmuring appreciation for the refreshments. Aggy's voice stopped her at the door.

"I'm thinkin' it'll be an adventure havin' you here, m'lady," the old woman said, with a glance that was remarkably like a leer. "'Twould be a verra great pity if you couldna find it in yourself to bide a wee." With a deafening clatter, she piled dishes on a tray. "The master's in the taproom, and will be wishin' for a word."

Lady Philippa proceeded thence, inspired not by a wish to meet her host but by a raging thirst. She paused on the threshold. Ancient oaken beams crisscrossed the room; blackened ceiling rafters retained a faint curve as if they had once served some other purpose; the windows were comprised of small panes of bottle glass. The over-all atmosphere was one of comfortable, almost austere, masculinity.

Few people were in the room. Unnoticed, for Nabby was comporting herself with all the conscious arrogance of one who served a gentlewoman of great rank, Lady Philippa observed them. A pale, dark-haired girl and a rugged man who sat at one small table caught her interest only briefly. Her appraising gaze moved to the tall and swarthy gentleman, perhaps forty years of age, who was the recipient of Nabby's harangue. His dark hair was longer than was strictly fashionable, and framed his harsh features admirably. He received the maid's instructions with courtesy and a lazy smile, an attitude that did nothing to dispel his aura of rakish manners and polished vice. The legendary Severin St. George, Lady Philippa mused, resolutely ignoring her sudden shortness of breath; as haughty as any of the previous Earls of Afton, and at least as dissolute. Udolpho, having inspected the inn to his satisfaction, chose that moment to make his presence felt and deposited himself at his host's feet.

"Good God," said Lucius, awed. Lord Afton gravely regarded the dappled apparition that stared up at him, tail twitching, then raised his eyes to the doorway where Pippin stood. A becoming hint of color rose in her cheeks.

"Lady Philippa." The Earl moved toward her, and she noted idly the easy grace of his carriage. "I am honored that you have chosen to honor my establishment. All arrangements for your comfort have been made." Those lazy eyes moved over her in a way that made of his words a mockery. "I pray you will consider my abode, and myself, at your disposal. If you require any additional service, you have only to ask."

Lady Philippa was given no opportunity to reply in kind to this generous, if double-edged speech. A slender, fair-haired young man detached himself from the fireplace and made his way to her side. "Pippin!" he cried. "By all that's wonderful! I protest, it's been an age since last we met."

Famous! thought Nabby, scooping Udolpho up in her arms. With two such attractive men on the premises, Lady Philippa would not be bored. Pondering the rival merits of the charming viscount and the dangerous earl, Nabby slipped from the room.

Lady Philippa was unaccountably cheered by her unanticipated reunion with a long-time friend and allowed him to possess her hand. Viscount Rockingham was an engaging rascal, with an ever-ready smile and merry brown eyes. "What's this?" she asked. "Avery, have you sold out?"

"My father insisted I resign my commission," the Viscount replied. "He didn't consider it fitting that his heir get himself shot to pieces in some damned foreign country. But I found town life dashed flat, so granted Severin the pleasure of my company."

Lady Philippa did not care to pursue this topic of conversation, for the Viscount's rash enlistment had resulted from her firm, if regretful, refusal of his suit. "Afton," she said, turning to that gentleman. "This is an unlikely setting for you." Unlike Avery, whom one might meet anywhere, Lord Afton seldom appeared in Society. Pippin did not find him greatly altered by the years that had elapsed since their last meeting and wondered if this fact would lead her to mourn or rejoice. A fitting place to ruralize, the perfidious Amanda had said. Lady Philippa experienced a sudden urge to throttle her friend.

"I might say the same of you," the Earl replied. "You seem to have developed a remarkable penchant for traipsing about the countryside." The blue eyes studied her in a manner that made Lady Philippa uncomfortably aware of her travel dirt. "Your girl told me of the accident; I instructed her to apply to my groom for aid. You appear a trifle the worse for wear."

"Nonsense!" interjected the loyal Viscount. "Pippin's in high bloom."

"Palaverer!" said Lady Philippa and dragged the bonnet from her tousled head. "It was the most harrowing thing." She accepted a glass of brandy from the Viscount. "We were accosted by the oddest girl—I'll stake my reputation she thinks I am a demi-rep!—and she warned us away from your establishment." She awarded Lord Afton her most dazzling smile. "I see, Severin, that the village is already familiar with your ways!" Gilly, blatantly eavesdropping on this conversation, clutched Lucius's hand.

"How unspeakably odious!" protested the Viscount. "Not only have you been put to a great deal of inconvenience, you have been offered insult." The brown eyes took on a different kind of gleam. "My God, those who are responsible shall pay for this!"

"Pooh!" said Lady Philippa, uncomfortably aware of the Earl's mocking interest, and of the futility of delivering him a snub. "You refine too much upon it. I continue very well and have suffered no great harm. You will vastly oblige me by forgetting this farrago of nonsense."

"It will be as you say, of course." Avery had the air of one determined to pursue an interrupted courtship, but Nabby effectively, and unwittingly, forestalled him by making a reappearance. She had zealously inspected the spacious chamber allotted her mistress and, finding no oversight or cause for complaint, was determined to bear that exhausted lady away.

"I believe you had best postpone these blandishments, Avery." Lord Afton deftly helped himself to snuff. "Lady Philippa has sufficient knowledge of the world to understand that your wish is her command—or so I gather from the various rumors concerning her that have reached me over the years."

"*That*," snapped Pippin, before Avery could voice the imprudent remark that was even then hovering on his lips, "is a supreme case of the pot calling the kettle black!" She awarded Lord Afton a haughty green-eyed look that would have done credit to Udolpho in a rage. "Or have you, with advancing age, abandoned your pursuits in the petticoat line?" The Viscount laughed aloud, and she smiled at him.

37

"Forgive me, Avery, but I truly am exhausted. May we continue our conversation at a later time?"

"With the greatest pleasure on earth!" retorted the Viscount, stifling his merriment as he bent over her hand. "I shall breathlessly await the event." A proper charmer! thought Nabby appreciatively.

"Now," interrupted Lord Afton, who had suffered Lady Philippa's direct hit with only a twitch of his lips, a reaction which she chose to interpret as outrage rather than amusement, "if I may, I will conduct you to your chamber before you, horselike, fall asleep standing on your feet." He dismissed Nabby with a single gesture, and so effectively that the little abigail was halfway to her chamber before she realized she'd been treated with no more respect than a kitchen slut.

Lady Philippa nobly refrained from several impolitic suggestions regarding where the Earl might escort himself and allowed him to take her arm. "And so, Severin," she murmured, as he escorted her down the hallway and up a narrow flight of stairs, "we meet again."

"*Not* one of your more brilliant remarks," Lord Afton replied. "Am I correct in assuming that you did not expect to find me here?"

"The deuce!" Lady Philippa withdrew from his grasp and turned to stare up at him. "Of course not. The inn's excellent accommodations were recommended to me, and it sounded perfect for my purposes. Unfortunately, no mention of the inn's owner was made."

"Unfortunate, indeed," the Earl agreed smoothly. "But you are not obligated to stay. Your carriage will soon be as good as new, and then you may proceed on your way."

"Oh?" inquired Lady Philippa, in whom this reasonable attitude had produced a towering rage. "And if I choose to stay? From what I have seen of Strachan, it will suit me admirably."

The Earl raised a quizzical brow. "You must suit yourself, of course—not that you have ever done otherwise! But I feel I must warn you that the village offers little amusement. You will find no diversion here to compare with your Marquis." The dimness of the upper hallway was playing tricks with Lady Philippa's eyes; before them danced angry little lights of various startling hues. "Were you of a temperament to welcome advice from old friends, I would tell you that the Marquis was the apex of a remarkably foolish career."

Only the reflection that Severin could, and would, have her

forcibly evicted from his premises kept Lady Philippa from conducting herself like a shrewish fishwife and throwing something, preferably large and very heavy, at him. "Beast!" she said. "I had forgotten that you make it a practice to be remarkably well informed. Tell me, since you cannot claim an equal ignorance, why did you not simply say the inn was full?"

"Curiosity." Lord Afton folded his arms and leaned indolently against the wall. "I wished to observe for myself the notorious Lady Philippa Harte." Observe her he did, and so thoroughly that she was left curiously shaken. The effects of long travel and little rest, Lady Philippa told herself firmly. And of no interest whatsoever to her was the opinion of a jaded roué.

"Now you have done so," she said at last, when he remained silent. "What next? Am I to be cast out to sleep in a haystack?"

"You look," and he moved from the wall to take her arm once more, "as if you have already done so. As I promised," and he threw open a door, "I have brought you to your chamber. I suggest you avail yourself of a decent night's sleep." The blue eyes were alight with mockery. "Despite your obviously unflattering opinion of me, I do not turn even ladies of shady reputation from my threshold."

Lady Philippa opened her mouth in preparation for a scathing comment regarding her host's long-standing preference for females of that variety, but her heel caught in the rug. Instantly, she found herself in two strong arms, being held firmly against a broad chest. "And then?" she asked, a great deal more faintly than she would have wished.

Severin set her away from him. "You may stay as long as you please." With an almost indifferent expression, he pushed back the red-gold curls that had tumbled onto her forehead. "I find it highly ironic that you should choose *my* roof beneath which to hide and lick your wounds. But understand this, Pippin! Strachan is a far cry from London. While you *do* remain beneath my roof, you will refrain from engaging in any such indiscretions as you committed with your Marquis."

Lady Philippa might well have erupted into wrath, for never in her entire lifetime had she been spoken to in such a manner, not even during her long-past association with Severin, but the Earl knew quite well how to silence an angry woman's tongue. He bent his dark head and brushed her lips with his own, light as a passing butterfly; then, while she stared at him in mute astonishment, shoved her back into her chamber and firmly closed the door.

Five

With dusk, the villagers withdrew into their homes, there to set about their pious Sunday evening pursuits. Andrew Macgregor's stern admonitions echoed all too clearly in their heads; the old minister lurked in his dark church and brooded upon the invasion of the heretic Sassenachs; Geilleis Graham sat down by her mother's bedside and thought wistfully of Lucius Cunningham and Edinburgh; while Lucius, alone in the cottage that served as his studio, thrust Gilly from his mind and applied himself to a painting of remarkable ferocity.

The inn saw little more activity. In its surprisingly modern kitchens, Nabby sat, determined in her mistress's best interests to make a confidante of the inn's housekeeper; in the taproom, Lord Afton and Viscount Rockingham, studiously avoiding any mention of Lady Philippa Harte, passed the time with a game of cards; and in an upstairs chamber, Lady Philippa lay wide awake upon her bed, her mind engaged with the ignoble character of the fifth Earl of Afton, and with how she might bring him to heel.

Nor were matters particularly different in the castle that towered above them all. Since this structure's furnishings were as venerable as the edifice itself, the great hall in which the laird and his lady sat was both inconvenient and bare. On the table before Lady Cassandra was set out a deck of gaudy cards.

"The nine of swords," she said. "Doubt and desolation, suffering and loss and misery. Or perhaps the loss of a loved one."

Duncan Galbraith observed his wife through small and bloodshot eyes. He could, with little effort, think of two such losses that he would little mourn—to wit, her ladyship's brothers, Bevis and Neville. Had he known more clearly the vagaries of his wife's family tree, Duncan might, despite her wealth, have thought twice about marrying her.

Oblivious to her husband's uncharitable thoughts, Lady Cassandra turned her attention to another card. "The Queen of Swords, reversed, which indicates an unreliable and narrow-minded woman who is given to deceit and malice."

"Valentine," said the laird abruptly, as with one hand he reached for the brandy decanter and with the other lifted his glass to his lips. Neville's wife found no greater favor with Duncan than did Neville himself, due entirely to the fact that Valentine had greeted her host's amorous overtures with mingled amusement and disgust. The laird pondered, not for the first time, a way in which he might be rid of the lot of them.

"Bosh," retorted Lady Cassandra uncordially. "Here's the Hanged Man, reversed. Arrogance, wasted effort, and false prophecy; absorption with the physical, and resistance to the spiritual. And the chariot, also reversed, indicating decadent desires, restlessness, possibly an unethical victory." She raised her faded, slightly unfocused gaze to her husband's face. "Severin to the life! Don't you agree, my dear?"

The laird, contemplating the dispatching of his dotty wife to some distant place where he might never have to set eyes on her again, merely grunted. So felicitous an act would not be easily accomplished; Lady Cassandra possessed a large number of surprisingly influential friends. "Something will have to be done," he said abruptly, "about Afton's influence on Valentine. I hope I don't have to tell you that it will not do."

Had Lady Cassandra been of a more coherent nature, she might have commented that Duncan, being a womanizer of notable degree, was in no position to throw stones. However, Lady Cassandra existed on an entirely different plane, and her sister-in-law's whims were of no more concern to her than the villagers' megrims. "Why should we concern ourselves?" she murmured, and looked once more at her cards. "I'm sure Neville doesn't mind. Ah, here's the High Priestess!"

"And just who," growled the laird sarcastically, "is that

42

supposed to represent?" Much more time passed in his wife's addlepated company, and he too would be driven mad.

"Why, Lady Philippa Harte, of course!" Despite her disassociation from mundane matters, Lady Cassandra managed to be well informed on events that transpired in the village below. "Just this day she arrived at the inn."

"Lady Philippa," repeated Duncan, with a great deal more interest than he had hitherto shown. He knew of Lady Philippa—indeed, who did not?—she had been the subject of tittle-tattle even since she went upon the town. The laird who, with an eye to his own skin, had been in the habit of reading his wife's correspondence for many years, now recalled with growing excitement a recent epistle from London. Lady Philippa had no reservations about dallying with married men, as evidenced by her ill-fated association with the Marquis. Had the laird possessed a mustache, he would have twirled its ends; as he did not, he sipped his brandy contemplatively.

"We must call on her," Lady Cassandra announced, and stacked her cards neatly on the table. "Tomorrow, if you agree."

"Why?" inquired Duncan, startled by his wife's sudden observation of the conventions. He was quite familiar with the inn, enjoying not only the company of his peers but the pursuit of the little barmaid Katy, whose extreme nervousness added excitement to the chase; but his wife had never before evinced the slightest desire to set foot across that allegedly haunted threshold. And that in itself was odd, he suddenly realized.

Lady Cassandra's process of thought could not by any yardstick be considered normal. "I wonder," she murmured, "if Valentine had anything to do with bringing him here." Her spouse goggled. "Valentine," she repeated irritably, "and Severin! You must surely know that they were once very close."

"From all appearances," growled Duncan, "they still are. I wonder that Neville will put up with it." A family of albatrosses, to be sure, and all of them hanging round his neck. Neville walked the earth as if it were his alone and took what he pleased without regard of consequence; Valentine suffered an overheated imagination and was forever kicking up a scene; Cassandra and Bevis both exhibited a sad lack of wit. Alas for the old days, thought the laird, when a chief's importance was measured by the number of his followers and not by the weight of his purse; when the Highlanders roamed as far afield as the Lowlands and Ireland, returning with looted cattle and corn and women; when the laird had the right of pit and gallows and could dispose of an unsatisfactory wife and her parasitic family with no ballyhoo.

"Perhaps," said Lady Cassandra, interrupting her spouse's fervent prayers for her speedy demise, "it concerns a wager. The English are notorious gamblers, as willing to lay odds on the antics of flies on a windowpane as on a horserace." She sounded very much as if she were instructing her husband in the ways of his betters, and the laird ground his teeth. "Afton may have a wager to win."

Duncan considered seeking out Neville for the purpose of getting up some diverting devilment, a pastime at which that indolent gentlemen excelled. "And Lady Philippa," he inquired in what he hoped was an idle manner, as he rose. "Have you any notion why she's come here?"

Lady Cassandra tapped one slender finger against the cards. "But of course! Lady Philippa is for Bevis, didn't I say? She is quite wealthy and worldly enough to overlook his little eccentricities."

Eccentricities! The laird gaped. Bevis was every bit as retiring as Neville was volatile, and hardly a fit match for a lady as dashing and reckless as Lady Philippa was rumored to be. "Might I point out," he said, "that your matchmaking efforts on your other brother's behalf weren't precisely felicitous? Neville and Valentine quarrel like cats and dogs. Further, Lady Philippa is known to be a heartless flirt, and a member of London's fastest set. A woman like that would make mincemeat of Bevis!" But not of himself, added the laird silently, a gleam in his beady eyes. He'd go to the inn tomorrow, certainly, and view for himself this infamous lady.

"You must not mock what you do not understand." With the visionary air of a lunatic beldame, Lady Cassandra caressed her cards. "It has been preordained."

Six

Aware that she'd lost her audience, Aggy waved her arms. She looked as though she'd be more at home stirring a cauldron in some dark cave than mixing up a mess of porridge in the inn's cheerful kitchen.

"What is it, gammer?" asked Nabby. This old inn left her with a queer feeling in her bones, a presentiment not alleviated by the unwelcome intelligence that a ghost was a fellow guest. It should not have surprised her, Lady Philippa was drawn to trouble like a bee to honey! Nor was Barney at hand to make light of this feeling of impending disaster; that falsehearted stalwart was bent on striking up an acquaintance with the homely female who'd taken fright at the sight of them. For Lady Philippa's sake, he claimed. Nabby was no credulous, damp-eared babe and had replied accordingly. "I was woolgathering."

"You young ones!" snorted Aggy, briskly whisking away Nabby's empty bowl. "Stravaiguin' about the country. What Black Douglas would think, I dinna know." Nabby received a sharp glance. "My late husband, that is."

Nabby didn't know whether the epithet referred to the deceased Douglas's coloring or humor, but was not inclined to take up the gambit. This old woman obviously wished to ascertain whether Lady Philippa could claim a husband of her own, and Nabby had no desire to enlighten her. The little abigail had come to ask questions, not to answer them.

Aggy was well versed in the use of herbs and other remedies, though she prudently refrained from advertising her expertise; and knew of more than one means to satisfy her

45

curiosity. She grasped the abigail's teacup and peered into its depths, then frowned. "This isna good, lass," she said beckoning Nabby closer. "Someone is plotting. There is need for caution. See the boomerang and the cup?" Nabby obediently stared into the cup, but saw nothing but soggy tea leaves. "A corkscrew, trouble caused by curiosity; a dagger, be careful of what you say and do; a giraffe, mischief caused by want of thought." She raised her eyes to scowl at her guest.

"Lud!" said Nabby, somberly.

"A rat," added Aggy. "It means a treacherous enemy. There will be scandal—see the bettle and the kite?"

"I hope you may be mistaken!" Considering Lady Philippa's penchant for falling into scrapes, Nabby thought it unlikely. But she had not sought out Aggy to have the future read. "Tell me," she whispered, leaning forward conspiratorially, "just who *is* Lord Afton and why is he here?" But Aggy only cackled maniacally.

Had Lady Philippa been so inclined, she could have conveyed to her curious abigail a staggering amount of knowledge concerning Severin St. George. Pippin was not feeling particularly agreeable, however, particularly after a night passed in sleepless contemplation of that annoying gentleman. She paused outside the taproom. This, her second day at the inn, she had hoped to spend in recovering from the rigors of her journey, plotting out her new book, and planning Lord Afton's richly deserved comeuppance. Instead, she had been forced from her bed by the arrival of the local laird and his family, an event which inspired her to swear mightily.

Whether prompted by her dislike for her host, or by her fondness for the irrepressible Viscount, Lady Philippa herself could not say, but she had allowed Nabby to take unusual trouble over her appearance. Her high-waisted morning dress of white French lawn had a stiff collar edged with lace and long loose sleeves that spread over her hand from a narrow wristband. Her hair was piled loosely atop her head, with errant curls skillfully framing their owner's face. Nabby had been rendered ecstatic by this rare opportunity to display her hairdressing skill. Lady Philippa drew herself up proudly, as befitted a gentlewoman of her reputation and alleged experience, and stepped across the threshold.

The taproom's inmates turned to stare. Lady Philippa ignored them and looked first at a timid, brown-haired girl who was washing glasses behind the bar, and then at Udolpho, curled comfortably in front of the fire. The Viscount stepped forward to take her arm.

"Lady Philippa," he said, and in a lower tone, "you outshine the sun today." Pippin smiled, despite her dislike of flirtations undertaken so early in the day. "Let me make known to you Duncan Galbraith."

"A true pleasure," said the laird heartily, grasping her hand. "I have heard much of you, Lady Philippa!" His eyes raked her with insulting familiarity.

"How kind." Lady Philippa was not unfamiliar with this reaction, and her tone was cold. The laird was a distinguished-looking but unfortunately vulgar man of approximately fifty years, clad in the Highlander's traditional tartan. This costume unfortunately exhibited a paunch that was not noticeably diminished by Cumberland corsets and extremely knobby knees.

Avery cleared his throat, and the laird released Lady Philippa reluctantly. "And Lady Cassandra," continued the Viscount, with an unfriendly glance at Duncan. "The laird's wife." This was an angularly ethereal Englishwoman of a comparable age. "Neville Alversane, Lady Cassandra's brother, and his wife Valentine."

"Lady Philippa," said Neville, a dissipated but attractive man of some forty-odd years, "you are a breath of sunlight on a cloudy day, and precisely the diversion we have sought. Will your stay among us be a prolonged one? Do say that it will!" His wife, Valentine, was a sulky-looking creature with auburn curls and discontented mannerisms.

"I cannot answer that," Lady Philippa replied. "It all depends."

"On what?" asked Valentine, with unamiable curiosity. Since Lady Philippa could not very well explain the curious state of hostility that existed between herself and her host, she remained silent.

The sound of shattering glass interrupted these amenities. Lady Philippa spun around, startled, in time to see the little barmaid run from the room, barely avoiding collision with her employer. Lady Cassandra gazed upon her husband's flushed features, and Lord Afton raised a quizzical brow. Pippin wondered why she should experience pleasure at sight of the detestable Earl, with his diabolical disposition and acid-dripping tongue.

"What ails the creature now?" snapped Valentine. She wore a cambrick frock buttoned behind with a Spanish vest;

her hair was dressed in the disheveled state known as "à la Titus"; and her dark eyes were fixed on Lady Philippa. "She's broken at least a dozen glasses since you hired her, Severin. I wonder that you tolerate such incompetence."

Loft Afton regarded his guests with idle interest. "You may leave Katy to Aggy."

"I suspect, Severin, that you are trying to humbug us all!" Lady Cassandra, with no time for trivialities, perched on the edge of a chair. "I don't believe the inn is haunted. It's no more than a tale you've invented to increase your business."

"Ah, but you forget," the laird interrupted. "Afton has seen the specter." Again he eyed Lady Philippa appraisingly. Amused, she looked away.

"Duncan's love for the ladies is a subject of much gossip here," Avery murmured into her receptive ear. "But Lady Cassandra seems to care little for his infidelities. It's rumored that only her fortune and aristocratic lineage enabled her to snare the impoverished laird. Rumor also claims that Duncan always refers to his wife by her title, even in their most intimate moments." Lady Philippa laughed aloud.

"If that's what Severin says, then it must be so." Valentine's tone was belligerent, as was the glance she cast at Lady Philippa. Pippin in turn observed that Valentine's intake of wine was far from genteel.

"Ghost?" she inquired idly. "This is a pretty thing!"

"William Macgregor, my darling," the Viscount explained. "Our Andrew's ancestor, a representative of divine justice during the witch trials. He hanged himself in this very house, and it appears his tormented soul cannot find rest."

"The deed occurred in Lady Philippa's room." Lord Afton leaned against the bar, suspiciously benign. "I trust, Pippin, that you will not allow the unfortunate event to interfere with your sleep." Valentine snickered maliciously.

"Pippin's not so poor a creature as to be frightened by a mere ghost," the Viscount protested. He smiled down at Lady Philippa. "Our William is not dangerous, just unattractive."

"Singularly so," said Severin, with more emotion than he had thus far exhibited. "He appears as he must have in his last moments of life, hanging in midair and gibbering, his eyes starting out of his head."

"William is said to appear in connection with evil," volunteered Lady Cassandra. "A continuation of his life's work."

"As to that," Lord Afton responded plaintively, "I cannot

48

agree. I see no reason why he should choose to grimace at me."

Valentine laughed again, and Lady Philippa uncharitably characterized her as inclined to hysteria. Nor did she fail to note that Valentine's gaze strayed often to the Earl, a fact which should have vindicated Pippin's poor opinion of him but instead made her furious. "Tell me, Afton," she said, "is it supposed to be sweet William who is so tastefully depicted on your sign?"

"To the life, if that's an appropriate phrase."

"Why did he kill himself?"

"Ah," replied the Earl, "that's the beauty of the tale. He was cursed, you see, by our leading local witch."

"For God's sake!"

"Precisely," said the Earl.

"My dear Lady Philippa," interjected Lady Cassandra, leaning forward with an anxious expression, "you cannot mean that you don't believe in the supernatural? Surely you do not discount the survival of the spirit!"

Pippin might utilize the macabre in her titillating narratives, but her feet were planted very firmly on the ground. "Arrant nonsense!" said she, but in a kindly tone. "I fear your so-called ghost will lead you on a wild goose chase." If they had been discussing the inn's otherworldly inhabitant before her entrance, it was little wonder that the nervous barmaid had fled.

"Allow me to introduce you," Lord Afton said, indicating a portrait on the wall near the fireplace. "Ailcie Ferguson. Strachan's chief claim to nefarious fame."

This announcement caused a stir of interest. "So that's the alluring Ailcie." Neville moved to study the painting.

"Where did you find this masterpiece?" Valentine asked, briefly forgetting both her sulks and her jealousy.

"Hidden upstairs," Lord Afton replied, amused. "This was Ailcie's home at one time."

Lady Philippa also crossed the room and regarded the portrait appraisingly. The painted woman was young and strangely appealing, with fair hair, pale eyes, and well-defined features. She was also voluptuous, with an air of bold mischief. Recognizing a kindred spirit, Lady Philippa was intrigued.

"Very well!" She turned to the Viscount, still at her side. "Why did William Macgregor hang himself in Ailcie Ferguson's house?"

"By that time it was no longer hers. The building was confiscated when its owner was convicted of witchery, and somehow Willian got hold of it. He used it to confine those awaiting trial. The torture chambers were in the cellars." The Viscount grinned. "You must ask Severin for the gory details."

"The deuce you say!" exclaimed Lady Philippa. Here, it seemed, was her story, complete with characters and details.

"Ailcie was a widow," Lord Afton explained, with unprecedented amiability. "Ferguson died under what came to be considered suspicious circumstances. Of course, he was all of seventy years of age, which might have had something to do with it."

"Old fool!" muttered Valentine, but her attention was on the laird. Duncan Galbraith flushed alarmingly. Aha! thought Lady Philippa, further intrigued.

"Ferguson left his wife in comfortable circumstances, I believe." Severin gazed impassively upon his newest guest. "Ailcie apparently wasn't popular with the villagers."

"At least not with the women." Valentine raised a hand to touch her immaculate auburn curls, in a manner that drew the attention of every man in the room, including that of her husband and the laird, embarking upon a game of darts.

"Fascinating, are they not?" murmured the Viscount, more interested in ice than fire. "There is yet another Alversane. Bevis, Neville and Cassandra's younger brother, is a confirmed recluse who has little in common with the other members of his family."

"A characteristic," responded Lady Philippa, witness to the sideways glance that Valentine bestowed upon the Earl, and his answering smile, "that I can only applaud." She protested only briefly when the Viscount drew her away from the others and into the hallway.

"Are you," he inquired, "trying to hold me at arm's length?"

"How unfair you are!" So the courtship was to be resumed. Lady Philippa played her part with expertise but, for the first time in her life, without any particular enthusiasm. "I have scarce had a chance to catch my breath since I arrived."

"I did not foresee your presence here and must hold it to be a piece of astonishingly good fortune." He firmly possessed himself of one of her hands. "You must know that I hold you in great regard."

50

"Avery!" But Lady Philippa made no effort to free herself.

"I have been too precipitate." The Viscount sighed. "I fear you will think I have presumed too much."

Lady Philippa fluttered her long lashes, not a bit deceived. Even had she not the advantage of previous acquaintance, she could not have missed the twinkle in those merry brown eyes. "If this is a declaration," she remarked, "it is the strangest I have ever received! Considering the number of hapless females you must have addressed in a similar manner, I should think your performance would be a trifle more polished."

"Cruel and unnatural!" cried the Viscount, stricken. "To taunt me with previous conquests while I have been sufficiently noble to refrain from mentioning your own."

"Your manner is quite ungentlemanly, sir!" Lady Philippa retorted coldly. Strange that this meaningless banter no longer had the ability to amuse her.

Avery dropped his head into his hand. "Good God," he uttered, in broken tones. "I am cast into despair, my heart broken, my hopes for the future in ruins." Despite herself, Lady Philippa laughed, and the Viscount lifted a mirthful countenance. "I swear, Pippin, you are a damned good sort of a girl!"

"Thank you!" Lady Philippa did not protest when he chastely kissed her cheek.

"Your misused coach," announced the Earl, causing them to spring apart, "is in working condition once again. You may depart, Lady Philippa, as soon as you please."

"What's this?" cried Avery, not at all dismayed at being caught in a situation that looked a great deal more compromising than it actually was. "Pippin, surely you don't mean to leave now!"

Lady Philippa was furious with herself for blushing like a guilty schoolgirl. "No!" she snapped and awarded Lord Afton a brilliant, sparkling scowl. "It appears Severin is laboring under a delusion. Nor, I might add, is it his first!" Without a word, the Earl turned on his heel and walked away.

"Heigh-ho!" softly said the Viscount, who knew both Lord Afton and Lady Philippa quite well, and who furthermore possessed a spirit of pure mischief. He had not expected to find, in this provincial village, entertainment better than a play.

51

Seven

Andrew Macgregor walked the night-time streets of Strachan, alert for signs of the evil that once more threatened the village, its foul presence invoked by the blasphemers and idolaters who frequented the inn. He could not deny a certain unchristian pleasure in his certainty that the mighty heathens must fall. The incomers had been warned and had chosen to disregard him. So be it. The responsibility for their rashness was theirs alone.

It didn't occur to the minister to be grateful to little Katy for the reports she made to him nightly. Instead, Andrew Macgregor was angered with himself for not thinking to utilize her unique position before. Katy afforded him a splendid opportunity to learn the extent of his foes' iniquities.

In the darkness, the old man's eyes gleamed. Perhaps he might yet be granted as harsh a challenge as his ancestor William had faced. His lips moved in silent prayer.

The minister was not the only person awake at that lonely hour. Long before daybreak, Lady Philippa had roused from confused, troubled dreams that dealt with Strachan's witch trials. The fire had reduced itself to ashes and the room was bitterly cold. She burrowed deep beneath the counterpane as Udolpho muttered fretfully and curled himself into a tighter ball at her feet. Pippin wriggled her toes under his comfortable bulk.

Sleep would not return, and she began to wonder what had wakened her. Lady Philippa usually slept deeply; Nabby had habitually employed three stentorian servants for the sole purpose of rousing her reluctant mistress from bed.

The night was still and quiet. Unaware of Andrew Macgregor's perambulations, Pippin thought resentfully that she and Udolpho seemed to be the only living creatures in the immediate vicinity who weren't lost in deep slumber. The inn maintained a vast number of retainers, including ostlers, yardboys, waiters, chambermaids, and boots; but even the pitiable creature who began her day's work by cleaning the hearths was still abed.

Lady Philippa scampered to the fireplace and found the floor almost unbearably cold. She struggled with the reluctant blaze, a task that was not familiar to her, and then froze motionless as she sniffed the pleasant scent of summer flowers. *"Flowers?"* said Pippin incredulously. Her curiosity aroused, she held a candle to the flames. With sleepy blinks, Udolpho emerged from beneath the covers and tottered to the fire.

The room was as Lady Philippa had last seen it, with the door bolted and no evidence of an intruder. The elusive, strangely provocative scent was still present, yet search as she might, its source remained undefined. Pippin began to wonder if this was one of the Viscount's tricks, designed perhaps to send her hysterically into his arms.

Maybe she had misjudged him. Lady Philippa wrapped herself in the counterpane and sank into a comfortable chair. There was more to Avery than appeared at first glance, despite his obvious ploy of regaling her with ghost stories designed to scare her out of her wits. The Viscount swore to strange knockings and footsteps, doorknobs that rattled as if some unseen visitor sought to enter the room, inexplicable shadows cast by no living being. Pippin smiled drowsily. Ironic that she should once again encounter both the Viscount and the Earl, and in this unlikely setting, and even more ironic that they should all three step so easily into their old roles. Never mind, she soothed herself. She would contrive that *this* drama ended differently.

Lady Philippa had almost resumed her slumbers, had indeed gained a foothold in some twilight land where Lord Afton conducted himself with quite uncharacteristic chivalry, when she was suddenly enveloped in chill that struck to her bones. A harp's music rang in her ears, and in her nostrils was the odor of the grave.

It was a full moment before Pippin could free herself from mindless paralysis; then, with an oath, she flung herself from the chair. Udolpho opened one orange eye in protest against his mistress's uncharacteristic gymnastics.

She stood by the small window, shivering and trying to collect her scattered wits. It was nothing more than a nightmare prompted by Avery's tales. Lady Philippa blinked, then leaned forward to stare fixedly into the darkness. It seemed, briefly, as if her thoughts of the Viscount had conjured up that gentleman. Pippin frowned. Whoever the mysterious man who walked the streets of Strachan when all honest folk were snugly abed, he had not been alone. Whatever lover's tryst she had briefly glimpsed, one thing was certain: sleep that night had fled.

Pippin glanced around the chamber, seeking some diversion for her lively imagination, then laughed aloud. The Viscount, if indeed he were responsible for this hoax, might have displayed more ingenuity. Who would believe that the deceased William Macgregor, the inn's alleged ghost, would herald his advent by the music of a harp or be caught, even in the hereafter, wearing a flowery scent?

The chamber had a sloped ceiling with exposed beams, and walls papered with a small print. The chair before the fire was covered in a fine green material that matched the window curtains and the hangings on the four-poster bed. A small table sat beside the chair, and an ornate mirror hung above the dresser. With a sigh, Lady Philippa took an intriguing-looking volume from the table and climbed back into bed.

The book she chose wasn't conducive to sleep, nor was it intended for the faint of heart. Lady Philippa scanned the small, privately printed volume of the inn's history with the vague intention of gaining information about her surroundings as well as further background for her new tale. It was curious that the town had not yet recovered from its ancient scandals.

Ailcie Ferguson's predominating crime was clearly that of being an attractive young woman, comfortably circumstanced, with an unhappy inclination toward indiscretion. The author was firm in stating that the wealthy widow had cheerfully dispensed her favors indiscriminately to all and sundry. Once the witchcraft mania struck, Ailcie's involvement was inevitable. She was not liked by the women whose husbands treated her with hopeful deference, and her husband's death was recalled. She was also accused of using magic to cause men to be unfaithful to their wives, and of selling strange concoctions to local girls. Ailcie protested that these mixtures were nothing more than beneficial creams and simple scents, but her demurs went unheeded. The villagers recalled that one of her customers had suddenly suffered a bloody flux, and another had miraculously recovered from a severe case of boils.

Ailcie labored under another grave disadvantage: pregnancy. Her determined refusal to name the father of this misfortune led the villagers, already half-crazed with fear and superstition, to attribute the thickening of her figure to familiarity with the devil. Nor did Ailcie deny the accusation; she regarded her questioners with startled contempt, then proceeded to compound her sins by a burst of manic laughter. When threatened and taken to view the torture chambers, she contemptuously spat on the floor.

Lady Philippa paused to stretch her cramped muscles. She thought very poorly of the villagers' credulity. Her sympathies were with Ailcie, whose morals may have been questionable but whose courage was not.

Outside the window, mist lay heavily on the countryside, and Pippin pulled the draperies tightly closed. Absorbed in her book, she joined Udolpho on the rug in front of the fire. The cat blinked at her and purred.

Ailcie Ferguson had proved herself an extremely unsatisfactory prisoner. When advised of the grave charges against her, she gave vent to such profane language that even the officials were shocked.

William Macgregor had taken a personal interest in the case. Due to Ailcie's advanced pregnancy, she was treated with unusual consideration, suffering only the application of the thumbscrew and the boot. Ailcie was not a native, but had been abducted from the Lowlands as a bride. It was not long before the villagers began to regard her as a manifestation from hell.

For reasons known only to himself, William Macgregor tried to insure that Ailcie was treated with comparative leniency, and his efforts were temporarily successful. Lady Philippa was surprised by his concern, and unimpressed; she saw little difference between having one's legs crushed and suffering the dislocation of one's joints.

The minister could not long prevail against general opinion, and Ailcie Ferguson was publicly stripped and searched for devil's marks. In the course of the examination, she was treated shamefully by the torturer's assistants. This ignoble act brought on the premature birth of her child. The minister took Ailcie's child and deposited it with a God-fearing family who resided several miles away. Pippin considered that this behavior might have been more laudable had William Macgregor informed his parishioners of the deed, but he did not.

Ailcie's fate, after that, was certain. There had been no hope that she might be proven innocent, but the sudden inexplicable cessation of her pregnancy made the villagers clamor for her death. William Macgregor ceased his petitions for leniency and watched the outcome impassively. As tongues of flame from the slow green fire licked her ankles, Ailcie Ferguson screamed and moaned. She cursed the villagers; she promised William Macgregor a death even more ignoble than her own, and endless suffering.

Pippin skimmed over the account of the witch's ordeal, having little heart for blood-curdling detail. Ailcie was buried in unconsecrated ground, with a stake driven through her heart and a boulder placed over her grave. Since she had neither confessed nor named accomplices, the matter ended there. Further action would have been nigh impossible, since most of the villagers had consorted with Ailcie in one way or another. Even King James might have boggled at the execution of an entire village.

Lady Philippa closed the book and, after dislodging Udolpho from his nest in her hair, sat up to thoughtfully regard the room where William Macgregor had hanged himself. It was Severin, of course, who had left the book for her to find; consequently, it must have been Severin who played the ghost. Pippin ruminated upon his various reasons for wishing her a speedy departure.

She wondered, too, though she would burn at the stake herself before ever admitting it to Lord Afton, if her journey to Strachan had been a grave error. And then she recalled the furor that even now swept London, occasioned by the philandering Marquis's divorce from his viper-tongued Marchioness. A witch-haunted village was preferable, she concluded wryly, and threw back the covers. Udolpho snarled.

Eight

The Highland morning was gray with clouds, an occurrence that did little to improve either Aggy's rheumatism or her frame of mind. When Lady Philippa appeared in the dining room at an unreasonably premature hour, Aggy surveyed her gloomily.

"Why so early, m'lady?" she inquired over the clatter of crockery. "Couldna' sleep?"

"I've been awake for hours," Lady Philippa replied blithely, accepting a cup of steaming tea. "Passing the time with a very interesting book." She glanced at her companion to see if this drew any response, but Aggy's weathered face remained blank.

"I suppose you'll be wishin' to break your fast now," the old woman muttered, somewhat belligerently.

"Lord no," Lady Philippa replied, with a gesture of distaste. "I can't tolerate the sight of food before noon." She noted that the room's massive furnishings were placed stiffly, oddly at variance with the inn's easy charm.

Aggy regarded her visitor sourly. "'Tis no wonder you're naught but skin and bones," she said. "If it's the master you've an eye to, you'd best plump up that skeleton of yours. That one has an eye for flesh."

Pippin choked on her tea and burned her mouth. "Indeed?" she inquired coolly, when she could speak again. "Lord Afton's preferences are no concern of mine."

"Hut!" growled Aggy. "I've no time for gossipin'."

This did not augur well for Lady Philippa's intended inquiries, but she bravely forged ahead. "Aggy?" she said. "Have you lived in Strachan long?"

"All my life, m'lady."

Lady Philippa thought a little subtlety might not be amiss. "Then I suppose you know all the old tales," she mused wistfully, and summoned a bland face to meet Aggy's suspicious glance. To her surprise, the old woman chuckled.

"Och, you're a sly one, m'lady," acknowledged Aggy, wiping her hands on her voluminous apron. "What is it you're wantin' to know?"

Lady Philippa smiled in the comradely manner that endeared her to servants everywhere, even those high sticklers who thought a lady should be more careful of her place. "Why did William Macgregor hang himself?"

Aggy eyed her inquisitor and involved herself with the preparation of another pot of tea. Pippin wondered if she'd been indiscreet but, just when it appeared that the old woman would remain obstinately silent, Aggy deposited herself and the teapot at the table.

" 'Twas the witch's curse," she replied, "and if you've any other thoughts in that red head of yours, you'd best keep them to yourself. People here don't take kindly to strangers pryin' into things that don't concern them."

"Aggy!" Lady Philippa protested. "You can't believe that nonsense."

"I can't?" inquired the old woman. "Even if I took it to be nonsense, as you say, I wadna be so foolish as to make a fuss about it. Let it go, m'lady. You'll do yourself no good."

But Lady Philippa was of a perverse character, and once set upon a course of action would not be dissuaded by anything so trivial as negative advice. "I suppose there are records of the trials?" she asked casually.

Aggy was not deceived. She set her cup down firmly. "Aye," she answered, "in the Macgregor's keeping. And I'll tell you as shouldna, m'lady, don't go fidgeting the Macgregor or you'll be bringin' down terrible trouble upon us all."

Lady Philippa wondered how the current minister inspired his parishioners with such varying degrees of emotion. Liberal thinker that she was—when she thought at all, which those privileged to claim intimate acquaintance with her ladyship unanimously agreed was not nearly often enough—threats of hellfire and eternal damnation held no terror for her.

"Is there really a ghost?"

Aggy sighed. "You've heard it said," she replied abruptly.

60

"I myself have heard the music of the harp, played by no earthly hands."

Lady Philippa experienced no urge to confess that she'd heard that same music. "But surely Ailcie Ferguson must be your culprit? She sounds a more likely ghost than the minister."

"Allelladay," murmured Aggy, into her teacup, then added with relief, "Here's Paddy with the post." Lady Philippa swore, silently but in a most disgraceful manner, at the appearance of a muscular young man with a shock of bright red hair. "Och, ye great lout!" scolded Aggy, but with a twinkle in her eye. "Trampin' in here in all your dirt and botherin' her ladyship! Where are your manners? Make your bow to Lady Philippa, lad!"

Upon recognizing the exalted nature of Aggy's visitor, Paddy blushed bright red and tugged awkwardly at his forelock. "Hello, Paddy," said Lady Philippa, charmed. "I believe you must be related to the small urchin who caused my coach to descend so abruptly into a ditch."

"Aye." Paddy allowed himself to be persuaded to join Lady Philippa at the table. And who would believe, he thought, dazed, that he'd drunk tea with a real lady? "It's sorry we are for the trouble he's caused you! Young Sandy's a right little scamp."

"Pooh!" retorted Lady Philippa, who didn't imagine that Paddy as a boy had been any better behaved. "No harm was done, after all, except to my coachman's sensibilities! Let us forget the matter, pray." In no time at all, she had drawn from Paddy his life story, or those portions of it that seemed suitable for a lady's chaste ears. The Macleans were a crofting family; they eked out a frugal existence from a barren area of land some three acres in size. The property did not belong to them, but was part of a large estate owned by Duncan Galbraith, the disreputable laird. "So your family pays a small rent for use of the land on which you've lived for generations," she mused, in unapproving tones. "It seems somewhat unfair."

"No, ma'am," Paddy disagreed, then blushed at his temerity. Lady Philippa was a new experience for him, a startling contrast to the local damsels, and he found it difficult to keep his mind on the conversation. "It's a way of staying on the land. I've no more wish to take up a profession in the city that did my father or grandfather before me."

"Hmm," said Lady Philippa, her opinion of the laird lessening appreciably, though it was a fact of life that the rich battened on the poor. "You should not condemn the city, Paddy, until you have sampled its delights." As if she had made an improper suggestion, Paddy shyly hung his head.

Aggy bustled about the dining room and regarded the two younger people with a tolerant eye. Her ladyship was a heedless madcap and should probably be turned over someone's knee and soundly thrashed, but Aggy saw no real harm in her. And who could blame Paddy for being dazzled by a creature that appeared as if she'd come straight from the pages of a storybook? Aggy only hoped Paddy had wits enough to refrain from blathering to his parents about his new acquaintance. They'd likely raise a terrible fuss.

The whole village had once thought that Paddy and little Katy would make a match of it, and a fine romantic tale it would have made, of childhood sweethearts growing up to wed. The old woman shook her head suddenly, realizing her indulgence in fanciful thoughts. Ah well, what harm did it do? She hadn't always been old, and Black Douglas had been a man to kindle the fire in a young girl's blood. Andrew Macgregor could bewail the weakness of the flesh but, so far as Aggy knew, he'd not developed the power to peer into people's minds.

As for Paddy and Katy, that romance had gone sadly awry. Katy's job at the inn had gone to her head. Aggy had little tolerance for such foolishness, but the girl gave herself airs and now had no time for Paddy. Aggy glanced at the boy, who certainly didn't seem to be suffering the pangs of unrequited love.

At that moment, Katy herself entered the room. She stopped short on the threshold, an expression of dismay on her features as she absorbed the sight of Paddy and the stranger absorbed in animated conversation. Aggy sighed. The fat was in the fire for sure. As if he shared her misgivings, Paddy rose abruptly to his feet, mumbled a word of apology, and fled. Aggy quickly followed him, with a sullen Katy in tow. Lady Philippa stared after them in surprise.

"Ah, Lady Philippa!" remarked Lord Afton from the doorway. "What cataclysmic occurrence has brought you so early from your bed? An anticipated tête-à-tête with Avery, perhaps?" His sardonic gaze swept the room. "Alas, you must be disappointed. Our fashionable friend rests still in the loving arms of Morpheus and will not stir for several hours yet."

Pippin refused to be drawn into an argument so early in

the day, particularly with one who could enforce her speedy departure from these fascinating premises. "Good morning," she said calmly, pouring him a cup of tea.

The Earl accepted the cup with an expression that might justifiably have been termed diabolical. His attire was as correct as if he had prepared to ride in Hyde Park; and the exquisitely cut blue coat with brass buttons, the leather breeches and top boots set off his splendid physique to advantage. Lady Philippa eyed his immaculate cravat, arranged impressively in the pristine folds of the Mathematical.

"Do I pass inspection?" inquired Lord Afton.

"We shall go on more prosperously," retorted Lady Philippa, who made a charming picture in a pale green muslin gown, "if you refrain from pinching at me. I have wished for the opportunity to speak privately with you."

"Lady Philippa!" The Earl's eyebrows rose. "Have you grown tired of poor Avery so soon?"

Pippin bit back an angry remark and contented herself with picturing the provoking Earl in various dire and painful predicaments from which she would refuse to rescue him. "Why are you so hostile, Severin?" she asked, with a flash of her disconcerting honesty. "I do not think you always held me in dislike."

The Earl smiled, an act which transformed his harsh features into something closely akin to beauty. "Perhaps not, when you were a schoolroom chit with no manners and an appalling tendency to fall into scrapes. But I insult you by referring to your harum-scarum youth! Now you are all that is proper, dignified, and staid."

"Moonshine!" retorted Lady Philippa, incensed.

There was mockery in Lord Afton's eyes. "True, alas. You have not altered one iota." The cruel lips twisted. "Conscience impels me to add that I once considered you a delightful child."

Lady Philippa was left in the unusual position of having nothing to say. She wondered why Lord Afton had never married; then concluded that any female forced to live in such close proximity to the Earl would murder him out of hand. "This is a very nice room," she commented casually. Severin regarded her quizzically over the rim of his cup. "The proportions are quite pleasing to the eye."

"The brilliance of your conversation overwhelms me," Lord Afton replied. "Have you developed a sudden passion for architecture?"

Pippin bit her tongue and smiled sweetly. "You must admit it's a charming old building."

"My good girl," Severin said plaintively, "you wound me beyond words. I've sunk a fortune into the restoration of this structure, only to hear you refer to it as interesting and nice."

Lady Philippa sighed. "I doubt you mistake my meaning."

"No," the Earl retorted. "Do you think that you might manage to be a little more direct? Does your chamber displease you? Have you some inexplicable aversion to your room?"

"No!" Pippin snapped. "And I refuse to engage in a brangle with you."

"Didn't you sleep well?" Lord Afton inquired solicitously. "Your temper seems a trifle short this morning." Lady Philippa glared at him, and he smiled lazily. "It would not be wonderful if you disliked *this* room, for our ghost is busy here." Pippin blinked as he indicated the chairs grouped around the fireplace. "No matter how we arrange the furniture, it returns to its original position in the dead of night."

"You jest!" Her words lacked conviction; Lady Philippa grew more and more convinced that Severin meant to drive her away with these foolish tales of ghosts. How much he must wish her gone! And how greatly he underestimated her.

"I am not given to jokery." The Earl appeared bored. "Ask Aggy, if you doubt my word. The matter drives her to despair."

Lady Philippa, again recalling her experience of the early morning, frowned. Lord Afton, who observed her expression with interest, appeared on the verge of speech. At that moment, the old oaken door that led to the hallway swung open of its own accord. Pippin jumped. Udolpho entered the room with great dignity and sat down on the hearth to bathe. The massive door closed silently.

"That, also, happens frequently." Lord Afton bent to scratch the cat's head. "Were not my housekeeper such a domestic tyrant, the servants would long since have fled. As it is, they fear Aggy more than any hypothetical ghost."

"Aggy is delightful," Lady Philippa protested. "How can you speak of her so?"

"I am a man of little sentiment," the Earl replied, stating the obvious. "Tell me, had you speech with my delightful housekeeper this day?"

"Of course." Pippin eyed him warily.

"I had begun to fear that her prolonged avoidance of this room," Severin explained, "indicated some calamity detrimental to my well-being. I find I simply cannot get along without that excellent creature. But you reassure me: Aggy is doubtless involved in nothing more ominous than matchmaking. She has taken quite a fancy to you."

Lady Philippa's piquant face was startled; Lord Afton's expression was bland. "I have told her that you are determined to have the charming Viscount, but she thinks Avery a poor match, for all he's heir to millions. Perhaps you should explain the matter to her."

That the Earl, in one of his all-too-frequent difficult moods, should taunt her with a youthful folly was entirely too much to bear. Lady Philippa rose gracefully and moved toward the door. She paused with her hand on the knob and wrestled with her temper. "Severin? Do any of the females of your acquaintance wear patchouli scent?"

Lord Afton's lean face assumed a thoughtful expression. "Patchouli?" he repeated. "I think not. Now if you'd said heliotrope—"

Lady Philippa's piquant face was startled; Lord Afton's ex-

Nine

The Viscount looked magnificent in a dark brown frock coat, buff kerseymere waistcoat, and light blue merino inexpressibles, but his cheerful countenance was unusually glum. Pippin eyed his face, noting the purple bruise that adorned one cheek, then tactfully lowered her eyes. It looked very much as if Avery had encountered someone's fist. She wondered who would dare treat him so.

The heavy mist had given way to a soft, gentle rain that could barely be felt on face or hair. Pippin, escorted by the silent Viscount, walked slowly along the road that led out of Strachan, savoring the magnificent scenery. Udolpho preceded them, his bushy tail waving gently as he inspected the area for something on which to exercise his mighty hunting skills. Nothing so mundane as a rat or mouse would do; Lady Philippa had a strange aversion to such creatures, even when presented as proud trophies of battle.

Lady Philippa paused on a small hillock. Before her lay patchwork crofts, great stretches of heather and golden bracken. Juniper bushes grew beside the dusty road that stretched to distant mountains. The scene was dreamlike and unreal.

"You are mighty discreet," the Viscount said suddenly. Pippin gazed at him quizzically. "Severin accused me of dallying with his serving-wench."

Lady Philippa bit back laughter, for Avery's tone was indignant. Whatever his peccadillos, the Viscount was surely not so unaware of his rank as to seek amusement among the lower classes. Or was he? She remembered the secret night figures that she had glimpsed. "That was very ungentle-manly," she agreed. "Lord Afton makes the error of comparing your manners with his own."

"Still on the outs with him, are you?" the Viscount inquired knowingly. "Severin's an unusual chap, but you mustn't think he's not quite the thing."

"I find him offensive," Pippin snapped. "It does not surprise me that he ventures so seldom into Society. So unconciliating a manner would soon cause him to be denied entrance to the best homes."

Avery refrained from reminding Lady Philippa that she was not known for her own conciliating ways. "Not a bit of it," he said cheerfully. "You allow yourself to be prejudiced by your sudden dislike. Severin is quite a favorite of Prinny's, and may at any time be seen rubbing shoulders with Brummell at Watier's. You must not think that because he seldom appears at the Opera or a ball, he is not accepted by the *haut ton*. Afton's appearance at a rout is enough to establish a hostess, you know."

Lady Philippa, who spared little thought for such matters, was inordinately displeased to be reminded that the Earl wielded such influence. "A man of fashion, then," she said disapprovingly. "I collect he spends his time in sporting pursuits, patronizing prize fights, and making ridiculous wagers."

"I've seen him win a fortune playing faro at Brooks," the Viscount replied. "But as to the other, no. The truth is that Severin has little liking for the gaieties of the metropolis."

Lady Philippa abandoned her pleasant fantasy of his lordship fallen on hard times. "Oh, curse the man!" she said. "Let us speak of other things."

Avery agreed, "Although I confess to the liveliest curiosity as to your displeasure with Afton."

"The merest trifle," Pippin replied airily. "Do not concern yourself." The Viscount shot her a sharp look but contented himself with speculating wildly as to why Lord Afton and Lady Philippa were at daggers drawn.

Aware of her friend's scrutiny, though fortunately not of his more bizarre speculations, several of which would have sent her into a towering rage, Lady Philippa glanced around her at the haunting scenery. The Highlands were immortal; their brooding majesty infused her with an uncomfortable consciousness of her own insignificant mortality. "Avery," said she, no longer able to contain her own curiosity. "If not a serving-wench, then who marked your face?"

68

"It was the oddest thing." The Viscount touched his cheek, a puzzled expression in his brown eyes. "And except for this, I would dismiss it as a dream. I heard a woman's laughter in the night, and a man's voice raised in argument, and when I rose to investigate, I encountered an intruder. I can recall no more." He shrugged. "When I awoke, it was in my own bed, and with this mark upon my face. A poor and lame explanation, you will call it, and I must agree; but I can offer no other."

"An intruder," mused Lady Philippa. Perhaps this intruder was responsible for her own strange experiences. "Have you any idea who it might have been?"

"No."

Pippin frowned. There was no doubting the Viscount's sincerity, and though she might suspect that the feminine laughter had issued from Lord Afton's rooms, her host's amours could not explain the welt on Avery's face, or how the Viscount had been returned to his own room. "Do you believe the inn to be haunted?" she inquired.

"After last night, I wonder." Avery's tone was wry. "Before that I was skeptical, though I have heard the harp, and Severin swears to the apparition."

"If ever a place merited haunting, that inn does." Lady Philippa wondered if she should, as Lord Afton wished, continue her sojourn elsewhere. Yet she had promised to meet her friend Amanda at the inn and longed greatly to give that interfering lady a piece of her mind. Then, too, this village had just the air that she wished to convey in her next book, and the only other accommodation was situated many miles away. It seemed the inn's advantages far outweighed its unsettling atmosphere.

"The inn has an interesting history," the Viscount volunteered. "It was once visited by Mary, Queen of Scots; and Bonnie Prince Charlie came close to capture there. He escaped through a trapdoor and onto his horse, which was kept in preparation for just such an emergency." But Lady Philippa still wore an abstracted frown.

The few villagers who were in evidence hastened, with downcast eyes, past the fashionable pair. Bullied by her maid into donning a pelisse of fawn-colored sarcenet trimmed with mohair, a fetching straw bonnet, and Limerick gloves, Lady Philippa mused wryly that Nabby's efforts had been in vain. The villagers could not have been more unappreciative had she worn sackcloth and ashes, and carried a dread and extremely contagious disease.

The Viscount pointed to the castle that towered above the inn. "One tale claims the inn to have once been the brewhouse for the castle. A warren of tunnels honeycombs the cliffs." He glanced at his companion's arrested expression and added quickly: "They are far too dangerous to use now. Some have fallen in, and an explorer could easily become lost. The castle and the inn were supposedly once connected in that manner." He smiled. "The cellars were sealed when we arrived: Severin opened them. We found an entrance that leads nowhere, and a bricked-up doorway that might once have been a tunnel entrance."

"Fascinating," murmured Lady Philippa, and determined to pay the cellars a surreptitious visit at the first opportunity.

"If you like such things," replied the Viscount, who did not. Pippin waved to small Sandy Maclean, who scampered across the road to grin shyly at her and take firm hold of Udolpho's tail, but the distant sound of Janet Kirk's voice sent him scuttling into one of the small cottages. "The place is riddled with secret passages and concealed cupboards and small windowless rooms." Lady Philippa decided that she must cultivate her host in the pursuit of historical research. It would not be an easy task; that enigmatic gentleman habitually greeted direct queries with sharp set-downs; but Pippin trusted she had sufficient wit to deal successfully with the difficult Earl.

These strangely stimulating reflections were interrupted by the dark-haired girl who had been present when Lady Philippa arrived at the inn. "This, my darling, is Miss Geillis Graham," said Avery gracefully. Gilly extended her hand.

"I was looking for you," she said, her abrupt manner appearing even more *gauche* in contrast to the Viscount's. "Perhaps you'd like to be shown around the village."

"How kind!" Lady Philippa was more than a little intrigued by Miss Graham's brusque manner. "We would be delighted, wouldn't we, Avery?"

"It is prodigiously thoughtful of you, Miss Graham." Exuding charm, not untinged with amusement, the Viscount scooped up Udolpho in his arms. Miss Graham regarded him with such enmity that Lady Philippa was taken aback.

"Very well," Gilly said, with obvious resignation, and Pippin's curiosity was further piqued. "The church first, I think. No doubt you've heard of old Macgregor's collection."

"Instruments of torture," volunteered Avery helpfully, and Lady Philippa eyed him askance. "Truly, my darling! You've an education in store for you." Pippin, aware that the mischievous Viscount was delighted at her discomfort, made a face at him. No matter! Perhaps Miss Graham might show them the records Aggy had mentioned.

Miss Graham led them through an archway made by the intertwined limbs of two rowan trees. The gate that once stood between them was gone, and the building itself appeared to be just another simple cottage. "Rowan was thought to be a safeguard against witches," she remarked with a searching look. Lady Philippa gave a small, amused smile and glanced at the old cemetery behind the church.

"Is William Macgregor buried there?" she asked. It was an idle question, but Gilly exhibited no surprise.

"Of course not; suicides can't be buried in consecrated ground. He's buried in yon glen." Miss Graham gestured. "We've a belief here in Strachan: if a suicide is buried within sight of cultivated land, the crops will suffer blight; if he's buried within sight of the sea, the herrings will desert the coast."

"Which must make the burial of suicides a wearing task," Lady Philippa interrupted merrily. She cast an appreciative eye on the wild roses that bloomed profusely in the churchyard and resolutely ignored Avery's growing glee.

Miss Graham nodded solemnly. "Aye. And the tools that make the coffin must be destroyed or never used again. Right after the burial, the bier must either be smashed or burned."

Lady Philippa began to wonder if she'd unwisely chosen her guide for this tour, but followed Miss Graham to the cellar door, above which a horseshoe was nailed. "Let us pray we don't encounter old Macgregor," the girl muttered. "He'd go off in an apoplexy if he knew I'd brought you here."

Pippin paused in the doorway as her dainty shoes encountered an alien substance. "What the devil is on the ground?" she demanded. "It sounds like sugar underfoot!"

"Salt," Miss Graham retorted wryly.

The helpful Viscount directed Lady Philippa's attention to the horseshoe that hung above their heads. "Old Macgregor's taking no chances," he said. "Salt and iron to keep the witches away?"

Miss Graham shrugged irritably, confirming Pippin's suspicion that the girl held Avery in less than the highest regard. "That's how things are done here." She produced a candle and lit it. "These people are very, very superstitious. They're also extremely suspicious of incomers. You'd be wise to tread carefully."

Lady Philippa was too engrossed in her surroundings to pay attention to forewarnings of doom. Avery helpfully explained the artifacts so lovingly displayed: caspie claws, iron vises utilized to crush the arms; Spanish boots, an ingenious invention which could be tightened to render a person's bones into pulp; pilliwinks, or thumbscrews, whose use accorded perfectly with their name. "I have the benefit," he added, "of previous acquaintance with these things, thanks to Miss Graham." He smiled at Gilly, but the gesture was not returned.

"Dear heaven," Lady Philippa said, with growing consternation, "I'd think they'd want to destroy these odious things instead of putting them on display."

"Not us," Miss Graham retorted, watching with disapproval as Udolpho leaped to the floor. "We take great pride in our heritage. Come along, you haven't seen the half of it." She continued around the small crowded room.

"Wretch!" hissed Lady Philippa to the unrepentant Viscount. "Is this your notion of passing an idle hour?"

"Any hour spent in your company," responded Avery and took her arm, "is sheer delight." He glanced about him. "No matter how morbid the surroundings, my dear!" Udolpho happily chased an eye-gouger across the stone floor.

"This," said Miss Graham, indicating a gruesome-looking object, "is a device limited to this country." She looked at the hair shirt with distaste. "It was steeped in vinegar before the accused person was induced to wear it. It stripped the skin from the body."

"How many people were killed here?" Lady Philippa's inquiry was faint.

"Twelve," Avery replied. "Our Ailcie was the third to die, then several years passed before the persecutions began again."

Lady Philippa swallowed hard, and the Viscount moved closer. A strange way to conduct a pursuit, Pippin thought wryly, and wondered at the precise nature of Avery's game. "It's difficult to believe that people could be so misguided. Were they allowed counsel?"

Gilly laughed mirthlessly. "Theoretically," she returned. "Who do you think could have afforded the fee?"

"Couldn't Ailcie Ferguson?"

"I don't think she took her predicament seriously, at first. There's no indication that she ever requested aid."

72

"Perhaps no one would have helped her anyway, lest he risk his own neck," Lady Philippa commented, thinking of the book she'd just read. The Viscount touched his own neck, thoughtfully.

"They used this room first." Miss Graham favored her guests with a strange look. "Before Ailcie's house became so conveniently available. Usually being in prison was a torture in itself. Many people died in the filthy places, before they had a chance to be brought to trial."

"I think," Lady Philippa announced firmly, having seen more than enough of the minister's prize collection, "that it's time I returned to the inn." She had no great liking for Miss Graham's vivid descriptions.

Gilly followed her into the sunlight, leaving the Viscount behind to capture Udolpho, currently engaged in combat with a branding iron. "I must speak with you," Miss Graham said quickly, with a hasty glance over her shoulder. "Privately! I took you there for a reason, honestly! Oh, pray don't refuse."

Lady Philippa regarded her companion doubtfully, but the girl seemed to have shaken off her unsettling mood. Miss Graham smiled shyly. But before Pippin could answer her request, Avery reappeared with Udolpho firmly clutched under one arm.

"I must go," said Gilly, and abruptly walked away.

"Do you know," mused Lady Philippa, gazing upon the Viscount with marked disfavor, "I don't think our Miss Graham particularly cares for you."

"It signifies not!" Avery made an eloquent gesture, nearly dropping Udolpho in the process. The cat hissed. "The only lady whose sentiments I regard is yourself." Lady Philippa wore a skeptical scowl. "In truth," he added, with every indication of reluctance, "it's not myself our Miss Graham disapproves of, but Severin. Which makes her a creature after your own heart, does it not, my darling?"

"Piffle!" retorted Lady Philippa perversely, turning away.

"What's this?" The Viscount raised his brows. "Surely *you* cannot also believe that Severin and I are cut from the same cloth!"

"I do not know," Lady Philippa retorted with feeling, "which of you is worse!"

"Oh, Severin, of course." Avery chuckled. "I could tell you tales!"

"Pray do not." Pippin retained her frown. "You may as well know, Avery, that old Macgregor's artifacts are a treat I could have happily been denied! I am quite out of temper with you." The Viscount followed her down the narrow street, in his brown eyes a thoughtful gleam.

Lady Philippa's temper was not the only one to be sadly frayed. Upstairs in his church, consulting his priceless books in preparation for his forthcoming sermon, Andrew Macgregor had heard her every word. The old man shook with rage.

Ten

Lady Philippa slipped inside the inn with a sensation of decided relief. She supposed Miss Graham's intentions had been praiseworthy, but the girl's company could hardly be called restful. Nor had Pippin found the church cellar's grisly contents or the Viscount's puzzling hints conducive to a cheerful frame of mind. Lady Philippa was quickly coming to consider the inhabitants of Strachan as superstition-ridden ninnies and the Viscount as a veritable snake in the grass. She had abruptly dispensed with his companionship when he cheerfully volunteered the information that her chamber was not only the scene of William Macgregor's shocking demise, but also the setting for Ailcie's none-too-discreet *amours*.

"Wretch!" Lady Philippa said aloud, then smiled despite herself. Avery, with his awesome nose for mischief, would never suffer from tedium. All the same, she wondered why Lord Afton had assigned her that particular room. Witchcraft, thought Pippin, alliances with evil and devil-worship, and traffic with Satan. "Poppycock!" she muttered and proceeded resolutely down the hall.

Aggy's voice was raised in anger, her brogue so thick her words were incomprehensible. Lady Philippa cautiously approached the kitchen.

"Such goings-on!" Aggy snorted, arms akimbo. She glared at a tearful Katy, huddled on a chair. Various other servants bustled about the huge room, ostensibly intent on their duties, but with ears pricked for every word. "I'll have no more of your fidgets, miss, or you'll find yourself without a place."

Katy sniffed abjectly into a dingy handkerchief. Aggy

75

snorted with annoyance. Nabby, engaged in the laundering of fine lace, glanced up with a sour expression as Lady Philippa stepped into the room. Pippin wondered what had cast her volatile maidservant so deep into the dumps.

"A regular watering-pot, you are." Aggy turned on Lady Philippa. "Have you ever heard the like, m'lady? Swoonin' and moonin' about the place, and tellin' me she'll nae help with the dinner because my cookin' makes her faint!" She scowled at Katy. "'Tis some buttercup she needs, to calm herself. Or some chrinostate in her tea, if it's her digestion that's upended, though I've my doubts of that."

Katy burst into loud sobs, interspersed with laments concerning her probable fate if she lost her place and apologies for her incautious behavior. Lady Philippa wasn't surprised to see Aggy immediately relent, having already determined that beneath that gruff exterior beat a heart of marshmallow. "Och, that's a'richt," soothed the old woman. Nabby followed her mistress out of the room.

"'Twas a black day," stated that young lady, after they had achieved a momentary privacy, "when we set out on this ill-fated jaunt! Nothing has gone right from start to finish. We should never have come!"

"What maggot do you have in your head?" inquired Lady Philippa, though she felt much the same way. "Were you an unwilling witness to that unpleasant scene?"

"Ah, that Katy's want-witted." Nabby shrugged irritably. "A silly miss, no better than she should be, and no concern of mine. Nor of yours, Lady Philippa! Don't be thinking to offer her charity."

Pippin raised her brows. These were harsh words even from Nabby, whose superior attitude befitted one whose rank entitled her to associate with no servants of less stature than the housekeeper and butler. "Pray tell me what it is that vexes you."

"Barnabas!" Nabby spat out the word with venom.

"Barnabas!" With difficulty, Lady Philippa repressed a smile. So Nabby was finding the pathway of true love far from smooth! "What has he done?"

"More like what hasn't he done!" Nabby's attitude would have shocked Aggy, a firm believer that all good servants were of quiet and regular conduct, but Pippin waited patiently. "As if I'd give a brass farthing for any of that!" Nabby paused judiciously. "Consider my own conduct! But

76

Lady Philippa, this time he's gone too far. Barney is making a cake of himself with that odious Janet Kirk."

"Janet Kirk!" Lady Philippa recalled that rather nondescript female and spoke with honest surprise. "But why! He must have some reason, Nabby. Surely you refine too much upon it!"

"Do I, ma'am?" Nabby's hazel eyes shot fire. "Forever underfoot, she is, and too forward by half. And Barney is such a gudgeon as to be taken in."

"Surely you don't believe he's developed a preference for her!" Lady Philippa was almost as bewildered as her abigail but a great deal less incensed. "Dear heaven, our fine Barnabas and a simple country maid?"

"Maid, Lady Philippa?" Nabby's features twisted ferociously. "Draggletail, I'd say! As for Barney's preferences, I can't dispute the evidence of my own two eyes!"

"Perhaps you mistake politeness for passion, Nabby." Unlikely, thought Lady Philippa wryly, as soon as the words were out. "It would not be like Barnabas to be rude."

"Polite?" Naby inquired. "Barnabas? The Lord only knows what he may be up to, Lady Philippa, but I'll wager you anything you like that no good will come of it."

Lady Philippa lowered her eyes and contemplated the evils of gambling as evidenced by her abigail. Nabby owed her mistress at least a year's salary already. "Why such great concern about Barnabas?" she inquired. "You've made it quite clear that, with you, he wastes his time." She did not imagine that the long-suffering Barnabas was engaged in anything more nefarious than repaying Nabby in kind.

"Lady Philippa," said Nabby, and her expression was grim, "I give you fair warning. If Barney's played fast and loose with me, there'll be murder done!"

At length, exhausted by her efforts to calm an overwrought and murderously inclined abigail, Lady Philippa ventured toward the taproom. She was not to receive the comfort of a glass of brandy, however; muted but angry voices indicated that others had reached the room before her. Lady Philippa, immune to the pangs of conscience, paused in the hallway and blatantly eavesdropped.

"I demand to see Severin!" Valentine Alversane was as imperious as any queen. Pippin heard the sound of a foot stamped hard on the floor. "Immediately!"

"As I have told you," the Viscount replied calmly, "I've no

77

notion where he is. You are, of course, free to search the premises."

Justifiably intrigued, Lady Philippa moved closer and peered into the room. Standing as she did in shadow, it was unlikely she would be seen.

"Fool!" hissed Valentine, dressed to kill in burgundy and white lace. "You know I cannot! I am forbidden these premises unless accompanied by my family, thanks to that damned meddling Cassandra." The Viscount looked interested, and she stopped, as if aware she had said too much. "Well, will you fetch Severin, or must I tell him you prevented me from seeing him?"

"And what," inquired Avery, amused, "do you think he'd do?" She flushed and bit her lower lip. "If you'll accept a bit of disinterested advice, you might do better to wait for Severin to come to you."

Aha! thought Lady Philippa, and wondered why she was not more pleased to have her suspicions proved correct.

"You are presumptuous!" Valentine's cheeks flushed the exact shade of her elegant walking-dress. "I had an appointment with Lord Afton that he failed to keep. Is it remarkable that I should wish to know why?"

"Not remarkable," replied the Viscount, contemplating his brandy glass. "Just a trifle ill-bred." Valentine drew back her hand as if to bruise his other cheek, but he caught her arm. "You make a great deal too many appointments with Severin, my girl!" said the Viscount, as angry as she. Lady Philippa wondered briefly if he meant to offer Valentine violence in return for hers, but instead he pulled her into his arms. Nor did Valentine protest. It was with a certain, and understandable, confusion of mind that Lady Philippa crept away.

She found Lord Afton in the small garden behind the inn, surveying two small animal corpses that lay at his feet, and discussing with Udolpho their relative merits. Lady Philippa, who was not fond of such spectacles, quickly raised her eyes to the vicinity of the treetops and contemplated telling her irascible host what she'd just seen. The reflection that it cast Avery's supposed infatuation with herself in an odd light indeed made her hold her tongue.

"You'll achieve nothing gazing heavenward, save a crick in your neck," the Earl remarked. "No wonder Udolpho doesn't think you fit to receive his offerings."

Lady Philippa didn't avert her gaze. "Avery said I'm sleeping in Ailcie Ferguson's chambers."

With laudable restraint, Lord Afton refrained from commenting on the Viscount's awareness of precisely where her ladyship slept. "I could have informed you of that interesting fact," he replied, "had you thought to ask me."

Then Pippin did glance at him—and not in a friendly manner. "Will you do something with those odious corpses, please? Why did you give me her room?"

Severin pushed Udolpho's mangled trophies aside with a superbly shod foot. "I thought the historical associations might please you," he remarked apologetically.

"Please me?" Lady Philippa demanded in honest amazement. "The room where a witch concocted her vile spells and a man hanged himself? You seem to have an odd notion of my preferences!" She glanced quickly away from his sardonic features and took stock of her surroundings. On the inn's back wall was a sundial that had marked passing time since the year 1600. Beneath it stood an ancient water pump. "I wonder if you and Avery do not mean to frighten me out of my wits with these tales of witches and ghosts! As if your efforts were not enough, then I must suffer Miss Graham and her positive mania for old Macgregor's collection! Call off your hounds, Severin. I do not mean to leave."

"Have I underestimated," Lord Afton inquired smoothly, "your strength of mind? I had thought the chamber's associations would amuse you. Would you prefer to have the use of another room?"

"No," said Lady Philippa, in a harassed manner that few of her swains would have recognized. The Earl considered her somberly.

"Tell me," he urged, "where did you encounter the fair Gilly? Surely she hasn't visited here already today. I didn't think she was quite that enamored of my inn."

"Or of yourself, it appears," Lady Philippa snapped. "Avery and I ran into her in the village."

"Not literally, I hope," Severin objected, with a pained expression. "I begin to think you shouldn't be trusted with a moving vehicle."

"Don't be an ass! We were afoot and so was he. She conducted us on a tour of the church cellar, which holds one of the most dreadful exhibits I've ever had the misfortune to view." Pippin touched the old pump handle and found it functioning. She brushed water droplets from her skirt.

Lord Afton was suddenly very still. "I suppose Macgregor was present to deliver the requisite oratory?"

Lady Philippa shook her head. "No. Miss Graham did that well enough herself. I think she, too, wishes me away!" She recalled the girl's request for a private conversation and wondered to what end.

"And I collect you chimed in with various blasphemous and irreligious comments?" Severin was even more than usually severe.

Lady Philippa frowned at his grave tone. "I suppose so. Why? Shouldn't I have?"

"My dear girl," said the Earl scathingly, "a babe in leading-strings would have more sense? You are speedily going to find yourself in trouble up to your pretty ears."

"If I do," snapped Lady Philippa, "you needn't fear I'll call on you for assistance!" She turned angrily away and collided with the water pump. "And furthermore," she added, as Lord Afton moved to extricate her, "I'm not your dear anything!"

"Of course you aren't," agreed Severin cordially. "It was a mere slip of the tongue."

So far was this from soothing Pippin that she grimaced horribly at him. "Do not let me detain you longer!" she said. "I only came to tell you that Valentine Alversane awaits you in the taproom—though, as I passed by, Avery was keeping her tolerably well entertained."

The Earl appeared, of all things, amused. "Jealousy doesn't suit you, Lady Philippa!" he remarked, and tweaked her nose. Whistling, he strolled out of the garden, leaving Pippin struggling with an errant desire to kick him in the behind.

Eleven

Lady Philippa had not passed a pleasant night. Her irritation with Lord Afton had induced her to while away several hours with retributory fantasies, in which he humbled himself and begged forgiveness for his misconstruction of her character. She finally fell asleep, only to see that gentleman take his seat in the House of Lords, there to animadvert wittily upon her appalling lack of intelligence while the Viscount laughed and applauded. Even that dream was short-lived; she was awakened by the sound of heavy footsteps pacing the floor of her room.

Pippin sat up in bed, wide awake and furious. Udolpho, in his customary spot at her feet, grumbled wearily. He didn't care for the restless nocturnal habits that his mistress was developing.

There was no scent of patchouli this time, and Lady Philippa knew she had bolted the door. She sat listening intently, but the silence was deafening. The brightening half-light revealed no signs of an intruder.

Muttering most improper profanities, Pippin dropped back on the feather mattress, hugging her pillow in a death grip. If it wasn't for her intense curiosity about Strachan's inhabitants, both dead and alive, and for the nasty debris left in the wake of her ill-fated association with the Marquis, she would be tempted to indulge her unhappy maid and return to England, taking up her customary summer residence at Bath. But there were too many Bath-regulars with long memories and longer tongues for Lady Philippa's peace of mind, just as there were too many inexplicable events connected with the

Hanging Man for the ever-curious Lady Philippa to depart without further investigation. Lord Afton was not the least of those intriguing, possibly dangerous, mysteries.

"The devil!" said Pippin aloud and clambered out of bed. Udolpho followed her grumpily as she unbolted her door and peered down the hallway, making a hideous face at the Earl's closed door. None of the servants were in sight, though Lady Philippa had the strange impression that someone had just whisked himself away. It was very puzzling, but she had little interest in the clandestine activities of her fellow guests and dismissed the matter from her mind. There was no sign of her faithful abigail, for Nabby had not yet grown accustomed to her mistress's newly developed tendency to arise at an early hour.

Lady Philippa grimly inspected her wardrobe. She had little enthusiasm for the finer details of attire; it was her custom to trust Nabby in all matters of dress. Left to her own devices, Pippin garbed herself in whatever came first to hand, with generally unfelicitous results. This day, however, she exercised unusual care. Lord Afton would at least appreciate her appearance, even if he did think her a garrulous half-wit. She yanked her utilitarian nightdress over her head.

Katy, begrudgingly obeying Aggy's instructions, carried the breakfast tray down the hallway. She paused outside Lady Philippa's door. Katy didn't know why any of the gentry would be so early up and about, not having to deal with any of the chores that brought the working classes so prematurely out of their beds, but Aggy insisted her ladyship would want her tea. Katy had protested, it wasn't her place to carry trays upstairs, but Aggy was adamant. Quite forgetting that she hadn't knocked, Katy pushed open the door and entered the room.

Lady Philippa, caught midway through the act of dressing, paused with a chemise around her neck and stared at the interloper with surprise.

Katy, struck momentarily dumb by the sight of an almost nude female torso, froze. She seemed unable to tear her eyes away.

"Do you think you might close the door?" Lady Philippa requested pleasantly, continuing her struggle with the chemise. Katy's eyes widened.

" 'Tis the mark of the devil!" she shrieked and dropped the tray. Pippin observed the fleeing girl with astonishment, then turned to regard herself with perplexity in the mirror.

"Fiend sieze the chit!" she said, observing the half-moon birthmark that was generally hidden by various articles of clothing. "The mark of the devil, indeed!"

There seemed little point in speculating about Katy's conclusions, so Lady Philippa finished dressing, piled the wreckage onto the tray, and descended the stair, bearing the tray precariously before her. Aggy apparently meant to add flesh to her slender frame, for the old woman had provided enough food to feed Wellington's troops for an entire week.

As Lady Philippa passed the taproom, the massive door swung inward. She paused, startled, as were the Viscount and Katy, who had apparently thought their privacy assured. The girl's face was swollen with tears, and Avery's hands firmly clasped her shoulders. Pippin was unable to determine whether the harassed Viscount sought to solace or scold the girl. Murmuring an apology, she hastily made her way to the kitchen. Avery's obvious intimacy with the various females of Strachan was a curious thing, but none of her affair, except in that he meant her to serve as yet another object of his philandering. How the Viscount had progressed in the years since their last meeting! Lady Philippa thought, with combined amusement and regret.

Aggy was alone in the kitchen. She surveyed the broken dishes with disgust, shepherded Lady Philippa into the dining room, and provided her with tea.

"Allelladay," the old woman mourned. "More of the good plate broken. That girl's a cursed nuisance, m'lady."

Lady Philippa sipped her tea. "You must not blame poor Katy—I gave her a fright."

" 'Tis her condition," Aggy replied. "I've seen it before. Foolish notions."

"Her condition?" Pippin repeated. Understanding dawned. "Good grief, is she in the family way?"

"As anyone with half an eye could see," Aggy retorted. "The young fool came to me for a potion, not that I'd give her one! I canna think what her people will say."

"She's not married?"

"Och, no." Aggy's tone was vindictive. " 'Tis her own fault for not takin' Paddy when she had the chance."

Lady Philippa abandoned all attempts to understand the working of Aggy's mind. "Is Paddy responsible?" she asked bluntly, remembering the engaging boy.

"I doubt it verra much, m'lady." Aggy handled the crockery with unnecessary force.

"Then who may the culprit be?"

"I wadna know," was the reply, "though I could make a verra good guess. Give me that cup, if you please, m'lady."

Aggy observed the tealeaves dourly. "A cross," she said with glum satisfaction. " 'Tis a sign of death, not necessarily for you, but concerned with you. And a snake, a verra bad omen. You must be verra careful." She glowered at Pippin's smile. "Scandal again, a monkey. Here's a needle, something you've done will be talked about. You're in danger, m'lady. Someone's a-plotting your downfall."

"The Marchioness, no doubt." Lord Afton stood in the doorway. Aggy left them alone together, muttering blackly to herself. "I hear we had a slight contretemps already today," the Earl added. "Why is it that you seem to wreak havoc wherever you go? I'd think it would be an exhausting habit."

"It wasn't my fault," Lady Philippa protested indignantly. The Earl's lazy gaze moved over her.

"On the contrary," Severin said. To her dismay, Pippin blushed. "I believe the responsibility lies entirely with you. Indirectly, if you will."

"You go beyond the line of being pleasing," Lady Philippa retorted, taking defense behind offended dignity. "In the future, instruct your servants to knock before entering a room."

"One can't think of everything," Lord Afton replied meekly. "Brush your hair, and get a wrap, and I'll take you with me to Inverness."

Although she would have preferred to deliver the Earl a stinging rebuff, Lady Philippa was too curious about his sudden amiability. No green girl, she did not in any way believe he was smitten by a sudden desire for her company. Thus she complied with his request, affecting a change of costume in something less than record time, and allowing herself to be helped into his sporty gig. But alas for her inquisitiveness: an explanation of Lord Afton's behavior was not forthcoming.

Lady Philippa stole a sideways glance at him: The Earl was the epitome of masculine elegance, in a rich green coat, silk waistcoat, and white doeskin trousers. His boots were so highly polished that they might double as a looking glass, and the snowy pleats of his cravat contrasted sharply with his dark skin. Once, mused Pippin, she had been entirely too fond of this cold and devious man. The Earl was a formidable opponent; he had cleverly drawn her affections away from the extremely eligible Avery and for no more noble purpose than his own entertainment. Lady Philippa frowned.

If Severin chose to cross swords with her again, he would gain neither amusement nor victory.

A muscle twitched at the corner of the Earl's mouth, and Lady Philippa spoke quickly. "I must compliment you on the inn," she said. "It is a splendid place, made even more interesting by its history."

"Yes," Lord Afton replied. "As I recall, you have said something of a similar nature before—not once but several times."

Pippin sighed. "You put me all out of patience with you. Must we always quarrel? I had not meant to be provoking, but merely to engage in harmless conversation. Surely it cannot be thought wonderful if I inquire about the inn?"

"Poor child." The Earl's smile was mocking. "You are grievously ill-used. What is it you wish to know?"

"Is the inn truly haunted? Avery has been quick to assure me that it is." So much for her hope, thought Lady Philippa, that Severin meant to be conciliating!

"And you distrust the Viscount?" Lord Afton wore his saturnine look. "You should not, you know. Avery is not given to prevarication, whatever his sins. I give you my word: the inn is haunted. Why do you ask? Have you been troubled by strange dreams?"

Lady Philippa thought of the nature of her night-time visions and flushed. The Earl regarded her speculatively. "I do not suppose," she said quickly, "that you would be inclined toward a discussion of what you call 'Avery's sins'?"

"No, Lady Philippa, I would not." Severin's teeth flashed in one of his rare smiles. "Consider the impropriety!"

"You are the most disobliging man." With effort, Lady Philippa retained her composure. "Very well, I will content myself with the ghost."

"So you mean to have Avery this time, providing you can bring him to the speaking point? Wise girl! But you'd best be quick about it, lest you are doomed to the fate of spinsters, leading apes in hell." The Earl appeared amused by Lady Philippa's indignation. "What gives you the impression that we have only one ghost?"

Wistfully, Lady Philippa contemplated adding Lord Afton to the inn's cast of unlamented shades. "It has puzzled me," she murmured. "From all accounts it is Andrew Macgregor who haunts the inn, but surely he did not play the harp or wear patchouli scent."

She had captured his attention, somewhat to her surprise.

"You are a most informative young lady." Severin's lazy blue eyes rested thoughtfully on her. "I had speculated upon that matter, but you have offered proof of a sort. I fear responsibility for the matter lies with me." He sighed heavily.

Lady Philippa did not trust this remorseful tone. "Pray explain."

"I meddled with what did not concern me, and witness the dire results. You might learn a lesson from it yourself!" Lord Afton shook his head. "And to further add to my improvidence, I had been forewarned. It grows increasingly evident that Aggy has the sight."

"You are in a very teasing mood." Pippin's voice was sharp. "What is this calamity that you have brought upon yourself?"

"Our local witch was buried with all due stealth, a stake driven through her heart, and a boulder placed over her grave. I assume its weight was sufficient to keep her confined." The Earl was glib. "But I, in my abysmal ignorance, ordered the removal of the stone, thus releasing Ailcie's power."

Despite her conviction that Lord Afton engaged in one of his monstrous jests, Lady Philippa shuddered. Severin might find his ghosts a source of amusement, but she could not forget the manifestations that she had experienced. It would not do to let her astute companion sense her apprehension, however, lest he increase his efforts to send her on her way. "I am not a child," she said plaintively, "that you must regale me with fairy tales."

"My deepest apologies," retorted the Earl. "I had briefly forgotten your advanced age."

"Toad," said Pippin, with emotion.

Inverness was a region of massive mountains and long sea lochs, vast tracts of country broken only occasionally by a straggling village or a tiny town. They approached the city itself, which lay at the mouth of the clear, swift River Ness. Inverness, according to the Earl, who appeared to know it well, was surrounded on three sides by hills, and on the other by the low-lying shores of Moray Firth. Lady Philippa thought of her town house in Cavendish Square, of Carlton House and Covent Garden, Almack's and White's, and marveled at the difference.

Lord Afton's business was speedily completed, and he professed himself at his companion's disposal. Blithely, Lady

86

Philippa demanded to be shown the town, and the Earl escorted her to a museum in Castle Wynd that housed a fine collection of Jacobite relics, and showed her the structure in Bridge Street that had been occupied by Mary, Queen of Scots in 1562.

"Furthermore," added Severin, with the air of one about to impart monumental information, "that very same lady was responsible for the change in the spelling of the royal family name. Stewart was too difficult a word for her refined tongue, so it became Stuart."

"You are amazingly well-informed," Pippin responded in admiring tones, and briskly adjusted her bonnet, tossed this way and that by the wind.

Lord Afton smiled complacently and spirited her off to view the town cross, vintage 1685, into the foot of which was built the ancient Clach-na-Cudainn, the stone of the tubs, where women bringing water from the river once paused to rest. "Are you in need of refreshment?" he inquired at length.

"Please." Lady Philippa's grateful tones masked her growing suspicion of his affability. The Earl left the carriage in the charge of his groom and escorted her through the streets. The townspeople appeared prosperous, and many could speak French, English, and Gaelic with equal ease. Pippin paused, caught by a bagpipe's mournful wail.

"A begging piper," explained Lord Afton and led her into the private room of a cozy pub. "They are still occasionally heard. Once, in the old days, the piper was as important a part of a laird's retinue as was his bard. The bards were historians, they kept ancient sagas and their clan's history safe in their memories. And the pipers had tunes for every event, from toothaches to festivals."

Lady Philippa arranged herself comfortably in a chair. "And does Duncan Galbraith have a piper?" she inquired. "To serenade his family?" She wore a bright green carriage dress that deepened the shade of her eyes, York tan gloves, and half-boots, laced with green.

"Those particular sagas," replied Lord Afton wryly, "are best forgot." He paused as their beaming host brought forth a huge slab of rich and mellow Dunlop cheese. "Our Duncan, alas, is typical of the line."

Lady Philippa studied her companion and fortified herself with wine. "Severin?" she asked, "why did you not prevent me from coming to Strachan? And don't tell me again it was curiosity! You might as easily have seen me in London, had you wished. For all you do not use it, Avery assures me you still have the *entrée* everywhere."

The Earl raised an eyebrow. "Lady Philippa, you are impertinent." He picked up the knife and deftly sliced the cheese. "Did you suspect I had involved myself in some hideous disgrace? I am sorry to disappoint you, but such debacles are your *métier*, not mine. But since you have made so bold as to inquire, I will tell you that I have little liking for town life, and consequently am not often in London."

Lady Philippa eyed the knife, lamentably out of her reach. "You prefer Strachan?"

"Consider the life of a man of fashion." Lord Afton's expression was one of distaste. "He passes his time in matters of dress, he consults with his tailor and his bootmaker, he spends hours in the tying of his cravat. When these weighty affairs are satisfactorily resolved, he exhibits himself in White's bay window, at Tattersall's, on Hyde Park Corner, in the fencing rooms in St. James's Street, or Gentleman Jackson's boxing saloon. Such fripperies may appeal to Avery; I find such an existence unbearably dull."

"You forgot to mention the gaming-hells." Lady Philippa was stung. Born into the enviable existence of the select few, she interpreted Lord Afton's remarks as deliberate provocation, despite an inclination to agree with him.

"Are you consigning me to a sponging house in Chancery Lane?" The Earl was amused. "I am not devoted to the board of green cloth. Nor am I content to idle away my time with Prinny at Carlton House, or avoiding matchmaking mamas and their insipid offspring at Almack's."

Pippin stared at her companion, startled. His lineage was impeccable and his wealth considerable, but she had never thought of Lord Afton as prey for fortune-hunting damsels. Perhaps his perverse disposition was not evident on slight acquaintance. Surely even the most rapacious of females would think twice before condemning her offspring to so sad a fate as must be that of Lord Afton's lady. "You have not answered my question," she said stubbornly.

"Nor do I mean to."

Lady Philippa glanced at the Earl's half-smile, then quickly away. She recalled a particularly flamboyant lady who had once lived under his protection, and who had doubtless been followed by an equally dazzling procession of high-flyers. But such thoughts were highly improper and oddly deflating outside.

"How odd!" she gasped, turning from the window to meet the Earl's quizzical gaze. "I swear I saw Andrew Macgregor pass by. Could he possibly have followed us here?"

"Your imagination grows overheated." Lord Afton's tone was cold. "It is the least felicitous characteristic of your sex." His face again wore its usual shuttered expression, and Lady Philippa made no demur as he guided her into the street.

"Then you don't believe he was following us?" she demanded.

"Don't be absurd," Severin retorted, handing her up into the gig. "Why should he do anything of the sort? I seriously doubt that it was even our Macgregor that you saw."

There was, in light of his lordship's damnable taciturnity, little point in argument. Nor was there opportunity. Lord Afton took the reins and whipped his horses to such a frantic pace that they swept out of the town as if the hounds of hell were in hot pursuit. Lady Philippa reflected that Lord Afton's methods of ending unwelcome conversation were as effective as they were unique.

"Severin!" she cried, clutching her bonnet to her head. "Have done with this! Or do you mean to kill us both, and your horses besides?"

The Earl obligingly slowed his steeds to a more decorous pace. Pippin inspected herself for bruises and broken bones. "Let us cry friends," she said. After all, one caught more flies with honey than with vinegar. "I concede that I am an unprincipled creature, entirely too inquisitive, and I crave your pardon. You see me chastened."

Lord Afton treated her to his charming smile, but it was offset by the watchful look in his blue eyes. "You appear the most complete romp." Lady Philippa took this as acceptance of her apology and docilely allowed him to straighten her bonnet. But any hopes of further cooperation was speedily abandoned; the Earl launched into an edifying dissertation on Inverness-shire. Lady Philippa's attention wandered during a particularly sonorous oration concerning mountain climbing, barley, turnips, and wheat. She didn't rouse until their arrival at the inn when, with a muttered oath, she sat erect and righted her bonnet. Lord Afton met her suspicious glance impassively, and removed his arm from around her shoulder.

"You have the distinction," he said, as he helped her to alight, "of being the only lady ever to fall asleep in the midst of my stimulating conversation."

Lady Philippa made an extremely rude noise. "What do

you expect?" she snapped. "When you talk so soothingly of sheep and cows? I'm not quite as goosish as you think, Severin. Why did you take me along today?"

"I suspect you attribute to me motives of the most ignoble." The Earl placed one hand beneath her chin and read the accuracy of his thrust in her expressive little face. He smiled gently. "I must disappoint you, my dear! I was inspired by nothing more exceptionable than an earnest wish to prevent you from tumbling into further mischief while I was away."

A worthy opponent indeed, mused Lady Philippa, as she resolutely refused to remember how comfortably she had slept against her enemy's chest.

Twelve

Still stunned, and more than a little confused by her traitorous emotions, Lady Philippa made her way slowly down the inn's hallway. It was what Lord Afton intended, of course, to engage her heart once more and thus decoy her away from the Viscount. Pippin's lips twisted ruefully. Was she of so scandalous a reputation, then, that Avery must be saved from her at any cost? Severin, at least, thought so. It did not occur to Lady Philippa, still suffering from her encounters with the irate Marchioness, that her reputation was not sufficiently tarnished that she would be considered ineligible for marriage with any lord in the land; or that even had her name been actually dragged through the mud, her vast fortune would have more than atoned for it. Instead, she pondered the enigma that walked beside her and vowed that the fifth Earl of Afton, no matter how mightily he contrived, would not prevent her from doing exactly as she pleased.

Lord Afton guided her to the taproom, filled with its usual customers plus the large and leonine man who appeared to be Miss Graham's exclusive property. Lady Philippa's startled gaze rested upon Aggy, behind the bar. The old woman didn't seem enthused by this task, and beckoned to the Earl wrathfully. Pippin hung back, eying the visitors, among whom were Valentine Alversane, now clinging possessively to the Earl's arm, and Lady Cassandra, staring somberly into empty space.

"My dear!" cried Lady Cassandra, glimpsing her. "When you have a moment, I particularly wish to speak with you." Lady Philippa nodded and smiled, and the laird sighed. His wife had not abandoned the notion that Lady Philippa would do nicely for Bevis, and Lady Cassandra's interest played havoc with his own plans.

The Viscount moved to stand behind Pippin, his breath warm on her cheek. "Severin's behavior is abominable!" he murmured, wounded. "I had hoped to have you to myself today, but he very neatly spiked my guns."

Lady Philippa swung around and smiled. "Never mind," she soothed. "We shall resume our flirtation at another time. I daresay you can find other things with which to amuse yourself." If not Valentine then Katy, the impudent scamp!

With no sign of a guilty conscience, Avery touched the bruise on his cheek. "You misjudge me." His tone was unusually sincere. "My object is not a fliratation with you." Lady Philippa glanced at him with surprise. "I fear, my darling, that you have misread my character! But I must enlighten you at some other time." He favored her with a bow so exquisite it would have done credit to Brummell himself, then strode from the room.

Lady Philippa frowned unseeing at the fireplace. Were the encounters she had witnessed not what they had seemed? Avery had made it clear that his intention was not dalliance. This startling revelation did little to ease the confusion that raged through Lady Philippa's mind. In hope of finding a reprieve from her warring emotions, Pippin slipped away to her room.

Sanctuary it may have been, but it was no more. Her belongings were strewn about in wild disarray, and the outline of her next book, complete with copious notes on Ailcie Ferguson and William Macgregor, were missing from their accustomed place. Lady Philippa flew down the stairs and burst into the taproom, attracting the surprised attention of everyone there.

"My room," announced Pippin, fixing Lord Afton with a belligerent eye, "has been turned upside down." So this was why he had lured her away from the inn, so that his henchmen might rummage through her possessions!

"Lady Philippa!" said Cassandra, with an animation that verged on ghoulishness. "Was anything taken!"

"Yes!" retorted Pippin, then could have bit out her tongue. How could she explain what had been stolen without announcing her secret to the world?

"I, too, have been robbed," offered Lady Cassandra, "and of my Tarot cards! Can it be the same culprit, do you think?"

"Pippin," interrupted the Earl, in kindly tones, "if you can bring yourself to tell us what is missing, I'll set inquiries afoot, and see if we can have the items returned."

"Papers," said Lady Philippa, somewhat ungraciously. "Just papers, nothing more." And that, she thought belatedly, was damned queer. What kind of thief would take a rudimentary manuscript and leave behind the jewel box that sat out in plain view?

"Valuable papers?" prodded Lady Cassandra, bright-eyed.

"No," said Pippin, and accepted a glass of brandy from her abigail, engaged in washing glasses behind the bar. "They were of no value whatsoever to anyone but me."

"What were they?" whispered Nabby, who had no idea that her mistress was the prolific Mrs. Watson-Wentworth. "Coo! What a horrid thing."

Lady Philippa regarded her abigail thoughtfully. "Tell me, Nabby, when is the last time you were in my room?"

"Not since this morning, my lady." Nabby grimaced at her reddened hands. "And you can blame Aggy for it! She's been working me like a slavey all afternoon." She pushed the hair off her forehead, leaving soapsuds in her curls. "Lady Philippa! You don't think *I* . . ."

"Of course not!" Pippin frowned. "Don't be daft, Nabby. You and Barnabas are the last people I'd accuse."

Valentine, who had been induced by Lady Cassandra's frown to release her grip on Lord Afton's arm, laughed merrily. "But don't you see what this means? How famous! Now we have further evidence of the ghost!"

"Ghost!" jeered Duncan Galbraith, with a unfriendly glance at his sister-in-law. "It's bound to be one of the servants, you know. Have them in and we'll put the question to them, one by one!"

Aggy stepped out from behind the bar, hands on her hips, and glared at the assorted company. "And that ye will not!" she cried. "As if I hadna trouble enough already gettin' anyone to stay. 'Tis honest enough the servants are, and ye can take my word that not a one of them would dare ransack Lady Philippa's room." She looked rather like a game little fighting hen. "And none but Katy had cause to be abovestairs."

Lady Philippa looked around the room. "Where is Katy?" she asked. "Hasn't she returned?" But why would the girl steal her notes? Lady Philippa doubted Katy could even read.

Valentine wore an arrested expression. "Return? Why did she leave?"

"We had a slight misunderstanding this morning," Lord Afton interceded smoothly. Lady Philippa noted that he had, with tardy prudence, moved as far away as possible from Valentine. "The girl's behavior grows progressively worse."

"You'd better turn her off and engage someone else," the laird suggested reasonably. "Damned if it's not hard to get good help these days!" Lady Cassandra sighed, wondering how she was to secure Lady Philippa for her younger brother when Bevis so steadfastly refused to be seen.

"I fear I shall have to do precisely that," replied the Earl, in tones that effectively forestalled further advice.

Lady Philippa moved closer to Ailcie's portrait, and subjected it to a harsh scrutiny. In the background of the painting stood a harp, the same instrument that now graced the taproom. Pippin wondered if Lord Afton counted among his abilities a musical talent.

"More trouble," said Gilly glumly to Lucius. "I tried to warn her."

"Of what, acushla?" Lucius growled, biting down on his pipe. "You worry yourself needlessly. The papers have doubtless just been misplaced."

"Not that." Gilly glanced over her shoulder and lowered her voice. "It's all over the village. Lady Philippa has a birthmark on her—her ladyship has a birthmark. Katy saw it and now everyone's convinced that Lady Philippa has a devil's mark."

Lucius gazed speculatively at the red-haired woman who caused Gilly such unease. "I must confess to a burning curiosity about the exact location of this interesting blemish." Gilly sighed.

Aggy leaned against the bar and longed for the comfort of her narrow bed. The day had been long and exhausting, as she had done the work of two. Nor were the day's trials over: Katy's mother, accompanied by Andrew Macgregor, invaded the taproom.

The old man looked about him and was aghast at what he saw. "Geilleis!" Gilly shrank back into her chair as if seeking shelter from the blast of his rage. "Is it to cavort with foreigners and idolaters that you absent yourself from church? Have you forgotten that you are cursed with tainted blood?"

"That," announced Lucius, rapidly coming to understand

94

Gilly's fixation, "is quite enough, old man!" He stood up, towering above everyone else in the room.

"It is, rather," agreed Lord Afton and casually flicked open his snuff-box. "Do you think we might be told the purpose for this visit? I hardly think it prompted by concern for our immortal souls."

The minister said nothing, literally choking with rage. This superior nobleman was solely responsible for the villagers' unrest, and Andrew Macgregor, though soothed by the conviction that the Earl must eventually fry in hell, found that day much too slow in coming. "Blasphemy!" he cried.

The Earl lifted a pinch of snuff to one arched nostril. "I am still," he murmured, "awaiting enlightenment."

But Katy's mother had no time to waste in verbal parrying, and furthermore, was of a disposition that immediately recognized, and bowed to, authority. "Oh, sir!" she cried, and Andrew Macgregor wondered with disgust if she meant to fling herself at Lord Afton's feet. "It's my Katy, sir, she's gone missing, and I'm that worried! I don't know what to think." And then she burst into noisy tears.

Missing? mused Lady Philippa, but said nothing, being more interested in studying Andrew Macgregor. Perhaps it was not he whom she had glimpsed earlier in Inverness, but to that man Andrew Macgregor certainly bore a startling resemblance.

"I imagine," drawled Valentine, displeased at being so effectively upstaged, "that you'll find the girl has stopped along the way to pass the time with one or another of her friends." Though her words were innocent enough, Valentine's tone was not, and provoked visions of giggling tussles in hay-filled byres. Lady Philippa recalled the encounter she had interrupted between Katy and the Viscount and frowned. Was Avery even at that moment with the missing girl?

"My Katy is a good, decent lass!" wailed Katy's mother. "And I'll thank you to remember it! Never before has she missed her evening meal." She wiped her nose on her apron. "Something terrible has happened, I feel it in my bones!"

"'Tis likely rheumatism," muttered Aggy sourly, drawing from Lady Philippa an amused glance. The laird, convinced that Katy had rebuffed his advances only to encourage someone else, drained his glass and wished that he'd stayed at the castle with Bevis and Neville.

"Enough!" said Andrew Macgregor angrily. "We know

Katy is still here. You will release her to us this instant or pay the cost!"

The old man obviously believed that the Earl held Katy prisoner for some vile, iniquitous purpose. It was too much for Pippin. "You absurd creature!" she said, half-choked with laughter. *"What* do you think Severin's done with her?"

Andrew Macgregor swung on her, with less than admiring regard. The shocking reputation that Lady Philippa was coming to heartily regret had preceded her to Strachan, and the resultant gossip had not escaped the minister's ear. Already Lady Philippa had proven a disruptive influence on the villagers. The younger men discussed her in furtive whispers, and Andrew had it on good authority that Paddy Maclean had so far forgotten himself as to engage in intimate conversation with her. Even small Sandy had fallen under her spell.

"I suggest," said Lord Afton, with an unappreciative glance at Lady Philippa's amused countenance, "that you conduct your inquiries elsewhere. No one here is inclined toward the abduction and imprisonment of foolish young females, particularly those who are obviously increasing."

Katy's mother gaped at this unexpected information, and the minister, prepared to denounce the lot of them in thunderous tones, paused open-mouthed. "Such a good girl!" mocked Valentine. "It's exactly as I thought."

" 'Tis true enough," Aggy said with melancholy pleasure. She'd have no part of these foolish accusations and was ready to swear that the master had never glanced in Katy's direction. Why should he, indeed? The Earl wasn't the sort of gentleman to take an interest in a simple country girl. "Katy hasna set foot in the inn since she flew out of here this mornin', and she needna bother to do so again! You may tell young Katy for me that her foolishness has cost her a place."

Katy's mother broke into renewed wails, and Aggy scowled. " 'Tis you that are responsible!" Andrew Macgregor cried, pointing an accusing finger at Lady Philippa, who blinked at him in surprise. "With your wicked ways you've frightened the lass out of her wits!"

Nabby made an irate noise and moved from behind the bar to stand protectively at her mistress's side. *"What* wits, old man?" she cried. Lady Philippa touched her arm, and Nabby closed her mouth on further speech.

Udolpho, disturbed by the noise, stretched and moved from his comfortable spot in front of the fire. He sat on Lady Philippa's foot and treated the minister to an appraising glare from his great orange eyes. Andrew Macgregor recalled what he knew of familiars, creatures dispatched by their mistresses on missions of evil and malice, and fell back a step.

" 'Tis deluded ye are, man," said Aggy. "Lady Philippa and Lord Afton have been gone from here all the day, and I myself saw your foolish Katy after they left." Her efforts earned her the minister's baleful glare.

"The heathens have you bewitched!" he proclaimed. Katy's mother shrieked and began to babble incoherently about spells and the effect of the evil eye.

"Hut!" Aggy commented contemptuously. "Ye've windmills in your head."

Udolpho, increasingly intrigued by all this strange to-do, rose and moved toward the minister. Andrew Macgregor, observing the approaching patchwork apparition with acute apprehension, stepped backward. Udolpho, delighted to find someone inclined to play, growled and leaped stiff-legged into the air. The old man also jumped and collided with a table. His mission forgotten and his dignity in shreds, Andrew Macgregor fled.

Thirteen

Lady Philippa was dressed all in black, and the hood of her cloak covered her shining hair. As she silently moved through the dark streets, she smiled to herself. Lord Afton would have several sorts of fits if he knew her current enterprise. The Earl had berated her soundly for laughing at Andrew Macgregor's discomfiture; doubtless he'd succumb to an apoplexy when he learned she had burgled the old man's church.

A dim light indicated that the minister was not yet abed, inspiring Lady Philippa with thoughts distinctly unsuited to such hallowed ground. But her ladyship was not one to be so easily deterred. She crept closer to the ancient building and risked a glance inside. The first article she spied was Lady Cassandra's missing deck of Tarot cards.

Andrew Macgregor held the cards gingerly, as if he feared contamination. Creations of the devil they were, he thought, with their gaudy colors and strange designs, and probably used for divination. How dare Lady Cassandra seek to know the future! He remembered her vague, unfocused stare. Mad! thought Andrew Macgregor. Mad—or possessed.

He dropped the cards, which attracted him in an unsettling way. Surely it was sinful of him to wish to know more of their meaning? Three cards lay before them, and he frowned at them, trying to penetrate their mystery. The cards bore legends: The Hanged Man, The Devil, The Magician. The minister selected another from the pile: Death. Katy was responsible for his possession of these pagan artifacts. He regretted her foolishness. Katy had been a useful tool.

Lady Philippa risked another glance through the window. She had amassed various useful, and unusual, talents during her twenty-odd years, and one of these was the opening of simple locks. If Andrew Macgregor was in possession of Lady Cassandra's cards, then perhaps he also knew the whereabouts of the missing notes and outline. Lady Philippa did not think he'd find her version of Ailcie's tale pleasant reading, biased as it was in the woman's favor. She suppressed a sigh and waited impatiently for the old man to tire of his investigations and go home, so she might enter the church in search of the old records. The air was cold; she hoped he would go soon.

There was the awful possibility that the minister might remain through the night. Lady Philippa doubted that his evangelical fervor would allow him to sleep in the church, though she knew nothing of his habits. Reckless as she was, Pippin lacked the audacity needed to attempt unlicensed entry in the presence of an antagonistic and suspicious man. In some instances she might have attempted such a feat, but not when the man was this one.

Andrew Macgregor shook his head, puzzling over the cars, then set them aside and pulled toward him a sheaf of papers. Lady Philippa ground her teeth with frustration as she recognized her manuscript. Her anger changed quickly to amusement as the old man's face became suffused with color, his expression horrified. But then he grasped the pages in his surprisingly strong hands and ripped them to pieces. Lady Philippa barely suppressed a cry of sheer rage. The minister blew out his candle and moved toward the door and she ducked into a bush, finding too late that it was liberally festooned with thorns.

When the old man's retreating footsteps had faded into the distance, Lady Philippa carefully disengaged herself from the thorns and looked around. It would not do to wait so long to avoid Andrew Macgregor, only to be observed by some villager's curious eyes. The cottages were dark, and no one was in view. Pippin set to work on the church's simple lock and in no time was inside.

The room held few hiding places. Lady Philippa made her way to the pulpit, hoping the minister didn't keep the records in his home. Unless the bare walls and simple seats held some fiendishly clever secret spaces, this was the most likely spot.

The pulpit at first offered no clue, though Lady Philippa didn't search as closely as she might have done. Night noises, and the fear of the minister's return, kept her nerves on edge. She saw the Tarot cards resting where Andrew Macgregor had left them, with her abused manuscript. With a smile for the minister's probable reaction to their disappearance, she slipped the stolen articles into the bodice of her serviceable dark dress. Her candlestick thudded against the rostrum.

Lady Philippa froze, anticipating instant discovery, then almost wailed aloud as her candle flickered and went out. It would be no fault of hers if she emerged from this enterprise unscathed!

No one came to investigate the noises that to Lady Philippa sounded as if they must waken the entire village, and she drew a breath of relief. The pulpit had a curiously hollow sound; she bent to investigate.

Undeterred by the lack of light, Pippin fumbled with the lectern. It was hollow; the entire back swung open as her fingers encountered some hidden spring.

Lady Philippa cursed the clumsiness that had left her without light. Her hands moved over several large volumes, some loose papers, then grasped a small book tucked away at the very back of the recess. She closed the panel. If a man of God could stoop to thievery, so could Lady Philippa Harte! If this book proved dull reading, she would return another time.

Pippin slipped out of the church, making sure the door locked behind her. It would be prudent to leave no trace of her midnight excursion. The sound of footsteps grew close and Lady Philippa ran, knocking over a large heavy object in her flight.

"Who goes there!" demanded Andrew Macgregor, sounding more than capable of dealing, single-handed, with all the countless demons of hell.

"Calm yourself, Macgregor," came a deep and unemotional male voice. "Surely you are aware of my addiction to late night strolls."

Lady Philippa peered from her hiding place behind a convenient bush. This tall, slender Englishman who stood mere paces from her could only be the mysterious Bevis Alversane. He had surely seen her; would he give her away? Pippin listened, taut as a violin string, as Andrew Macgregor muttered that he wished to retrieve an article left in the church.

"What a pity," said the stranger. "It must be important indeed to bring you from your bed at so unreasonable an hour. Allow me to assit you." He waited politely by the church door.

The minister was in a quandary. He remembered the items left so conspicuously on the pulpit, and knew that this man must not be allowed to glimpse them. "It will wait till the morning," the old man retorted ungraciously, and trudged toward his home. Bevis Alversane followed him.

Lady Philippa crouched motionless, afraid to breathe. Surely there was no place such as Strachan for those who walked abroad in the dead of night! She listened to the retreating footsteps, then cautiously rose. The careless placement of a foot caused a twig to snap, and she froze. She'd made enough noise during this endeavor to awaken the dead.

It seemed, for one horrified second, that she had accomplished that very feat, for a strong arm grasped her shoulders and a hand was clamped over her mouth. Lady Philippa was dragged further back among the concealing shrubbery.

"Hist!" came an amused whisper, as she struggled to free herself. "I've no wish to manhandle you, my darling; only promise me that you won't scream." In an excess of relief, Lady Philippa collapsed against the Viscount's chest.

"Avery!" she murmured weakly. "How dare you treat me so roughly? You frightened me half to death!"

The Viscount was not inclined to release her, and smoothed her tumbled curls. "Little pea-goose," said he. "You are as pale as death. Were you trembling lest the Macgregor discover you?"

"You will admit it to be a quelling prospect." Lady Philippa found herself enjoying the half-forgotten sensation of being enfolded in a gentleman's arms.

"I will admit," retorted the Viscount, "that this is dashed irregular. What havey-cavey dealings are you now involved in, my girl?"

Pippin drew away. "I might ask the same of you." Avery was as impeccably attired as if engaged in pursuits no more exceptionable than a stroll down St. James's Street, but an air of suppressed excitement hung about him. "You are big with news."

"What a confoundedly curious wench it is," the Viscount remarked. "Let us call a truce! I will leave you your secrets if you will refrain from prying into mine."

"Agreed." Reluctantly, Lady Philippa gave her word. She would have given much to know how Avery had spent his evening, and the precise nature of the relationship between

102

her friend and the missing Katy. *Was* Katy still missing? she wondered. Avery placed a finger beneath her chin.

"You are a vixen," he said, "and your madcap conduct would drive a more prudent man to despair." Lady Philippa sighed, sure that now Avery meant to lecture her on her reckless conduct. "But you have quite stolen my heart away, and I find that less unconventional ladies now bore me excessively." He smiled at her bewilderment. "Tell me, do you think you might consider my suit?"

"Avery!" Pippin's voice was faint. "Are you making me a declaration?"

"I am trying to do so," the Viscount retorted. "Is the thought of marriage so repugnant to you?"

"Marriage?" repeated Lady Philippa, who'd suspected that Avery might have a liaison less acceptable in mind, an understandable enough assumption considering his recent conduct. She thought of Katy and Valentine. "Repugnant, no. I am truly sensible of the honor you pay me."

"Rot!" interrupted the Viscount, and Lady Philippa found herself being ruthlessly kissed. Her thoughts were in such turmoil that she offered no resistance.

"I am not," remarked the Viscount as he released her, "to be cast into despair, then." His tone was one of satisfaction. "You are not indifferent to me—a promising omen!" Words eluded Lady Philippa, and Avery drew her arm through his. "Come. I will escort you back to the inn."

Fourteen

Safely in her own room, Lady Philippa bolted the door and wearily pulled off her dark costume. Udolpho, curled up in the green chair, was studiously aloof. Pippin cast an eye upon the tail that was afflicted by slight irritable twitches and concluded that the cat resented his exclusion from her nocturnal expedition, numbered high among his favorite things. She retrieved the Tarot deck and mutilated manuscript and tossed them carelessly into a drawer. The small book received more deferential treatment: it accompanied her to bed.

Lady Philippa opened the volume and stared in dismay. It was written in an almost illegible hand. Enlightenment would have to wait; Pippin was too tired to make the necessary effort. She shoved the book under her mattress, snuffed the candle, resolutely put all thought of the evening's unexpected proceedings from her mind, and was instantly asleep.

Another night's rest was doomed to be disturbed. When awakened again by the sound of footsteps, Lady Philippa groaned and pulled the pillow over her head. That gesture did not suffice; a clammy hand brushed her shoulder. Pippin sat up abruptly and peered into the darkness. Her mouth dropped open at the sight that confronted her.

Illuminated by the dying fire, a scowling man stood by her bed. He was dressed in long-outdated clothes, a noose dangled from his furrowed neck, fanatic eyes burned in his emaciated face.

Strangely, Lady Philippa felt no fear. "Avery!" she snapped. "You go too far!" And then she realized that this man was both taller and less muscular than the Viscount.

If a joke this was, it was a macabre one. The apparition's mouth fell open and it gibbered dreadfully; saliva dribbled down its chin. Lady Philippa swallowed hard. One thin finger raised to point at her.

"What do you want?" she asked weakly.

The wraith made beckoning motions.

"To the devil with this!" cried Pippin, as she leaped out of bed and raced down the hallway to Lord Afton's room. He was fast asleep, buried beneath his bedclothes. She shook him violently. The Earl opened one eye.

"I hope you've a very good reason," he murmured wrathfully, "for this untimely intrusion." Lady Philippa's speech was impeded by the chattering of her teeth. Lord Afton sat up and reached for a candle.

"My good girl, what is the matter with you? You look as though you'd seen a—Aha! Comprehension looms. Sit down over there and avert your maidenly gaze while I clothe myself. Which poses a problem: just what is the prescribed attire for comforting a female besieged by ghosts?"

Pippin huddled in a chair, listening to the oddly soothing sound of Severin's voice uttering inanities. He held out a glass. "Drink," he ordered. She did so and shuddered.

"Now," demanded the Earl, wrapping himself in a magnificent dressing gown, "tell me precisely what has stricken you with such terror? I assume that you've been visited by my tame apparition?"

Lady Philippa hugged herself. "I thought at first it was Avery," she said, "set on frightening me." Severin quirked a brow and earned her wrath. "How can you remain so calm? Someone is masquerading as a dead man—and in your house!"

"Are you sure," inquired Lord Afton, "that it *is* a masquerade? I'll confess that I haven't given much thought to the matter. Consider the profit I stand to make on this enterprise with old William intact."

"Profit?" Lady Philippa looked at him blankly. Surely the Earl could not believe that she had truly seen a ghost! But Avery could not have been the specter, and Severin, as she herself had seen, had been sound asleep in his bed.

"Never mind." Deftly, Lord Afton built up the fire. "Tell me exactly what drove you to invade my chaste bedchamber at so improper an hour."

"You won't believe me." Why should he? Lady Philippa could barely believe it herself.

106

The Earl studied her practical nightwear sardonically. The muslin peignoir and petticoat might have been made of the rudest burlap. "My dear child," he remarked, "I can only think of two reasons for your presence here, and your attire is an excellent argument against the first."

What was the man talking about? Lady Philippa stared.

"Your wits seem to have deserted you," Lord Afton observed. "Even so, I cannot imagine you attempting a seduction while covered from chin to toe in voluminous draperies." Lady Philippa, who had never in her life attempted anything of the sort, flushed. "This avails us nothing!" remarked the Earl. "Tell me what you saw."

Pippin, reduced to the status of a recalcitrant child, obeyed. Severin's haughty face wore an expression of extreme interest. "You've made yet another conquest, it seems," he said.

"Wretch! How can you jest about it?"

"I do wish you'd rid yourself of the notion that I am perpetually in jest," Lord Afton commented plaintively. "I was entirely serious. I suspect that William was trying to convey some information, and I propose to discover what that information was."

"Why *me?*" Prompted solely by a desire for companionship, Lady Philippa trailed him down the hallway.

"You are not the first to ask that question." Lord Afton opened the door to her room. "Although I cannot applaud William's estimation of your intelligence."

Pippin wrinkled her nose, wrapped herself in a concealing cloak, and dropped into the green chair. Now that the Earl was involved, the experience was taking on an air of adventure. "Fraud!" she remarked scornfully to Udolpho, who opened an inquiring eye. "Cats are supposed to be extremely sensitive to things supernatural, or so I've always read." Udolpho blinked. "They're supposed to yowl and run furiously from the room when a ghost comes to call. And their fur is said to stand on end." But Udolpho merely yawned and resumed his interrupted slumbers.

The Earl put out the light. "William may be shy," he explained. "While we wait, you might tell me where you were earlier."

"I went for a walk," Lady Philippa replied irritably. She might have known Lord Afton would notice her absence, no matter how absorbed he might be with his own affairs.

"Apparently you didn't hear me state my conviction that it

107

would be extreme folly for you to venture unescorted beyond the inn."

"You have no right to dictate to me," Lady Philippa retorted, grateful for the dark.

"No." There was a faint hint of amusement in his voice. "A fact for which I hope you are properly grateful. I should probably beat you at least once a day." Pippin was sure that he smiled. " 'If a woman's eyes are green, whip her with a switch that's keen.' You behold in me the results of Lady Cassandra's influence." His voice took on a sterner tone. "But as long as you are here, you will abide by my advice."

"And if I choose to disregard you?"

"Then I shall be sad to see you leave." Severin's tone suggested that further argument would be mere wasted effort. Pippin sighed.

"No one saw me," she meekly lied. Having saved her from the minister, Bevis Alversane would hardly betray her to Lord Afton. And the Viscount obviously had his own reasons to keep their encounter a secret.

"I wish I might be sure of that. Did you discover what you sought? I admire your enterprise, but I feel I should inform you that breaking into locked buildings borders on the lawless."

The Earl, at times, was uncannily omniscient. "I found the Tarot cards and my missing papers." Pippin offered, hoping he wouldn't press her for further detail. "They were on the pulpit." She chuckled. "I'd give anything to see old Macgregor's face when he discovers that they've disappeared."

"Idiot!" said Severin.

Further conversation was inhibited by the apparition's reappearance. He was vague in the darkness, his hideous features obscured, but the urgency of his beckoning gestures was unmistakable. Despite the Earl's strongly masculine presence, Lady Philippa experienced a reawakening of unease. She clutched at Severin's arm, and he clasped her hand reassuringly. The ghost suddenly vanished into what appeared a solid wall.

"What are you doing?" Lady Philippa inquired irritably as Lord Afton pressed his hands to the wood. Ignoring her, the Earl continued his explorations. Pippin heard a slight noise, such as might be made by the manipulating of a spring, and a section of the wall slid noiselessly aside. "Severin! A secret passage?"

Lord Afton fastidiously wiped his fingers on an immaculate

handkerchief. "This structure is honeycombed with them." He peered into the opening. "I confess I did not know of this one, but it does not surprise me to discover a hidden access to Ailcie's room." His dark features twisted into a smile. "Witch she may or may not have been, but her fondness for gentlemen is not in dispute."

Lady Philippa moved to stand beside him. A narrow staircase wound downward, between the walls, into darkness. "Where does it go?"

"I have just told you that I do not know." The Earl lit his candle and lifted it high. "But I intend to discover precisely that, as William Macgregor doubtless intends that we should." He regarded her. "Perhaps you would prefer to remain here. This is not a ladylike pursuit."

"Nonsense!" retorted Pippin, stung. "I would not miss this for the world."

Severin smiled, an act which caused his companion to experience a queer wrench somewhere in the vicinity of her heart. "Very well." He stepped into the opening. "William! We await your guidance." Pippin pinched him.

"This is no time for levity," she hissed, and promptly tripped on the top stair. The Earl caught her before she fell, then preceded her down the steps. Lady Philippa reflected that Severin St. George, despite his abominable temperament, was a fascinatingly contradictory gentleman. He was on whim exquisitely polite or appallingly rude, a gentleman or a barbarian; he was heartless, but with a curious sensibility, and capable of inspiring either deep friendship or violent enmity. An enigma, decided Pippin, and a most provoking one.

The vision flickered before them, at times visible, at times not. They stumbled through the tunnel and Lord Afton uttered a blasphemous oath as his elbow encountered a wall. At length they found themselves in the cellars. Lady Philippa glimpsed a bricked-up doorway that might have once been a tunnel entrance, but the damp and stifling atmosphere of the place squelched any desire to explore. The Earl paused to point out a tiny aperture, the mouth of a speaking tube once chiseled out of the rock and connected with the castle above, then they stepped out into the fresh air of the small garden behind the inn.

"William seems to have deserted us," Lady Philippa said, hopping from one bare foot to the other. The ground was pebbled with small sharp stones.

"Alas, poor ghost!" murmured the Earl absently. "I believe

there's an old storage room in the immediate vicinity. Yes, my amazing intellect has proven itself once again." He pointed. "Behold!"

Pippin observed a small and ancient doorway set into a mound. Her teeth were chattering again, this time from cold. "You'll never get it open," she stuttered. "It's warped."

"Strive for a little more faith!" Severin put his shoulder to the door, which opened with surprising ease. "You see?"

Lady Philippa put one icy foot on top of the other and hugged herself tightly. Her unease was growing apace with the Earl's enjoyment of the escapade. "Can we postpone this until the morn?" she asked. "I'm about to take my death of cold."

Lord Afton withdrew his head from the opening. "I think not," he said quietly. "Why don't you go back?"

Lady Philippa's suspicions were instantly aroused. "What is it, Severin? What did you find?"

He had turned away from her and stepped inside the shed. "Katy."

"Katy? Is she hurt?" Pippin hurried to the small door.

The Earl's voice was muffled. "She's dead. You'd be well-advised to look the other way."

Lady Philippa was wise enough to obey, but she wasn't quick enough to miss glimpsing the little barmaid's battered head. She gulped and Lord Afton set down his burden to grasp her shoulders.

"I am not going to succumb to the vapors," Lady Philippa announced stiffly.

"Of course you're not," the Earl agreed. "You're going to return to your room and wait for me." Their voices were mere whispers, barely audible.

"What are you going to do?"

"I'm going to tamper with the, uh, evidence."

"Severin!"

He shook her. "Use your head! What do you think will happen if she's found here?"

Lady Philippa envisioned several unpleasant possibilities. "Severin," she said faintly, "it wasn't an accident?"

"I'm afraid not." His tone was somber. "Murder most foul, as in the best it is." He bent and dropped a light kiss on her ladyship's lips. "Go on, now. To your room."

Fifteen

Lady Philippa opened one eye cautiously. She suffered a moment's confusion as to why she was sitting, cramped, in the green chair. Then the events of the night assailed her wakening memory and she groaned. She had fallen asleep while awaiting Lord Afton's return.

Udolpho, sole occupant of the bed, yawned and stretched luxuriously. Only the tip of his magnificent tail protruded from beneath the covers. It was sheer ecstasy indeed to have slept alone; his mistress had lately developed an unsettling tendency to toss and turn. However, much as he deplored her new habits, Udolpho's devotion remained steadfast. He emerged from his burrow, dropped heavily to the floor, then settled himself in Pippin's lap.

Her ladyship sat quietly, ignoring her aching muscles and absently scratching Udolpho's chin. The cat purred and kneaded her leg. His sharp claws pricked her flesh, but Lady Philippa was oblivious. She was busy with thoughts of the previous night.

Those events seemed incredible when reviewed in the lucid light of day. Pippin wondered why the morning's small hours lent themselves so well to things fanciful and macabre. Carried away by imagination and local history, she had evoked a ghost, and Lord Afton, with an unprecedented abandonment of his habitual languor, had so far bestirred himself as to indulge in a treasure hunt with the specter as guide. It was a scene so improbable as to boggle the imagination. If not for the discovery of the body, Pippin would have suspected herself of dreaming the whole thing.

No nightmare, however, could call forth the ghastly terror of that graphic memory. Lady Philippa forced away an image of Katy's pallid, shattered face, and wondered who could be responsible for such an atrocious act. At least Katy wouldn't have to suffer the results of her foolishness! Pippin frowned. She knew little of murder and couldn't imagine why anyone would destroy so timid a creature as Katy, a threat to no one unless by her pregnancy. It was difficult to envision the timid girl as inspiration for the more violent forms of either love or hate.

But the Viscount's behavior suggested otherwise. Lady Philippa could not explain away the encounter that she'd seen, for it had left her with a strong impression of intimacy. She wondered if anyone but herself knew Avery and Katy had been on more than casual terms. If so, the Viscount was in the devil of a fix!

Nor could Lady Philippa rid herself of the suspicion that Avery was entangled up to his neck in the night's proceedings. All London would be a-twitter with scandalized speculation if the Viscount had to stand his trial for murder.

Pippin shuddered. At least the Earl's subterfuge might prevent that particular catastrophe. She only hoped he and his grim burden had not been observed.

Marriage with Katy would have been unthinkable for a man of the Viscount's rank; it would have meant utter ruin. Perhaps Avery had seen in Katy's death the easiest solution to a distasteful, and dangerous, dilemma. Had he indeed fathered the girl's child, the villagers could not have been expected to accept the information with equanimity. Lady Philippa sighed. If harm came to Avery, it would not be by her hand. She would voice her suspicions to no one. Whatever else the merry Viscount might be, and Pippin had begun to suspect that was far more than at first appeared, he was her friend.

It occurred to her that a woman might have the strength necessary to strike the blow that had caused Katy's death and that, due to Andrew Macgregor's hostility, suspicion might also fall on her. To complicate matters, Pippin had been out that night as had the Viscount, Bevis Alversane, and probably Severin. Who else had been wandering Strachan's dark streets?

Lord Afton's actions were understandable; it would be disastrous if the girl's body was discovered anywhere near the inn. Ill will was already strong enough to be frightening.

Then there was the matter of the ghost. Despite the testimony of her own senses, and the terror she had experienced, Lady Philippa found it difficult to accept the credibility of a specter. A human was behind this haunting, and furthermore a human who'd known not only of Katy's death, but where her body lay.

Lady Philippa pushed Udolpho from her lap and rose. She was in the last stages of her preparation for an assault upon the nether regions of the inn, and upon the village itself if necessary, when the Earl appeared at her door.

"Where have you been?" Pippin cried. "Why didn't you come back last night?"

Lord Afton winced. "Your concern for my well-being," he said, carefully closing the door behind him, "naturally fills me with delight, but I would infinitely prefer that you lower your voice to a more moderate tone. It would profit us both greatly to have our neighbors think us abed with the sleep of innocence in the wee hours of this morn."

Lady Philippa ignored his gentle leer. "What have you done with Katy?" she demanded. Severin raised a hand.

"No names," he said firmly, "and no mention of our, er, little escapade to anyone." He regarded her severely. "Do you understand, Pippin? I wish no stirring narratives of last night's adventures, no matter how fascinating a tale it may make."

She nodded, too relieved by his reappearance, hale and apparently in one piece, to rebel against his assumption that she was sufficiently bird-witted as to speak of what they'd seen.

"As far as our various acquaintances are concerned," Lord Afton continued, "you and I never set foot from this place after the departure of last night's guests. We will, of course, exhibit the natural reactions of shock and polite dismay."

"I wish you'd tell me what you've done."

The Earl moved to the window and idly glanced outside. "Acquit me of deliberately adding to your suspense," he replied. "By the time I returned, you were sound asleep. I must admit to a certain disappointment! I'd thought you found the evening's entertainment as stimulating as I." Lady Philippa glanced at him with extreme annoyance and began inexpertly to brush her hair.

"The village," said Lord Afton calmly, "is in a uproar. A most unfortunate event has transpired." He paused, with good effect: Lady Philippa was tempted to hurl her hairbrush at him. "It appears our Katy fell from the foot bridge last night at some unspecified hour."

Pippin's mouth opened, and he removed the hairbrush from her nerveless hands. "Here," he murmured, "you're making a sad botch of that. Death was instantaneous, I'm told; the poor child struck her head on the rocks. I've often commented on the unstable condition of that structure, by the bye. There seems to be some question of why Katy should have been so careless as to fall, but that's being attributed to a combination of things—among them her agitation at the discovery of your birthmark."

Lady Philippa groaned as Lord Afton made a ferocious assault on her curls. "Yes," he agreed thoughtfully. "I'm inclined to regret that she had an opportunity to apprise the world of that particular piece of information, but one can't be expected to think of everything."

Pippin stared with horror, for the first time seeing Lord Afton as a monster of inhumanity. He had seen, had actually touched, Katy's lifeless body! How could he remain so aloof?

The Earl was not unaware of her reaction. "I apologize for any damage to your maidenly sensibilities," he said impatiently, "but I find it difficult to maintain a sorrowful role in the present trying circumstances." His glance fell on the peignoir that she had tossed thoughtlessly aside. "I suggest you dispose of that," he added. "It might lead someone to unfortunate conclusions."

Lady Philippa surveyed the gown with dismay. Its hem was stained with dirt and spotted with blood. "How?" she said faintly.

"She was dragged, of course." Severin looked slightly intrigued and lay down the brush. "Which suggests that our villain wasn't strong enough to carry her. That narrows the field considerably; our Katy wasn't a heavy girl."

Lord Afton showed signs of engaging in pleasant speculation, and Pippin quickly reclaimed his wandering attention. "Severin? What do the villagers think?"

"Not a great deal, I daresay; they seem to suffer a collective limited intellect. A result of inbreeding—I shouldn't be at all surprised to find some of them actively insane." He appeared surprised at Pippin's impatience. "I've sufficient intelligence myself to understand that your frowning countenance betokens a disagreeable emotion of some sort, and I find it extremely unnerving. Could it be that you are out of temper with me?"

"You," retorted Lady Philippa grimly, "are the most exasperating person I've ever known!"

Lord Afton sighed. "Endeavor to cultivate a little patience," he begged. "Let me give you a perfect example of the sort of woman I most admire. She never frowns, nor does she raise her voice, nor does she plague one with questions."

A delicate way of informing her, thought Lady Philippa ruefully, that embraces inspired by dark hallways and the discovery of corpses signified nothing to the Earl at all. "Would you prefer that I ask Aggy?" she asked, with commendable self-control.

"Well," said Lord Afton thoughtfully, "I rather think I should. However, Aggy is in a state of considerable agitation, and I imagine that exposure to you would result in the absence of any breakfast for me, so I shall nobly offer myself to you. What did you want to know? Ah, the villagers."

Even in her current state of extreme confusion, Lady Philippa was far from obtuse. "What's wrong, Severin? Were you seen?"

"Certainly not," responded the Earl with wounded pride. "I never fail in my endeavors." Then he dropped all pretense, and treated Lady Philippa to a deprecatory smile. Lady Philippa was enchanted. "Truth is," he said, "I'm not as clever as I thought—a mortifying discovery, I assure you! The villagers accept Katy's death as normal, to an extent; I've succeeded in preventing the suspicion of murder from falling upon one of us."

"What's wrong, then?" Despite herself, Pippin was rapidly succumbing to the charm of that smile.

"In a word, witchcraft." Lord Afton's swarthy features were grim now, as grim as the subject of which he spoke. "Rumor claims that the girl was cursed, bewitched."

"Good God!" cried Lady Philippa, released by shock from her own bemusement. "By whom?"

"Rumor is not certain on that point." The Earl looked bleak. "It fluctuates among the lot of us, including Valentine and Aggy."

"That is totally ridiculous!" But Pippin's protest was weak. Severin shrugged.

"You're the current leading choice, but I wouldn't take it to heart. I must insist, however, that you refrain from wandering around the town until this uproar dies down. Irksome as you may be at times, I am not enamored of the thought of bodily harm being done you."

"Don't worry," Lady Philippa replied, watching with irritation the Earl's progress toward her door. "I'm not quite the fool you think me."

"No?" inquired Lord Afton skeptically, his well-shaped hand already on the doorknob. "I shall be delighted to see evidence of my error. And for all our sakes, mind your wretched tongue!"

Sixteen

Lady Philippa slipped cautiously outside. It had not been an easy matter to outwit her watchdogs, and though her mission did not delight her, it was necessary. Intrigue came naturally to one who had successfully traversed the testing-ground of Almack's; hopeful mamas with daughters of marriageable age resorted to incredible subterfuges to gain footing within that sacred temple of the *ton*. Lady Philippa wondered what Lady Jersey or Princess Lieven would say to her latest exploits and hoped fervently that those august ladies might never know.

Fortunately, the cottage that Miss Graham shared with her mother was not far from the inn. Lady Philippa spared the small building no more than a cursory glance as she prayed fervently that Miss Graham herself would come to the door. The stone house had small windows that helped to conserve warmth in the winter and a thatched roof insulated with moss.

Miss Graham no more than discovered the identity of her visitor than she dragged the unresisting Pippin inside. "Did anyone see you come?" Gilly whispered. "Hist! Keep your voice down. It won't do to have my mother hear you. Come in here."

The cottage was immaculate. Lady Philippa followed Miss Graham into the tiny kitchen and wrapped her hands gratefully around a huge mug of steaming coffee.

"Nasty stuff, that," commented Gilly, pouring herself more of the same, "but I've a fondness for it. Another thing to be laid at Lucius's door. I suppose you've heard about Katy?"

Lady Philippa nodded, not trusting herself to speak.

"Then what are you doing here? It would only take a glimpse of you to touch off violence, and much as I dislike them, I've no wish to see my neighbors turned into lunatics."

Lady Philippa didn't need to be told that the people were in a mood to disregard the law. A miasma of suppressed emotion hung over the village. "Have I come at a bad time?" she asked. "You said you wished to speak to me."

"Too late for that, now." There were dark shadows beneath Miss Graham's fine eyes. "I only meant to warn you about the villagers. They are very superstitious and take their superstitions seriously. I hoped you would not laugh at them, as the others do." She shrugged. "But perhaps it would have made no difference—in the end."

Lady Philippa did not care for this fatalistic tone. "Did you see Katy?" she inquired, again visited by the horror of that dead face.

"Aye, and an ugsome sight she was. The village is rife with speculation about her leman." Gilly refrained from adding that Lord Afton and Neville Alversane were the prime contenders for this unenviable position, due to Katy's mother's recollection of her daughter's reference to a fine, but nameless, foreign gentleman.

"How terrible," Lady Philippa said. Gilly glanced at her visitor's pale face and deemed it wise to offer some distraction.

"It's a pack of nonsense," she retorted briskly and refilled Lady Philippa's cup. "And it's foolish to dwell on it. Katy was a very silly girl, and one explanation of her accident is as good as another. It's my own belief that a stray kelpie did her a mischief, not recognizing her as one of his own."

Pippin managed a weak laugh. "That's better," Gilly approved. "You should know by now that we Highlanders cannot accept commonplace explanations for anything. We spend our time straining our imaginations for outlandish reasons, and the more improbable they are, the more likely we are to accept them. Did you know that multiple births were once viewed with suspicion? The mother of twins was believed to have been dallying with two men, the mother of triplets with three. Rather embarrassing for the poor ladies, wouldn't you agree? But that's the way we are."

Lady Philippa's laughter was more sincere, and Gilly persevered.

"Some of our beliefs are rather charming. For example, we

have a proverb that the sea will search the corners of the world for its children." Gilly realized that this wasn't a happy choice of subject matter, but her guest looked interested. "A body washed ashore was buried as near the high water mark as possible so that the sea might easily reclaim its own, if so inclined. It was also the height of impropriety to bring a drowned person into a house; they usually awaited burial in the barn. Which has always struck me as being a trifle lacking in dignity, though I don't imagine the corpses minded."

Lady Philippa traced patterns on the table. "What will they do with Katy?"

"She'll be buried with all due pomp," replied Gilly. "I suppose I shall have to go, though I'd almost rather brave old Macgregor's wrath. I find funerals abominable."

"I agree." The villagers, it seemed, were sufficiently aroused to take justice into their own hands. Would there be other funerals? wondered Lady Philippa, chilled.

"Don't you be thinking of attending!" Gilly protested anxiously. "Go back to your inn and stay there until this uproar wears itself out."

Aware that her presence in the little cottage was rendering Miss Graham acutely uncomfortable, and that the girl either could not or would not tell her more, Lady Philippa rose. Gilly inspected the street, then pushed her visitor out the door.

"Thank you," Pippin began, but the girl shook her head.

"God be with you," Miss Graham murmured somberly and closed the door.

Lady Philippa darted across the street, only to meet the tall Englishman who had acted as her champion of the night before. "Hello!" she said, with her most charming smile. She might as well have grimaced at him for all the effect it made. "Are you going to the inn?"

He nodded, and she fell into step beside him. Various London gentlemen might profess willingness to expire for a smile from the enchanting Lady Philippa Harte; Bevis Alversane, for all the appreciation he displayed at being in her company, might have had Medusa at his side.

"I'm grateful to you," Lady Philippa said as they entered the inn, "for your assistance last night. I shudder to think of Macgregor's reaction had he discovered me out at that hour, and unescorted."

"Don't mention it," Bevis Alversane replied stiffly. He would have been a handsome man if not for the nervous tic

119

that afflicted one eye. "Such foolishness, I believe, is common to members of your sex."

Lady Philippa stared, amazed. Bevis Alversane's quixotic behavior of the previous evening had led her to vague speculations about a possibly romantic nature hidden behind his haughty mask, but the man's lack of warmth did not suggest any such hidden tendencies. Pippin concluded—not for the first time—that interpretation of character was scarcely one of her strong points.

"Well, Alversane," drawled Lord Afton, stepping into the hallway, "to what do we owe this unexpected pleasure? Is it the local scandal that so inspires you?" He shot Lady Philippa an unreadable glance. "Or could it be the dubious charms of my distinguished guest?"

Bevis flushed unbecomingly. Pippin wondered at Severin's patent dislike.

"Cassandra wants you to come to the castle," Bevis said, grudgingly including Lady Philippa in his glance, "tonight. She's gotten hold of some fool notion about a séance. Damned idiocy, if you ask me."

"Ah, but I didn't," the Earl replied. "Are we to take it that you don't plan to attend this convivial gathering?"

"No." The man's voice was brusque.

"Then by all means tell Cassandra that we shall be delighted to attend." Severin watched the man's departure impassively, then turned his attention to Lady Philippa. "And now, my girl," he said sternly, "you will be so good as to tell me where you've been."

Nor was Lord Afton alone in questioning Lady Philippa's activities. Andrew Macgregor, as was his custom when struggling with serious thought, walked idly through the village, arriving unwittingly at the detested inn.

He stared up at the structure with angry, red-rimmed eyes. The discovery of the barmaid's body, combined with the disappearance of the strange deck of cards and Lady Philippa's notes, caused him great displeasure and a conviction that the forces of evil were more powerful than he had initially assumed. He frowned. His villagers were shocked, but not inclined to question the circumstances of Katy's death, and it was his responsibility to prevent them from discussing it as mere accident. Andrew Macgregor knew the girl had not experienced a natural death, though he had yet to discover whose hand had sent her tumbling into the water. He paused

120

to consider whether his parishioners would benefit from the exercise of bier right, which utilized the amazing capacity of a corpse to bleed on the approach of its murderer, then decided against the ordeal. It would have been dramatic, but eminently impractical.

The old man sought cautiously to arouse the villagers. He was anxious to take action, but his devout followers were not yet prepared for events as drastic as those he had in mind. Katy's death had come at an opportune time; properly handled, it would enable him to put into action the beginning stages of his plan. It would be extremely advantageous if further events increased the villagers' suspicions and ill will, but Andrew was content to preach and wait. Evil would not be allowed to rampage unchecked. It was not in the nature of things.

He wondered how best to utilize Lady Philippa's birthmark. Even the most skeptical of his flock could not easily dismiss that discovery, for it was common knowledge that Satan's compact with his witches was sealed with just such a mark. Made by the Devil's talon, the scar was inconsistent in design, and signified its bearer's allegiance and subjugation. The old man smiled mirthlessly. The best proof of involvement in witchcraft, the devil's mark, justified torture and death. There was a special manner for testing such marks, notoriously insensitive to pain: the point of a bodkin was applied to each scar or unusual area of skin.

Approaching footsteps startled him, and he quickly stepped behind concealing shrubbery, then peered cautiously through the bushes. A man and a girl, known to him as Lady Philippa's retainers, were engaged in fierce argument.

"Are you queer in the attic?" demanded Barnabas, who wore what could only be described as a Friday-face. "How did you come to let her give you the slip?"

Nabby tossed her sandy curls. "That's fine for you to say," she snapped, "but I'd like to see *you* stop Lady Philippa when she'd made up her mind. I thought her safe in her room."

"Aye." Barnabas released her, and Nabby rubbed her arm. Despite her sulky expression, she wasn't averse to an occasional demonstration of masculine strength. "Lady Philippa is damnably hot-at-hand." He smiled, reluctantly. "No one shall say she's wanting in dash! But she has not made herself a favorite among the natives."

"Why should she, pray?" demanded Nabby. "A lot of cantankerous gapeseeds!" She sighed. "I tell you, Barney, I wish

I'd never set foot in this place, but nothing I can say will persuade her to leave." The hazel eyes narrowed. "And I think I know why."

Barnabas, who had fallen into the habit of skulking about the village, had a much clearer notion of local opinion than his companion. Barnabas's romantic appearance was an invaluable asset; many were the village maidens who, though distrusting Sassenachs, gazed upon that handsome countenance and were smitten with emotion that found outlet in excessive garrulousness. Great, thought Barnabas, were the risks he took for Lady Philippa's sake! "If you mean to tell me she's set her cap for the Viscount," he said, "you're sadly out, my girl."

Nabby chose to overlook this familiarity. "How can you say that?" she cried. "He has taken a marked fancy to Philippa, for all she's almost on the shelf!" She frowned. "Barney, he's surely not dangling after a rich heiress!"

Barnabas shook his head. "I don't deny the Viscount's dancing attendance on her, and I don't doubt he'll come up to snuff, but I can tell you now that Lady Philippa will have nothing to say to him."

"A lot you know about it!" Nabby would have spoken again, but he frowned.

"We've more important matters to discuss! One girl is already dead."

Nabby blanched. "Barney! You don't think Lady Philippa is in danger?"

"Of course I do," Barnabas retorted. "Use your head! Why else would I be kicking up such a devil of a fuss? You'll watch your mistress carefully, unless you wish to see her end up like poor Katy, with her head smashed in."

" 'Tis more than one person can do," Nabby commented glumly. "Like quicksilver, the mistress is, here one moment and gone the next, and me never knowing what she'll take it in her head to do."

Barnabas was too astute to be deceived by this sudden helplessness. "Do your best," he advised. "I'll assist you as best I can, but I've other fish to fry."

"I'm sure you do!" Nabby stamped her foot, incensed. "What's it to be this time? Dallying with Janet Kirk? And what would Lady Philippa say to *that*, I wonder!"

"Not a word. Her ladyship is mightily discreet." Barnabas's tone indicated that the virtue was not shared by Lady Philippa's maid.

"The devil," said Nabby, gloomily. She preferred Barnabas in the role of devoted swain, a part which he had not seen fit to play for some time. "What must I do?"

"Keep Lady Philippa in your sight at all times," Barnabas replied. "Sleep at night on a pallet in her room."

Nabby thought of her soft bed, and sighed. "Very well." She gazed upon that incomparable face. "Barney, why are you so cross with me?"

"You are an unprincipled minx," Barnabas said, with a noticeable softening of his expression, "but I am not cross with you." With no scruples whatsoever, Nabby allowed herself to be embraced. She gazed up at Barnabas, expecting a romantic declaration. "Some of the villagers can remember the last witch to burn in Scotland," he said somberly. "She was found guilty of riding to a witch's sabbat on her daughter's back." Depressed, Nabby allowed herself to be led away.

Andrew Macgregor emerged stiffly from his hiding place. The meeting had been fortuitous, though he had not learned as much as he hoped. He hurried toward his church to consult that witch hunters' handbook, the *Malleus Maleficarium*. The blessed volume never left that building, where it had resided for hundreds of years. Andrew was not the first to receive guidance from those brittle pages. Nor did he conceive of himself as the last.

The minister's senses were fine-tuned instruments, unerring detectors of wickedness. It was obvious to him that the red-haired woman was a witch, evil to such magnitude that she corrupted all who had contact with her. Proof lay in the shocking behavior of her servants, so godless as to court in public. The evidence of Lady Philippa's satanic mark and that malevolent cat, her familiar, would perhaps convince the villagers of her guilt. Andrew Macgregor himself had no need of such proof. First, he would deal with her ladyship, and then with her ladyship's accomplice, the dangerous Earl.

Seventeen

━━━

Janet Kirk was suffering an agitation of the nerves. Her teeth had an uncontrollable tendency to chatter, her knees knocked painfully together, but she would not let mere physical terror sway her from her purpose.

Nor had Janet needed Andrew Macgregor to point out the importance of this undertaking. Janet was no one to shirk her duty, even when that duty might shatter her hopes of the breathtaking Barnabas, whose devotion to Lady Philippa was both puzzling and unshakable. Janet had tried to dissuade him from this misguided sense of duty, expounding upon duplicity and ungodly behavior, but Barnabas had only remarked that such notions were daft.

Katy had been her friend. Janet knew as well as the minister that there was something extremely strange about Katy's death, for Katy would never willingly have set foot on the precarious bridge. Katy had feared heights; one glance at the rushing stream would have brought on one of her attacks of giddiness.

It was possible that Katy's wits had been addled as a consequence of the discovery of Lady Philippa's betraying mark, and she had tumbled off the bridge all unaware, but Janet was reluctant to accept that general opinion. Whatever her shortcomings, and even Janet had to admit they were multitudinous, Katy has possessed a strong instinct for survival. It was far more likely that the red-haired stranger with the heathenish name had bewitched poor Katy with a glance from those slanting green eyes.

Andrew Macgregor had explained the phenomenon of the

evil eye, a gift granted by the powers of darkness to those so debased as to have signed, in blood, the devil's pact. Janet's imagination took fire; the minister had told her, with a notable lack of regard for her maidenly state, just what allegiance to Satan involved. It was not difficult for Janet to envision Lady Philippa as paramour to the Dark Prince; life in a country village had left her with very decided notions of what such a relationship might entail. Janet imagined herself in such a position and shuddered. Her conception of evil personified bore a startling resemblance to Lord Afton.

Small Sandy seemed to suffer no ill effects from his encounter with her ladyship, but his family was watching him carefully. The Macleans had at first been inclined to dismiss Janet's prophecies of danger, but Katy's fate had made them realize their error. Janet's face wore a small vengeful smile. The Macleans would need to be vigilant. Their younger child exhibited an alarming attraction to Lady Philippa's hideous, multicolored cat, just as their elder showed an equally strong attraction to Lady Philippa herself.

Alas, Katy had not confided the name of her lover, even when Janet had pointed out the enormity of her sin. Such things as childbirths unhallowed by wedlock were not tolerated in Strachan. Janet was briefly envious of Katy's luck in snaring a wealthy gentleman, but stifled so unworthy an impulse. It was selfish enough Katy's fine lover had been; he'd given her nothing but a swollen belly, not even a brass ring.

Katy had been patently unworthy in her position as the minister's tool; Janet would achieve more satisfactory results. She shared Andrew Macgregor's conviction that Lady Philippa was responsible for the village's misfortunes, but further proof was imperative. The villagers were a bunch of foolish old maids who would not be convinced by a mere devil's mark.

Janet thought of that mark somberly, secure in the belief that Katy's discovery had led to her downfall. It seemed that Lady Philippa should have long since been struck down by a lightning bolt from above, but the ways of the Lord were mysterious. Retribution would come. Janet hoped to be present on that fine occasion, when even Barnabas would be forced to admit that he had misjudged his employer's nature. Having regained her courage, Janet marched boldly into the kitchen of the inn.

Lady Philippa, meanwhile, was sunk in gloom. She cared for her current position in the village no more than she cared

126

for the Earl's harsh lecture concerning her thoughtless conduct, for he had learned somehow of her surreptitious visit to the Graham cottage. Both Nabby and Barnabas were consequently in disgrace, though neither of them would admit who the talebearer had been. Lady Philippa knew perfectly well that her loyal retainers went to great lengths to keep her under their eyes. She had her revenge in denying Nabby's request to share her room.

Confinement to the inn was tedious in the extreme, but Lady Philippa had no desire to brave Lord Afton's wrath, and the villagers' resentment, by venturing outside again. She could not leave William Macgregor's mystery unsolved, nor could she leave the Earl in so disapproving a mood. She would have to redeem herself, a task that loomed monumental at the present time. Thinking that Aggy might be able to offer diversion, Pippin made her way to that worthy's realm.

Aggy had a visitor, and Lady Philippa paused unseen in the hallway to eavesdrop. Her brief glimpse of Aggy's guest enabled her to identify the female dragon who'd been present at their nearly catastrophic introduction to young Sandy Maclean.

Aggy appeared skeptical. "Is it work you're wantin', Janet Kirk?" the old woman inquired waspishly. "Or is it a chance to be snoopin' around like yon Katy was? The master's a good man, for all his foreign ways, and I willna hold with what's bein' said about him."

"You know good positions aren't easy to find," was all Janet offered in defense.

" 'Tis months I've been here," Aggy said, "and I've seen nothing untoward. 'Tis rocks you have in your head if you think you'll find proof of your foolish suspicions here."

"Does that mean you'll have none of me? You need help here and there won't be many to ask for the place. Not after what happened to Katy." Janet did not need to add that the Earl's reputation was not one that would encourage many to seek the place. A young girl of the lower classes embarked upon a perilous course when she entered domestic service, particularly in an establishment where the masculine element was of the rakish sort.

"What happened to yon foolish Katy is nothing to do with the inn, and you may tell Andrew Macgregor so." Aggy's tone was irate. " 'Tis the biggest pack of nonsense I've ever heard."

Janet cleared her throat. "The minister is not pleased with

you, Aggy Campbell," she murmured. "He fears you've been corrupted and thinks it would be best for you to avoid this place hereafter."

"And leave the master with no one to serve him, pray? I wadna think of it." Despite her belligerent tone, Aggy was shaken. Andrew Macgregor's influence in the village was formidable. "The Macgregor need have no concern for my soul, and you may tell him so."

"Very well," replied Janet. "Am I also to tell him that you sent me away? Don't be a fool, Aggy! You know me to be a good worker."

Aggy favored the girl with a penetrating stare. " 'Tis not your qualifications I'm doubtin', 'tis your motives."

"Those needn't concern you." Janet sensed the old woman was weakening. "I'll do the work, and do it well. What else I may do won't interfere."

" 'Tis not my decision," Aggy said gruffly. "You'll have to speak with the master, and I wadna be surprised if he'll have naught to do with you. Himself is a verra discernin' man."

. Aggy did not care for the situation in which she found herself. She knew the villagers' superstitious convictions were the work of their fanatic minister, and she also knew Lord Afton and his friends to be blameless of the charges leveled against them. However, she had lived in Strachan too long to underestimate the seriousness of the present situation. If she declared herself too firmly on the side of the foreigners, she'd be ostracized by her neighbors, which wouldn't be all that bad a thing. But the foreigners would eventually depart, and then she'd be alone.

"Andrew Macgregor will be pleased with you." Janet had followed the old woman's changing expressions with fair accuracy.

Aggy wiped her hands on her apron. "I'll take you to the master." She glared impotently at the placid girl. "But dinna expect me to recommend you, because that I will not!"

Lady Philippa barely had time to duck into the dining room. A hand grasped her arm, pulling her farther into the darkness. Pippin gasped.

"Hush! Close the door." Lady Philippa recognized the voice of Paddy Maclean and obeyed, intrigued and slightly gratified. It was no small feat for a lady so stricken in years as to be considered nearly on the shelf to inspire a halfling with calf-love! Heavy curtains covered the small windows; she could barely distinguish his features in the shadows.

"What in heaven's name are you doing here?" she whispered. "You've startled me out of a good year's growth."

The young man appeared extremely nervous. "I came to warn you," he said. "You must leave."

Lady Philippa perched on the edge of the table and regarded him with amusement. Yet another person wanted her out of Strachan, it seemed. "Why must I?"

Paddy literally wrung his hands. "They're saying you killed poor Katy." At her gesture, he sank into a chair.

"What?" Lady Philippa's first horrified thought was that someone had seen through Severin's ruse.

"They say you were angered because she saw your mark." Lady Philippa wondered if Paddy knew the exact location of that mark. She would have been even more amused had she known that Paddy's blushes were hidden only by the gloom.

"This is utter absurdity!" she replied. "It's nothing more sinister than a birthmark. I'm amazed that you can credit such fairy tales. As for Katy, I'd no reason to wish her harm. I barely knew the girl."

Paddy took a deep breath. "They also say that you consort with the fairies, and that you've caused Mora Graham to sicken and my young brother to disregard his parents' words."

Lady Philippa was diverted. "And does he?" she inquired.

Paddy stared. "What?"

"I wouldn't worry about it," Pippin said kindly. "It's probably only a phase. Go on, tell me what else I'm thought to be responsible for."

Paddy was extremely confused. Had he been in Lady Philippa's place, he'd have been terrified, but this strange woman was uncannily free of fear. He experienced grave qualms. Paddy couldn't imagine what retribution would fall upon him if his traitorous behavior became known.

"They say," he continued obediently, "that you can do all sorts of wondrous things, that you can cause milk to sour or the hens to stop laying, and that you can bring thunder and lightning or hail and drought."

"Is that all?" Her eyes had adjusted to the darkness and she could see Paddy's face, which revealed terrified resolution. Pippin appreciated the impulse that had brought him to her and pitied him for his obvious dilemma, but she was also extremely impatient with him. It was incredible that any sane person could accept such inanities.

"Nay," said Paddy, "I disremember the rest." He rose and

shuffled his feet, anxious to be gone. "You see why you must go. It's dangerous for you to stay here."

"Nonsense," retorted the disillusioned Lady Philippa. She pulled aside one of the curtains and looked outside. The storm that had threatened all day was upon them. A demon of mischief took hold of her.

"If I can control the elements," she observed, "what have I to fear from puny mortals?" An obliging clap of thunder punctuated her words. Paddy turned corpse-white and stared with horror. Lady Philippa awarded him a heavy-lidded smile.

"I daresay I can cause other intriguing phenomena," she mused. "Perhaps a swarm of locusts or a visitation of the plague, though I'll admit that does seem a bit extreme." Paddy sidled toward the door.

"I only wanted to warn you," he mumbled, sweat breaking out on his forehead. Lady Philippa felt a twinge of remorse, but she was also furious at the predicament she was in.

"Don't tease yourself; I appreciate your concern. I won't ill-wish you." Inspiration struck her. "But tell your friends to cease meddling in my affairs or they will suffer my wrath."

Paddy fumbled with the doorknob; his hands were icy cold. He knew he'd been a fool not to listen to the minister; Lady Philippa was obviously everything she was purported to be.

"Don't put a curse on me!" he cried. "I meant you no harm."

Pippin stared at him, aghast. "Paddy," she said quietly, "where is your sense of humor? I was only playing a senseless game. I'm no more a witch than you are, and I had nothing to do with Katy's death."

Unconvinced, Paddy fled.

Lady Philippa was heartily ashamed of herself and regretted the impulse that had prompted her to be so tongue-valiant. Nabby had been correct in predicting that her mistress would one day go too far! Perhaps she'd done no serious damage, if only Paddy would refrain from repeating her thoughtless threats. Disaster would result if the Earl learned of the interview, no matter by what means. He would doubtless request her to disappear straightaway and never, if she could avoid it, to let him see her again.

Had Lady Philippa but known it, she had nothing to fear from Paddy. He would not reveal his visit to the inn, for it would cause him endless trouble. Too, Paddy suspected he'd made a cake of himself. He plodded gloomily up the muddy road, kicking inoffensive pebbles and damning his own good intentions.

Janet Kirk, however, was an entirely different piece of goods and had spent a profitable few minutes with her ear pressed to the closed dining-room door. She was chagrined to learn that Paddy, whom she'd known all her life, was so deeply caught in the enchantress's snares.

Eighteen

"It all began with the Spanish Inquisition," Gilly said. "That set the pattern for all the later trials. Any person who fell under suspicion had to prove his innocence or suffer punishment."

Had not Lucius been an unusually patient man, his affection for Gilly would have expired long since. The lady, however, was becoming obsessed. He could not consider Strachan a beneficial influence. "I wonder what fine things are transpiring in Edinburgh," he said wistfully.

Gilly might not have heard. "The Inquisition was responsible for some truly ingenious horrors," she continued. "People were roasted on spits over fires, or had their bowels transferred to basins. Sometimes their arms and legs were tied to horses, which were then driven in four opposite directions."

"Have a heart, lass!" Lucius protested. Gilly turned her brooding gaze on him.

"Germany was the worst," she added. "The law demanded torture there." She smiled gravely at his expression. "Aren't you intrigued, Lucius? You should be. You see here in Strachan precisely the mentality that allowed such barbarism to occur. Imagine, the witch seldom knew who her accuser was. And great pains were taken to keep her alive until she revealed her accomplices. Physicians were kept in attendance and the torture was stopped if the accused showed indications of an early demise."

Lucius muttered something indistinguishable and Gilly shot him a puzzled glance. They were seated in a secluded corner of the castle's great hall. Comfortable furnishings were scattered about, but did little to relieve the overwhelming and inhibiting dimensions of the structure.

Gilly twisted the glass in her hand. "They were fed salted food and their water was mixed with herring pickle, so that they suffered constant raging thirst. Their feet were cut open and boiling oil was poured into the wounds; their tongues were pierced."

"Acushla!" Lucius groaned.

"I'm sorry," Gilly said, and sighed. "I'm being a terrible bore. But I can't rid myself of the notion that it's all going to happen again. Our Scottish witches were serious and dangerous creatures who had the power of prophecy. They raised storms and beset vessels at sea."

Lucius glowered. "You've a wealth of best-forgotten information," he complained. "But I fail to see why the sight of me should inspire you to such gloomy oration. Can it be there's a flaw in my charming character, a flaw of which I've been hitherto blissfully unaware?"

Gilly smiled. "I'll be good," she promised. "Not another word on the subject shall I utter, not even if Lady Cassandra manages to conjure up Katy herself."

"You do my heart delight." Lucius beamed. "Ah, there's your winsome friend."

"Use the word sparingly," Gilly pleaded, glancing across the room to where Lady Philippa, the Viscount, and Lord Afton stood. "Call her my friend in the village and you'll make me even more enemies."

Unaware that she herself was an object of interest, Lady Philippa gazed about her with delight. Originally a peel, a stone tower house built by some long-ago laird to protect his lands and shelter his people, Galbraith Castle had been extended into an L-shaped structure by the addition of a wing. The original entrance, which could be reached only by a ladder to the first floor, had been abandoned for a ground-level door in the newer wing.

Lady Cassandra condescended to conduct her fascinated guest on a tour, talking all the time of her latest discoveries. "I've found a recipe for incense used in amatory spells," she exulted. "It consists of musk, lignum aloes, red coral powder, tincture of ambergris, and rose petals, mixed with a few drops of pigeon's blood and the desiccated brain of a sparrow."

"A sovereign remedy," murmured the Viscount, who stood behind Pippin. "My dear, you're looking fine as fivepence."

134

Lady Philippa determinedly set aside her suspicions and allowed him to take her arm. She wore a gown of sea-green sarcenet with tiny puffed sleeves and a narrow skirt trimmed with a double pleating of ribbon. Another matching ribbon was wound through her curls.

A staircase in the newer wing led to the first floor; above that, the steps disappeared inside a turret, allowing more space in the individual rooms. Stone vaulting removed any danger of fire, an iron gate stood behind each wooden door, and gratings protected the windows. The royal standard of the old Scottish kingdom, a flag bearing a scarlet lion on a field of gold, was also in evidence.

Lady Philippa was in unaccountably high spirits. Aggy had defiantly feasted them with cloutie dumplings, a hot dish lavish with currants, sultanas, and orange peel; and it was furthermore a great relief to escape the inn. To add to her sense of well-being, Pippin had patched together her abused notes, and now saw the plot for her next book in its entirety. Since that plot dealt so largely with Ailcie Ferguson and Strachan, Lady Philippa was more than ever determined to see the current troubles to their conclusions. She was quite out of charity with Lord Afton, who had not altered his opinion of her imprudence, but this was not a matter to plunge her into despondency, nor were his polite arguments in favor of her departure. As they returned to the others, Pippin stole a glance at him, engaged in quiet conversation with Miss Graham. Lucius Cunningham did not appear pleased.

"I must speak with you," murmured the Viscount, drawing her aside. "I feel I owe you an explanation of my conduct, in light of recent developments."

Lady Philippa wondered if those developments were his recent declaration of his intentions toward her or Katy's untimely death. She had little doubt that her friend referred to his relationship with the dead girl.

"Fiddle!" said she. "Our secrets were to remain our own." To her relief, Avery did not take advantage of this proffered generosity.

"It was the most trifling thing, but I know how it must have appeared." The Viscount wore an expression of such charming ruefulness that Lady Philippa immediately suspected she was to be fobbed off with a Banbury tale. "Katy was a pudding-heart! It was my misfortune to come across the girl just after she'd glimpsed your birthmark. She kicked up the devil of a fuss."

"So I've been informed," Lady Philippa remarked wryly.

"I sought to calm the wench, with a notable lack of success." Avery possessed himself of one of Pippin's hands. "Heaven knows what you must have thought when you saw me with her."

"Moonshine!" said Lady Philippa. It did not seem politic to add that she had considered Katy a straw damsel who wasn't beyond casting out lures. "It is not necessary for you to explain."

"I adore you," the Viscount retorted. "I would not have you think the worst of me. To continue: our encounter in the streets of Strachan on the fateful night also has an innocent explantation. I saw you leave the inn and followed you."

Lady Philippa did not respond to this pretty speech as her suitor might have wished, for she had been visited by a notion that was a source of considerable chagrin. Avery's devotion was nothing to cavil at, if only one might be convinced of his sincerity, but Avery was also possessed of a great regard for his own skin. Only Pippin suspected that the Viscount had been on more than intimate terms with the girl, and should she marry him, her silence would be assured. Avery's next words confirmed her fear.

"I trust," he said, "that you are aware of the consequences should these matters be noised abroad. I find I do not fancy myself cast in the role of murderer."

"You may trust me." Lady Philippa firmly withdrew her hand from his clasp. "I assure you that I shall do everything in the world to prevent the story from becoming known."

If the Viscount remarked her coolness of tone, he was too much the gentleman to question its cause. Lady Philippa reflected that she was in a sad fix and did not know how it was to be resolved. It seemed she must discover the extent of Avery's involvement with Katy. For friendship's sake, she would protect him, but even so freethinking a lady as Pippin would not consider marriage with a murderer.

At Lady Cassandra's insistence, the group was seated around a circular table. None of them seemed particularly enthused: Valentine was petulant, Neville bored, and the laird obviously wished himself elsewhere. Lady Philippa found herself seated between the Viscount and Severin.

Lady Cassandra turned down the lights and placed a screen in front of the fire, then seated herself in the remaining chair. "Place your hands flat on the table, please," she

136

said. "Thumbs together and little fingers touching those of the person next to you."

Then she raised her voice in song. Avery winced. "I had thought she meant to call up ghouls and ghosties," he murmured, "but this is a great deal too much to bear!" He sounded offended, and Pippin grinned.

"I cannot think," Lady Cassandra protested, "that the atmosphere is right. We must all concentrate."

Pippin had little hope for the success of Lady Cassandra's endeavors—not subscribing to the effectiveness of attempted communications with the dead—and concentrated instead on the Viscount's flattering attentions. A confirmed flirt Avery might be, but he was not in the habit of lavishing such devoted attendance upon the objects of his fleeting interest. Had this interesting courtship taken place in London, all of their acquaintance would be eagerly scanning the papers for the announcement of their betrothal. Lady Philippa was too fond of the Viscount to gloat over her unexpected conquest. Instead, she wondered if she really wished to end her days in the unenviable state of spinsterhood; she cursed the unlucky accident that had allowed her to see the little barmaid as near as made no difference to being clasped in Avery's arms.

In a reedy voice, Lady Cassandra called the dead girl's name. Pippin felt Avery shake with barely suppressed merriment, and then the table began to rock, accompanied by an odd rapping noise.

Lady Philippa experienced exasperation. It seemed that Lady Cassandra wasn't sufficiently high-minded as to avoid indulging in cheap stage effects. The table began to rise. "I shall split my seams," the Viscount gasped, "if this silliness does not soon cease!"

Gilly was not equally amused. With a faint cry, she gripped Lucius's hands. "Hush, acushla," he rumbled. "It's only a trick." His voice was almost lost in the growing din.

Lady Philippa did not award the table's gyrations the attention they deserved. She heard Valentine's startled exclamation, but she was gripped by a deadening chill.

"I could swear," Gilly murmured, "that I heard a harp!" Lady Philippa sat as one frozen, unaware of Avery's hand on her arm.

"Come to us, Katy!" cried Lady Cassandra, above the rappings and thuds and heavy footsteps. "We wish to help you!"

Gilly could tolerate no more. She broke away from Lucius and ran to light the candles. "Perhaps you'll believe me now," she said, shoving aside the screen that dimmed the fire. "It's dangerous to meddle with things you don't understand." She turned to face the startled group, then stood rigid with shock.

The attempt to contact dead Katy had been unsuccessful, but their endeavors had not been entirely in vain. The Hanging Man stood among them.

Valentine screamed and knocked over her chair in her hasty flight; Lucius took one look at the apparition and moved quickly to Gilly's side. Lady Cassandra stared in stark disbelief; Neville and the laird exchanged a glance, then moved stealthily toward the intruder as if to take it captive. Lord Afton sprawled negligently in his chair, a sardonic expression on his face; and the Viscount hovered about Lady Philippa protectively.

It was at Pippin that the ghost stared. Its mouth opened in terrible speechless contortions, and its gestures were frenzied.

Neville and the laird moved quietly closer to their uninvited guest. The specter, with a final agonized grimace, stepped backward several paces, then disappeared.

Lord Afton regarded Pippin, whose face was ashen. "Do you think you might do something about your beau?" he inquired. "His attentions grow a trifle marked. Do you think it kind to encourage him?"

It was not seemly for a well-brought-up young lady to employ vulgar expressions. "Hell and the devil confound it!" cried Lady Philippa, thereby shocking everyone, with the possible exception of the Earl.

Nineteen

Andrew Macgregor opened the huge Bible to Leviticus, chapter xx, verse 6, and read aloud: " 'And the soul that turneth after such as have familiar spirits, and after wizards, to go a whoring after them, I will set my face against that soul, and will cut him off from among his people.' "

Aggy, upon whom the minister's gaze rested, schooled her features into a pious expression. She had no desire to incur further disfavor; awesome was the Macgregor's wrath.

The minister moved to verse twenty-seven. " 'A man also or woman that hath a familiar spirit, or that is a wizard, shall surely be put to death: they shall stone them with stones, their blood shall be upon them.' "

Aggy, maintaining her pious mask, thought she'd never heard such arrant nonsense. She wondered that Janet Kirk would miss the service, and tried unsuccessfully to dismiss her nagging unease.

Paddy Maclean, too, had noted Janet's absence and hoped the girl wasn't at the inn. He remembered his interview of the day before and suppressed a shudder. It was not clear to him whether Lady Philippa did or did not possess unearthly powers, but he intended to henceforth avoid her.

Andrew Macgregor paused for brief explanation. "The devil, having entered into a compact with a witch, gives her a small demon in the shape of a domestic animal to advise her and perform errands for her. Such errands include murder." The old man watched impassively as his parishioners' faces registered varying degrees of comprehension. He was pleased.

They'd begun to realize the significance of the red-haired noblewoman's malevolent-looking cat.

That was not all the villagers realized; some of the more discerning among them had begun to wonder if their minister was mad. Yet there was the manner of Katy's death, which seemed less and less like an accident. And who was there but Andrew Macgregor to see justice done? Certainly not the laird! Duncan Galbraith would have exhibited more concern over a dead sheep. The villagers would wait, then, and see what next transpired.

"We have a long and glorious tradition to uphold," said Andrew Macgregor. "In 1537, Lady Glamis burned for using charms against the king; in 1576, Bessie Dunlop roasted for receiving herbal cures from the Queen of the Fairies; in 1588 Allison Peirson burned for prescribing magic potions derived from converse with the Queen of Elfhame."

Paddy Maclean was rendered acutely uncomfortable by the minister's theme. The Macgregor's piercing eyes seemed able to peer into his soul, and Paddy had no wish to reveal the indiscretions that lay hidden there. It promised to be a long sermon, and he inched forward, seeking some elusive comfort from the hard wooden seat.

"Consider our history!" Andrew Macgregor demanded. "In 1590 the North Berwick witches invoked a tempest to shipwreck their king! In 1597, the Aberdeen witches danced with the devil around the town cross. In 1607 Isobel Grierson caused sickness and disease. Margaret Barclay caused the ship bearing her brother-in-law to sink. Isobel Gowdie changed herself into a jackdaw and flew to the sabbat, leaving behind a broom in her bed to delude her husband. The wizard Thomas Wier repented of his infamous behavior and confessed to incest, adultery, and bestiality!"

Adultery! Aggy thought that extremely unfair. What was she if not the keenest of chaperones, not that the Earl and his guests had failed to comport themselves with anything but the greatest propriety. The Quality could not be measured by the same yardstick as common folk, yet even the irrepressible Viscount could be trusted not to go too far. And Lady Philippa might be a green girl, despite the fact that she was almost beyond marriageable age, for all the worldly wisdom she displayed. Aggy returned her attention to the minister. Heaven knew what tarradiddles he would come out with next.

Andrew Macgregor glowered at his wide-eyed congregation. "In 1727 Janet Horne was burned for using her daughter as a flying horse. Do not be so foolish as to underestimate the threat of such iniquitous beings as these!" He leaned forward, eyes blazing. "Know you that there is such a one newly come among us, one and maybe more! Will we allow evil to walk these streets, to plunder and murder and rapine? To teach our youth the pathways of sin?" He gazed pointedly at the Maclean family and Paddy squirmed uncomfortably. Thanks to Katy and Janet Kirk, the entire village knew of his conversations with Lady Philippa. He glanced down the bench to where his young brother should have been, but small Sandy was gone.

Aggy could tolerate no more. She rose with great dignity and marched down the aisle. At the door she met small Sandy, who sidled past her and resumed his seat with an expression of cherubic innocence.

The minister watched the departure of one of his flock with a vindictive expression. He had long suspected the old woman's loyalty; again his intuition had been proven correct.

"The stranger among us employs evil fascination," he lamented as Aggy closed the door behind her with a determined thwack. "There are those who can bewitch by a mere glance from their eyes. The Bible tells us of such people." He opened the book to Mark. " 'From without, out of the heart of men, proceed evil thoughts . . . an evil eye.' "

Andrew had not anticipated Aggy's defection, but it fell in well with his plans. He turned to the verses of Matthew. " 'If thine eye be evil, thy whole body shall be full of darkness.' " Paddy glanced down at his small brother suspiciously, but Sandy's guileless countenance was meant to dispel such doubts as his elders might entertain.

Aggy strode wrathfully away from the small building that housed Strachan's religious element. If there was a God, which she had lately come to doubt, then He must be growing mighty impatient with His humble servant, Andrew Macgregor. If He was not, then He possessed a great deal more tolerance than did Aggy.

Aggy was not alone in Strachan's streets on that Sunday morn. Lady Philippa's brindled cat peered cautiously around the corner of a building, then skulked along the street in the old woman's wake. Udolpho was the picture of indignation, whiskers a-twitch and fur on end, as befit one who had been kidnapped and released, all within one short hour. The big cat snarled, causing Aggy to jump and look over her shoulder nervously.

Janet Kirk, having locked herself in one of the inn's smaller bedrooms, carefully applied medicine to her numerous wounds. Who would have thought that the cat would scratch so fiercely, especially after she'd befriended it with saucers of milk and choice pieces of meat? Fortunately, her sleeves could be pulled down to hide the marks. Janet inspected herself in the mirror and was satisfied. She exhibited no signs of strife.

Janet was unaware of the minister's plans concerning Udolpho, and had experienced misgivings while forcing him into the wire cage, for she was fond of animals and knew Andrew MacGregor meant the cat no good. After her bloody experience, however, she had suffered a change of heart. It would have been a pleasure to see the cursed creature dead. She had no doubt it was a demon sent from hell.

She had not liked to miss the service, but it had been an opportunity too rare to be by-passed. With Aggy in church, and the Viscount, Afton, and Lady Philippa gone on a sightseeing drive, she had been free to search the inn, and profitable that enterprise had been, so much so that she had ceased to brood upon the significance of Lady Philippa's retainers' absence from their posts.

Janet had been disappointed at first, for the Earl's belongings had included nothing of interest, but her spirits rose when she began to search Lady Phiilppa's room. Already she had found a deck of strangely marked cards, copious notations that dealt with the infamous Ailcie Ferguson, and more important, a blood-stained nightgown. Had it not been for her sudden thought that her scratches might fester if not properly cleansed, she might have discovered more. There was still time; she returned to Lady Philippa's room.

Janet would have been interested to learn of the forgotten book that rested beneath Lady Philippa's mattress; she might have found a study of that volume an undertaking of extreme interest to her. She might also have exercised more caution had she known that even then the expedition was returning to the inn.

"I cannot credit it," Pippin lamented, limping along the road. Her shoes, not designed for excessive walking, had rubbed a blister on her heel. "These things do not happen to you."

142

"I regret your disillusionment," Severin replied. "As you have discovered, occasionally they do."

Lady Philippa didn't doubt that her companion's pleasant mood was due in part to the argument they'd just had, which he'd won. "I fail to see," she said pettishly, "why you left poor Avery with the rig."

"Why should I not?" the Earl inquired, catching her as she stumbled over a rock in the road. "He may thank me yet. I suspect the temper of my abused beasts is more equitable than yours."

Lady Philippa lapsed into silence, her attention concentrated on her sore heel.

"Don't sulk," Lord Afton murmured, his swarthy features amused. "We shall resume our explorations another day."

"It would be no more than you deserve," Pippin replied grimly, "if that wretched girl has torn the inn to pieces."

"Janet Kirk is too clever for that," said the Earl in bored tones, having already expressed a disinclination to again cover this all-too-familiar ground.

"You're asking for trouble! You know quite well she took that position at the inn so she might poke and pry. Severin, she jumps like a scared rabbit every time someone speaks to her."

"You insult my intelligence," Lord Afton replied plaintively. "I am fully aware of the girl's motives, and have therefore given her ample opportunity to, er, 'poke and pry'. Her endeavors will accomplish nothing, and then we'll be left in peace. Ah, here we are. Shall I carry you over the threshold?" He paused suggestively.

Lady Philippa, stifling an unmaidenly desire to be lifted in those strong arms, limped past him with dignity. She paused to remove her shoes, then staggered up the stairs as gracefully as possible, aware that he watched her halting progress.

Janet Kirk stood peering intently into Lady Philippa's jewel box when its sorely tried owner entered the room. Pippin's temper flared; she yanked a locket from the intruder's hand and swore. "Draggletail!" she cried. "The devil fly away with you!"

Janet, prepared for such emergencies, lashed out viciously and ran from the room. Lady Philippa stared at her scratched and bleeding arm, then began a frenzied search of her belongings. Thus the Earl found her, sitting on the floor with her head in her hands, amidst chaos.

"What on earth is happening here?" he inquired, settling

himself comfortably in the green chair. "Janet is downstairs indulging in some very queer antics. She cut off her nails and threw them into the kitchen fire, then she washed her hands and threw the water into the fire. The kitchen, I hardly need add, is filled with smoke."

Lady Philippa revealed a pale face and pushed the curls out of her eyes. "I cursed her," she said defiantly. "Don't lecture me, Severin! I'd do it again."

Lord Afton regarded his immaculate footwear. "Of course you would," he agreed calmly. "Do you mind telling me why?"

"She was snooping, just as I said she would. When I came in, she had my locket." Belatedly she realized this was not a felicitous admission to make.

"The locket." Severin's expression was amused. "Your indignation was so great when you found Janet with the thing that you erupted into unwise speech?"

"You gave me that piece more years ago than I care to recall," Lady Philippa retorted, and hugged her knees, "and I happen to have a fondness for it."

Lord Afton wore an enigmatic expression and Lady Philippa glowered at him. "Don't look so smug!" she said. "I don't keep it for sentimental reasons." She dropped her eyes. "Its value is not inconsiderable. I see no reason to allow an ignorant half-wit to make off with it!"

Lord Afton gave no indication of having received a quelling set-down. "Since you're so attached to the bauble, I'm surprised you didn't have it on."

"I don't sleep in it," Lady Philippa replied sharply. "I'd probably strangle myself. Anyway, you ordered me awakened at so early an hour that I was fortunate to even accomplish the act of dressing."

"A pity," murmured the Earl, with a thoughtful glance. Lady Philippa ignored the insinuation and raised frightened eyes to his face.

"Severin, she took Lady Cassandra's cards." And, she added silently, pilfered my papers again. It would be little short of miraculous if *this* book was ever done!

"And that's inspired this face of woe? They're Lady Cassandra's responsibility, not yours."

"I realize that, but what will the minister think? He doesn't know I took them from the church! At least, I don't think he knew that I was the culprit."

"I share that sentiment with you," Severin interrupted. "I

quake to imagine his wrath. The cards, however, need not trouble you. By no stretch of the imagination can they constitute proof of anything."

Lady Philippa sighed. "There's more."

"Do you know, I thought there might be?" Lord Afton was at his most beguiling. "Make me the recipient of your girlish confidences, I beg! You perceive me in an unusually mellow mood."

Pippin doubted that unusual state would prove of long duration. "She found my nightgown," she said meekly. "It's gone, too."

"Marvelous," murmured the Earl. Pippin looked at him anxiously.

"What are we to do?"

Severin's face was transformed by a sudden smile. "I have it!" he announced, "though it will mean irreparable damage to both our reputations. I, for one, will never again be able to hold up my head after it becomes known that I have so far forgotten my hostly precepts as to have ravished a maiden visiting my own demesne."

"And thus we passed the crucial time?" Lady Philippa laughed, no whit discomposed by such frank manners and, if truth be known, not at all averse to the idea. "And how will you explain the dirt on my gown?"

Severin shrugged. "I have perverse tastes. You struggled; I overcame you in the relative seclusion of the back yard."

Pippin wore a rueful expression. "I could think of countless more amusing ways in which to ruin myself."

"One must make sacrifices," the Earl replied.

Further conversation was made impossible by a discordant symphony: the anguished cries of a girl mingled with the irate snarls of a cat. "Udolpho!" gasped Lady Philippa and sped from the room. Lord Afton followed at a more decorous pace.

The scene that greeted them afforded Pippin great satisfaction. Udolpho and Janet Kirk were locked in a frenzied embrace, and Udolpho was very much in control. Lady Philippa began reluctantly to remove her pet from its noisome prey.

"It's a demon," Janet gasped, wiping blood from her face.

"It is," agreed the Earl, with a fond look at the beast, resting complacently in its mistress's arms. Udolpho was delivering a disgruntled diatribe on his various uncomfortable adventures. "You would be wise to avoid him in the future."

145

Janet agreed heartily with that advice and departed to bathe her wounds for the second time that day.

"Severin?" asked Pippin, when they were once more alone. "What about Katy?"

"My dear child," replied the Earl, with an airy gesture, "you may leave that matter safely to me."

"Do you mean you know who killed her?"

"Let us say, instead, that I entertain strong suspicions." He gazed at Lady Philippa's expression. "And no, my charming nitwit, I do not intend to share those suspicions with you."

Twenty

Nabby looked charming in a walking dress of white muslin, a sarcenet scarf, kid halfboots, and lilac gloves, but Barnabas exhibited little appreciation of the picture that she made. Nabby sighed and touched the ribbons of her gypsy hat. The ensemble had once belonged to Lady Philippa, who swore it made her look like a simpering miss, and Nabby's nimble fingers had altered it to her shorter frame.

Barnabas was not unaware of his companion's finery, but he had more serious matters on his mind. His devotion to his employer equaled that of her abigail, and Barnabas had a much clearer notion of the danger that threatened Lady Philippa. A curate's son, intended to follow in his father's footsteps, Barnabas had early perceived that only the most outrageous behavior would dissuade his pious, and stubborn, sire from that course. Hence, since he had little wish to enter orders, and even less fondness for his rigid and moralistic parent, Barnabas had run away from home. Young as he had been, and with little knowledge of the ways of the world, Barnabas had soon fallen in with bad company and countless times barely avoided being caught, not only by the irate husbands of the women who so consistently pursued him, but by the law. With no wish to end up dangling from a gallows, and with an excellent set of forged references, Barnabas had gone into service instead. Those glowing references would have done him little good, and perhaps a great deal of harm, with an employer astute enough to check them out, but Lady Philippa had never bothered to ascertain their veracity, believing her own instincts a reliable judge. It was not the first time, Barnabas thought, that his mistress had been led astray by a pretty face.

Barnabas was not sorry that more reckless part of his life had ended, for it had been fraught with danger; he regretted only not knowing his father's reaction to his flight. No matter, the breach would not be healed. Barnabas had been driven to desperate measures, though to none so extreme as some of his compatriots, one of whom had ridden from Gravesend to York in a remarkable fifteen hours to establish an alibi.

But Barnabas had not forgotten his early years, nor the stern parent to whom Andrew Macgregor bore more than a passing resemblance. Barnabas knew the power of such a man and the influence he wielded over his congregation. Right or wrong had little to do with that influence; the parishioners followed blindly where their minister led. Lady Philippa made a great error in dismissing Andrew Macgregor as a crazed old man.

Disgruntled by this indifference, Nabby pleated her skirt and thought viciously of Janet Kirk, in whose company Barnabas was all too often to be found. He sought to hoodwink Nabby with tales that this perseverance was for Lady Philippa's sake, but Nabby was not so easily bamboozled. Had Barnabas explained that Janet began of late to drop hints concerning Andrew Macgregor's plans, Nabby might have been appeased, but Barnabas was not a confiding man. Nabby's spirits were not raised by her rival's almost constant presence at the inn. She wondered glumly if Barnabas had truly developed a *tendre* for the girl; if so, there was nothing to do but wish him happy, and then go drown herself.

"I think," she said mournfully, "that the Viscount has proposed. It's the queerest thing, for Lady Philippa appears sunk in gloom, yet I'll swear she hasn't refused him."

Barnabas looked startled, for his thoughts had proceeded upon an entirely different vein. "She will," he retorted. "I told you before, they'll never make a match of it."

"And that pleases you?" Nabby cried indignantly. "Are you willing to see her dwindle into an old maid?"

Barnabas scowled. "You're so anxious to marry her off that you'll settle for anyone of decent birth. I trust Lady Philippa has more sense!" His expression did not indicate any great hope of this.

"What have you against the Viscount, pray?" Nabby reluctantly turned her steps toward the inn since her escort exhibited an unflattering eagerness to return.

Barnabas shrugged. "He's not the man for her ladyship."

"Then who is?" Nabby wailed. Barnabas made no reply. This utterance of cryptic remarks was not one of the habits that endeared him to her. "Jackanapes!" said she and determined at that moment to prove him wrong. If Lady Philippa didn't have the Viscount, it would not be because Nabby had neglected any opportunity to further that gentleman's cause. This contradictory attitude heartened her so considerably that she entered the inn cheerfully, with no thought for the detested Janet Kirk. Barnabas caught her arm.

"Tell me," he said, "has there been any word of Lady Viccars? She was supposed to arrive several days ago."

Nabby's hazel eyes grew round. She approved of Lady Viccars, that most generous of Lady Philippa's friends, but recalled that Amanda was solely responsible for their presence in the village. Belatedly, Nabby wondered why. "No. Barney, you don't think anything's happened to her?"

Barnabas released her with a short laugh. "It's not Lady Viccars that worries me! That one always lands on her feet." A brooding look clouded his handsome features as he recalled the various escapades into which Amanda had led his mistress. "But I'll be out-of-reason glad to see her again."

Nabby's pleasant mood abruptly vanished, for mention of Lady Viccars brought back unpleasant memories of the Marquis, to whom she had introduced Lady Philippa. Too, Amanda fussed over Barnabas a great deal more than was proper. Silently, Nabby trudged up the stairs.

The inn was suffering a visitation of Alversanes and Galbraiths. "Suffering" was the appropriate word: Valentine and Neville were quarreling.

"You must admit," murmured the Viscount into Lady Philippa's dainty ear, "that it's a tenacious lass." He surveyed Janet Kirk, briskly busy behind the bar. "A female of less purpose would have been moved to give notice before the end of this day."

"She may yet," offered Lady Philippa hopefully, with an unfriendly glance at the object of their conversation.

Avery shook his head. "Not this one. Thus far she's stuck it through your curses and Udolpho's attack. I doubt she'll leave us now."

Lady Philippa watched the bustling girl with a critical eye. The Viscount had been more entertained than surprised by the account of her misadventures with Janet Kirk. "I'll swear she's washed every glass in the place at least three times."

"Efficiency." Avery's brown eyes twinkled. "Katy could never be persuaded to work on the Lord's Day."

"Efficiency, my foot!" snorted her ladyship, albeit delicately. "It's vulgar curiosity. At least Aggy will keep an eye on her."

Aggy was doing precisely that, and with a persistence that would have been amusing under other circumstances. The old woman had moved firmly into the enemy camp with an enthusiasm that was endearing and contagious. She was prepared to withstand a siege, and Lady Philippa would not have been surprised to find her engaged in the preparation of boiling oil!

"Avery!" Valentine interrupted her harangue against her husband long enough to beckon them. "You are keeping mighty aloof! Have we incurred your displeasure?"

The Viscount, who had kept Lady Philippa at his side all the evening, took hold of her hand and drew her to him. Pippin knew that some ulterior motive lay behind this unusual solicitude and speculated as to what it might be. The Earl watched their approach cryptically.

Neville bowed and pulled out a chair, apparently having decided that Lady Philippa was worthy of his attention. She listened to his slightly indelicate compliments with a flattered and somewhat foolish air. The man was undeniably attractive, and she didn't trust him an inch.

"You waste your time, Neville," Valentine said spitefully. "It's obvious that Avery is Lady Philippa's current favorite."

"My dear," retorted Neville, "conversation with a beautiful woman is never a waste of time." His gaze caressed Lady Philippa, whose discomfort was not relieved when the Viscount dropped a proprietary hand on her bare shoulder.

"Take a damper, Avery," the Earl remarked into the sudden silence. "Pippin will think you damnably hot-at-hand."

Lady Philippa remembered Avery's interest in Katy—indeed, that puzzle was never far from her mind!—and wondered if Severin suspected him of complicity in the girl's death. But Katy, despite her timidity, had been a lass with a wandering eye. The laird had paid her marked attention, Neville had flirted indolently with her, and, Pippin suddenly remembered, Katy had once been courted by Paddy Maclean.

"What's this?" Valentine inquired, her bright gaze upon Lady Philippa and the Viscount. "A new development? Do

150

we at last see you *serious*, Avery? Are we to wish you happy, then?"

"You must not expect an announcement yet," the Viscount murmured, with a caressing look. Lady Philippa flushed, mortified by the realization that this loverlike role was for Janet's benefit. Avery needn't appear a doting idiot, she thought resentfully, nor was Lord Afton's amusement well timed. A spirit of rebelliousness moved her to touch lightly the hand that rested casually on her shoulder. She was startled to feel a momentary tightening of the Viscount's grip.

"How intriguing!" Valentine's quick eyes were malicious. Neville grimaced and moved to talk to Janet at the bar. Valentine stared after him, and her lips twisted viciously.

Lady Cassandra cleared her throat and bestowed upon Lady Philippa a meaningful glance. "My dear," she murmured, "I understand you have met my brother Bevis at last. You were fated to do so, of course! I read it in the cards." Duncan, with an irritated expression, led the reluctant Viscount away for a game of darts. Udolpho, deprived of his admiring audience, sat up and viewed the scene thoughtfully. Rats deserting a sinking ship, thought Lady Philippa ruefully, as even Lord Afton moved away.

"Have you found them?" she asked cautiously. "Your missing cards?" Folly, not to have returned the wretched things to Lady Cassandra immediately. Pippin cursed her laggard memory.

"No, but it doesn't signify." Lady Cassandra, not pleased to be sidetracked, fluttered her slender hands. "I have others. Bevis, my dear, was quite taken with you!"

"He was?" Lady Philippa sounded no more astonished than she felt. If Bevis Alversane was smitten, he chose a damned odd way to show it! She could only hope he had not told his sister the precise circumstances of their meeting, for Lady Cassandra had no more discretion than a suckling babe. If *she* knew Lady Philippa had broken into old Macgregor's church, the whole village must share that knowledge by now. It was not a particularly soothing reflection.

Lady Cassandra leaned closer. "You must not mind Bevis's reticence, you know. He must be brought to speak of his feelings to you. Believe me, the feelings are there!"

"He told you," Pippin inquired subtly, "how we met?"

"Of course!" Lady Cassandra's faded eyes were puzzled. "When he delivered my invitation to the inn." She frowned.

151

"A pity that séance was brought to so untimely an end. We must try to contact poor Katy again."

Having little desire to discuss the dead girl, Lady Philippa chose Bevis as the lesser of two evils. "Has your brother always been shy?" Valentine, she thought, was regarding her husband and Janet Kirk with an expression that was positively murderous. Another possible villain? wondered Pippin.

"He has." Lady Cassandra sighed. "I've been reading about natural talismans, and some might benefit Bevis. Mandragora, for example, inspires love, as does powdered toad. The ruby calms excited senses, while hyena skin lends invulnerability." Lady Philippa hoped she didn't look as bored as she felt.

Valentine interrupted them abruptly with a harsh obscenity. She glared at her husband, who appeared unconscious of her rage. "You see how it is with Neville?" she hissed. "He is the greatest beast in nature, so desirous of cutting a figure with his fancy-pieces that he must flaunt his indiscretions in front of his family." Lady Philippa thought it ironic that Valentine should so bewail her husband's rakish tendencies when she herself was not above reproach. Did Neville's behavior prompt his wife to console herself with Avery and the Earl? Or was it the other way around?

"Oh, no," Lady Cassandra protested. "Neville's not like that at all. You mustn't mind his little flirtations; the poor boy gets bored. I've often thought it would have been kinder of Papa not to leave Neville *quite* so much money. It's ruined him, you see."

"His manner is abominable!" Valentine cried. "It cannot but give every genteel female a disgust of him."

Lady Philippa wished herself far away from this nasty little scene. Despite Neville's calm demeanor, he couldn't help but hear Valentine's every word, as could the laird and Avery, apparently oblivious to all but their game of darts. Janet Kirk's cheeks were flushed, and her gaze fixed firmly upon the bar. The Earl, despite the unappreciative look that sat on his harsh features, did not attempt to intervene. Perhaps, mused Pippin, this squabbling was an accepted part of entertainment at the inn.

Udolpho, long enough ignored, rose to his furry feet and paced the length of the room. Lady Philippa watched him idly but didn't interfere. The cat leaped onto the bar, a graceful feat which brought Janet Kirk's horrified face onto a level with his own.

152

Udolpho was not one to bear a grudge. He reached out, claws sheathed, and patted the girl's pallid cheek.

Janet's nerve deserted her. She shrieked and ran from behind the bar. Neville caught her and shook her soundly.

"Stop it!" he roared. Janet subsided into weak sobs.

Valentine, incensed by the sight of another woman in her husband's arms, hurled her glass to the floor and marched across the room.

"Oh, dear," said Lady Cassandra, with a regretful glance at the breakage, "I fear we're in for it now."

"Neville!" Valentine's face was contorted with rage. "I demand that you escort me home!"

Neville observed his wife's irate countenance, but didn't relinquish his armful of trembling femininity. "You must please yourself," he replied. "I prefer to remain here." With an oath, Valentine turned on her heel and stalked from the room.

Odd, thought Lady Philippa, that neither Avery nor Severin offered comfort or assistance. She wondered, not for the first time, which of those unchivalrous gentlemen was Valentine's chosen cavalier.

Twenty-One

"Surely you jest!" Gilly exclaimed, horrified. "It would be the greatest folly."

"Not at all, my dear," Lady Cassandra replied. "It is the perfect thing. Neville will be distracted and recover from his anger with Valentine, and Valentine will find the festivities entertaining."

"Have you told the others of this plan?" Lady Philippa inquired, glancing around the inn's dining room. They were alone, Aggy having led Janet Kirk sternly away so that they might talk undisturbed.

Lady Cassandra shook her head. Her enthusiasm for her new idea was so great that she had lain awake all night planning details. "Duncan and Neville took it into their heads to go fishing late last night, and Valentine had not yet come down when I decided to call on you."

"And Bevis?" Pippin poured more tea.

"One never knows about Bevis." Lady Cassandra presented a dazzling appearance in a promenade dress with gathered sleeves and a high arched collar, and a Spanish coat of fine orange merino with lapels and epaulets and a border of raised white velvet. "Smitten as he is with you, I don't think we may rely on him. You will help with the arrangements, will you not, Lady Philippa?"

Pippin smiled, as much at Gilly's astonishment over Bevis's alleged infatuation as with enthusiasm for Lady Cassandra's plans. "Certainly, as much as I can. I haven't had a great deal of experience with these matters."

Lady Cassandra obviously did not believe that any lady of

Pippin's social standing could be totally ignorant of al fresco parties. "You're far too modest, my dear."

Gilly followed this disagreeable conversation, thunderstruck. She had come to the inn early, hoping to persuade Lady Philippa to the wisdom of immediate departure from Strachan, but Lady Cassandra's presence swayed her from that purpose.

"Lud!" Gilly said, banging her cup on the table in a most inconsiderate way. Lady Cassandra winced. "Can't you see how dangerous this scheme must be? I do not scruple to tell you that the villagers are in high fidgets about Katy's death, and most fervently wish you all to the devil. Dear heaven, I don't know *what* they'd do if they found out you were holding a picnic!"

"This does not concern your villagers," Lady Cassandra pointed out, somewhat acerbically.

Gilly tried reason. "Why don't you postpone your plans, at least until the fuss dies down?"

Lady Philippa was inclined to agree that Lady Cassandra's suggested entertainment was not an altogether felicitous idea, but she suspected also that Lady Cassandra possessed an unexpected stubborn streak.

"Nonsense!" Lady Cassandra was firm. "It's not as if we'd be doing anything exceptionable!"

"Old Macgregor will not remain uninformed," Gilly said ominously. "That man knows everything that happens in this place."

Lady Cassandra's laughter was light and tinkling. "I'm sure you overestimate him," she replied. "Surely he doesn't possess supernatural powers! You must join us, Gilly, you and Lucius. It will be diverting, I promise you."

"Pray accept my excuses," Gilly retorted. She had a hearty wish to avoid further involvement. In truth, she took great enough risk in just coming to the inn. "Lucius and I have a previous engagement."

Lady Philippa knew perfectly well the girl was lying and wished she might do the same. Al fresco parties, with the attendant discomforts of insect bites, poisonous plants, and crumbs, were not among her favorite pursuits, particularly when held, as Lady Cassandra intended, at twilight.

"Are you out of frame, Gilly?" inquired Lady Cassandra. "It is not like you yet, unless I mistake the matter, we have made you excessively cross. If you do not care to join our party, we shall contrive without you, but we would be glad of

156

your company. The invitation remains open, should you change your mind." She sighed. "There is little enough amusement in these wild parts. I daresay our picnic will be the social event of the year."

"I don't like it above half," Gilly repeated, "but I see I cannot dissuade you." It was becoming apparent that Lady Cassandra's understanding was not great.

Lady Philippa wondered why the girl was so set against the idea. Little harm could come of the party, despite Gilly's protests; Lady Cassandra certainly planned nothing even the least witchlike. "Where will you have the picnic?" she asked.

"Does it matter, dear?" Lady Cassandra's pale brows rose. "I thought the open field near the castle. Unless someone has a better idea?"

"I'd suggest," contributed Gilly with little enthusiasm, "that you get as far from the village as possible." If she couldn't stop this insanity, at least she might be able to prevent it from getting totally out of hand.

"What fun we shall have!" Lady Cassandra exclaimed, clapping her hands. "Duncan will surely know of an appropriate site. What else? Oh, we'll want a bonfire."

"Must you?" Gilly asked glumly.

Lady Cassandra nodded. "Certainly."

Pippin's spirits were not raised, it would take a roaring volcano to combat the Highland chill. Lady Cassandra gathered together her various belongings, including shawl, gloves, and reticule, and rose to leave. "I wonder," she said, "if Lord Afton will attend."

"I consider that unlikely," Lady Philippa retorted, amazed at her own disappointment. "Lord Afton will probably consider it a foolish waste of time, and beneath his dignity."

Lady Cassandra left them then, apparently well pleased. Pippin suspected she would meet Bevis again at his sister's party, even if it was very much against his wishes.

Gilly dropped her head into her hands. "A picnic!" she mourned. "You had much better not engage in this reprehensible scheme."

"Do not trouble yourself," said Lady Philippa, privately concluding that Miss Graham's nerves were perilously close to being overset. "I could not dissuade Lady Cassandra even if I wished to do so, for my word weighs little with her. Come, do not be so glum! There will be little harm done."

"We shall shortly see." Gilly foresaw that she would soon achieve the melancholy satisfaction of having her suspicions proved correct. "I only hope you may not find yourselves with the devil to pay over this business." Lady Philippa only laughed.

Janet Kirk, at that moment, walked briskly down the inn's dark hallway. She was pleased with her success as an informer. Katy had been inept, wasting time with romantic foolishness and overlooking obvious evidence, and as a consequence, much proof had doubtless already been destroyed. There would be no more to escape the watcher's eye!

Andrew Macgregor had actually expressed his satisfaction with Janet's efforts. It had not been easy to slip away long enough to deliver the parcel to him, but she managed to snatch a moment while shopping for Aggy, who was understandably reluctant to show her face in the village. Not for anything would Janet have been in Aggy's place, for the old woman had revealed herself to be one with the idolaters. Janet herself might consort with heathens, but Janet was engaged in the Lord's work. And if the Lord didn't choose to protect her, then Janet could protect herself. Already, by prompt action, she had withstood the malignancy of a curse.

The minister was pleased with the contraband. His eyes had widened at the sight of the blood-stained nightgown, and he had very gingerly inspected the strange cards and the hand-written notes. Janet applauded his quick appreciation of those articles. Andrew Macgregor might be of advanced age, but his wits were still keen.

Nor had he berated her for her failure with that infernal cat, not that the blame was truly hers. Only an imp from hell could have escaped that stalwart cage. It was a miracle that she captured the creature at all, and Janet was relieved to learn that she wasn't expected to repeat the feat. There were limits to even Janet's dedication. She had no wish to lay eyes upon that wicked creature again.

Janet regretted that she had not been able to confiscate the locket, for she remembered Lady Philippa's violent reaction when she saw it in Janet's hand. Andrew Macgregor agreed that this was curious and that possession of the locket was of paramount importance. He trusted Janet to obtain it for him. Despite Aggy's constant supervision, Janet was confident that with patience and vigilance the opportunity would again come her way. She pushed open the kitchen door and dropped her parcels on the table.

"It took you an unconscionable long time," Aggy muttered

suspiciously, moving to deal with the purchases. "Now I'll be late with the master's meal."

"It won't hurt him," Janet retorted flippantly. She saw nothing in the dark foreigner to inspire devotion; indeed, on closer acquaintance, she found him positively sinister. "I came back as quick as I could. There's a terrible uproar in the town." She neglected to add that she wasted precious moments in idle conversation with the bedazzling Barnabas.

Aggy paled. "What now?"

Janet related the news with relish. "One of the Macleans' sheep was found this morning with its throat cut wide open."

Aggy stared in bewilderment. "Its throat? 'Twas a dog, surely! You know how they go when they've had a taste of warm blood."

Janet grasped a broom and began to sweep the floor. "It was no dog. Or any other animal unless one's learned to carry a knife. Its throat wasn't mangled, it was slit clean."

"Leave that!" Aggy busied herself at the stove. "Don't you know better than to be raisin' the dust when I'm tryin' to fix food? Sit down and keep out of my way. You can carry that tray when I'm done."

Janet hadn't missed Aggy's shaking hands. "What about Lady Philippa?" she asked casually. "Doesn't she break her fast?"

"That one doesn't eat enough to keep a bird alive." The old woman assumed an elaborate nonchalance. "And what do they say about the sheep? Surely 'twas some half-wit's idea of a joke?"

"That's not what I heard," Janet replied. "No one rightly knows what to make of it, but no one's talking of a prank. The Macleans are very wroth—it was their prize ram."

"Then they shouldna let it roam."

"It didn't roam," Janet said placidly. "It was safe in the pasture, and no one heard a thing." She glanced at the old woman. It wouldn't do to push Aggy too far. Janet chose her words carefully. "I don't hold with it myself, but some say that it's a punishment on Paddy for being too friendly with yon Sassenach."

"Hogwash!" cried Aggy vehemently.

Janet shrugged. "And the cows' milk has gone sour."

Aggy was shaken; to a family that depended on their livestock for the major portion of their livelihood, these were catastrophic events. She shoved the tray to Janet.

"Take this up to the master," she said. "He'll be in his room."

Janet obeyed, thinking it was a lazy man that stayed in his chamber until well past noon. She could not know of the explorations that took the Earl stealthily about the town while the villagers were asleep.

He was not communicative and merely told her to leave the tray. Janet was relieved; the man made her uneasy. Not one to let a chance go by, she paused and put her ear to Lady Philippa's door. There was no sound, and Janet carefully stepped inside.

The red-haired woman was not in her room but a mound of black and orange fur lay in the middle of the bed. It opened one orange eye, inspected the intruder, twitched one black ear, and began to wash its feet.

Janet paused, undecided, but the cat didn't appear interested in her. She took a cautious step into the room. Udolpho looked up and wriggled his multicolored nose. Janet's courage deserted her. She quietly closed the door and proceeded down the hall.

Twenty-Two

Lady Philippa had rebelled against the tedium of the inn. Surely, with the exercise of caution, she might enjoy the brisk fresh air without being accosted! A grumbling Nabby had been persuaded to accompany her.

But Fate, in the form of Andrew Macgregor, was to prove Lady Philippa's assumptions incorrect. Never had the minister imagined that he would be so fortunate as to meet this disturbing female face to face. He broke into frenzied speech.

"Thou shalt not suffer a witch to live!" he cried, raising a fist to the heavens. "Neither shall ye use enchantment, nor observe times."

"Poppycock," replied Lady Philippa, indignant at having her aimless perambulations thus disturbed. "Don't quote your Bible at me!"

The old man shook with rage. "What peace, so long as the whoredom of Jezebel and her witchcrafts are so many?"

Lady Philippa regarded him with contempt. What magic did this mad old man possess that he held an entire village in thrall? "Can you talk in nothing but Scripture?" she jeered. "Old man, you are fast becoming a tedious bore!"

Andrew Macgregor opened his mouth in protest, but Lady Philippa had the bit between her teeth. Nabby closed her eyes and prayed. "Witches!" said Lady Philippa, with fine scorn. "Open your eyes, Macgregor! The times of witches are gone. No one with the least claim to intelligence could believe in such things today."

"For rebellion is as the sin of witchcraft!" bellowed the minister, combatting impiety with verse. But the evil woman

161

was so hardened that she did not even flinch. "Stubbornness is as iniquity and idolatry!"

Lady Philippa seriously hoped the minister, whose face had assumed an alarming hue, wasn't going to expire at her feet. Nabby plucked anxiously at her sleeve.

"I strongly suggest, for your own sake," Pippin added firmly, "that you try to overcome this preoccupation with the past! It is decidedly unhealthy, and extremely contagious besides. This entire village has been infected with your mania." The old man's eyes bulged, and he struggled for breath. Judging that he'd taken her point, Lady Philippa turned away. "*I'd* recommend," she added, as an afterthought, "a good dose of mineral water! It would take your mind off these ridiculous pursuits."

"Prophets that speak in the names of other gods shall die!" Andrew Macgregor screamed at her retreating back. "A woman that hath a familiar spirit shall be stoned to death!"

Oddly refreshed by this encounter, Pippin walked briskly toward the inn. Nabby drew a deep breath. "Gave me a nasty turn, he did," she gasped. "I thought that you would come to fisticuffs! Mighty hoity-toity that one is, for a commoner! Lady Philippa, it would suit me fine if we were to set out for London today."

"I am not so poor-spirited!" Pippin replied. She then whistled a jolly little tune and broke off only when Nabby sniffed disapprovingly. "Consider Amanda's displeasure if she were to travel this great distance to find us already gone."

"Prudence, I'd call it," Nabby muttered. "Lady Viccars will give me a terrible scold for not taking better care of you." And that in spite of the fact that their current difficulties were entirely Lady Viccars' fault. Nabby glanced sideways at her headstrong mistress. Or, she amended, at least partly.

Rapidly approaching hoofbeats interrupted them, and Nabby glanced nervously behind her. The minister had disappeared. Only Neville Alversane was in view, riding hell-for-leather on a lathered horse. Nabby raised her hand to wave at him. It was then that a rock struck Lady Philippa's temple, knocking her senseless to the ground.

Pippin surfaced from darkness to the sound of Neville's voice. She lay face-down on a very hard and prickly sofa. Horsehair, she thought, and correctly deduced that she must be in the inn's little used drawing room.

"I tell you I saw no one else," Neville protested irritably.

"I had other matters with which to concern myself! I saw Lady Philippa fall, and I brought her in here."

Pippin wasn't yet prepared to face the inhabitants of the inn, particularly Lord Afton, with his inclination toward violent wrath. How furious he would be with her! She kept her eyes firmly closed, no great deception since her head was racked with pain.

"It's not serious," the Earl commented, as a weeping Nabby applied compresses to her mistress's brow. "I doubt there's danger of concussion." His fingers explored the area, and Lady Philippa suppressed a strong urge to yelp with pain. "Find me some scissors! I'll have to cut her hair."

Pippin sat up abruptly, pushing Nabby aside. "I'll see you hanged first," she announced faintly, clutching her head. "You'll do no such thing." The room danced, and she clenched her teeth against nausea.

Lord Afton folded his arms and looked amused. "A miraculous recovery," he remarked, "though you still look a trifle green. Does your head ache abominably?"

Lady Philippa groaned and fought futilely to retain her dignity. At the Earl's gesture, Nabby picked up the basin and withdrew.

"I'm sure it is no more than you deserve," Severin said callously, "but my tender heart can't bear the sight of a woman in pain." He shook two tablets from a small bottle and handed her a glass of water. "Take these."

Lady Philippa raised her head and inspected the offering suspiciously. "What are they?"

"It's refreshing to find a member of your sex that doesn't exhibit an overwhelming addiction to panaceas!" Lord Afton commented acidly. "But you do choose inappropriate times to exhibit your scruples."

Pippin still hesitated. Was he so angry that he sought to poison her? Surely not! Yet Lady Philippa had to admit that her conduct, at least from the Earl's point of view, was far from commendable.

"Don't you trust me?" Severin inquired, with marked impatience. "They will deaden the pain. I've no desire to commit vulgar mayhem on your unconscious body, and, despite what you may have heard, the white slave trade does *not* flourish in Scotland."

Lady Philippa managed a weak smile and swallowed the pills. Neville appeared with two glasses of brandy, of which the Earl received one. She sighed.

"Yes," said Severin, with a softened expression, "I realize you've had a trying experience. If you behave, you may remain here while we talk. It is a shame that Avery chose this particular time to go riding; he would make a much more attentive nursemaid than I, and without lacerating your tender sensibilities."

So he *was* furious with her! And with Avery, too, it seemed. Lady Philippa remained prudently silent, wondering what misdeed the merry Viscount had committed.

"What brings you here in mid-afternoon?" Lord Afton's voice expressed nothing but idle curiosity, but his gaze at Neville was razor-sharp. Pippin glanced at Neville in time to see him swallow a sizable amount of whiskey. The man was pale and his hands shook. "Surely not a fondness for our company?"

Neville's face was haggard. "Valentine," he said bluntly, "is dead."

Lady Philippa gasped, but Lord Afton impassively regarded the other man. Perhaps it was mere imagination, but Pippin thought Severin stiffened as Neville grasped his arm.

"She did away with herself," he insisted. "I swear to you, Severin, I had nothing to do with it!"

The Earl gently removed himself from that clutching hand. "How?" he inquired softly.

"An overdose of laudanum," Neville replied despairingly. "She took it frequently, even though I disapproved."

Lady Philippa thought the whole thing was very strange, but maybe this sense of unreality was due to the tablets she'd swallowed. Valentine was dead, but why should Neville offer Severin explanations? They should be offering him sympathy.

"I'm sorry . . ." she began, but she was ignored.

"What happened after you left here last night?" Lord Afton asked. Neville raised tortured eyes.

"Nothing. I didn't even see her. Duncan can vouch for that, we were together." They had left the inn together, after Neville had charmed Janet Kirk out of imminent hysterics, so that much was true. Pippin fought against increasing giddiness.

"I discovered her body this morning when we returned." Neville's voice was anguished. "It doesn't make sense! Things were no worse than usual; she had no reason to put a period to her existence!"

Lady Philippa thought that a sad epithet for a marriage, if an all-too-ordinary one. "Did she leave a note?" The men turned to stare at her, and she smiled innocently. "Isn't that what suicides do?"

"The note doesn't make sense either," Neville groaned. "She said she couldn't live with the knowledge. And I don't know what the deuce it means."

"Maybe she thought you were indulging in an *affaire*," Pippin offered brightly. Whatever the tablets Lord Afton had given her, they had a speedy effect! The Earl sat down, choosing a chair facing both of them.

"That wouldn't have bothered her," Neville replied bitterly, with a glance at Severin. The Earl shrugged.

Lady Philippa saw her opportunity. "Maybe," she said, carefully choosing her words, "she thought you had something to do with Katy's accident."

Neville glowered. "Her condition, you mean?" He shook his head. "I know what they say in the village, that I was her fine foreign gentleman, but I swear I never did more than talk to the girl." He glanced again at Severin. "I'm not the one with low tastes."

Lady Philippa was suddenly, and inexplicably, irate. "You're implying that Severin—"

"Quiet!" demanded the Earl. "He's implying nothing of the sort."

"I can't understand it," Neville repeated. "Why would Valentine kill herself? I denied her nothing that she desired."

Lady Philippa opened her mouth, but Neville forestalled her. "I know what you're thinking, but you're wrong! For all her foolish jealousy, Valentine had all she wanted of me."

"I don't think," said Lady Philippa faintly, her words slurred, "that I'd want a marriage like that." Her eyelids felt as though they were weighed down with sandbags, and she fought desperately against drowsiness. Severin had tricked her, the brute, insuring that during this most exciting of all evenings she would be safely tucked away in her bed. But his next words brought her wide awake again.

"If you don't learn to mind your tongue," said Lord Afton, "you'll have no marriage at all." Ignoring her owl-eyed stare, he turned to Neville. "How are the others?"

"Cassandra is prostrated," Neville retorted with fine irony. "I think you'd better come."

"I shall accompany you!" announced Lady Philippa, struggling to rise.

"No, my little termagant, that you will not!" Firmly, the Earl pushed her back down on the sofa, then moved to the

165

door and called for Aggy. The old woman promptly appeared, a teacup in one hand.

"Remain here," Lord Afton said to his housekeeper, "until I return. Don't leave this room for any reason at all, and allow no one to come in."

Aggy nodded, a grim sentinel.

"Severin?" said Neville plaintively. "What happened to her? She used to be so frivolous, so gay."

But the Earl closed the door, and Lady Philippa missed his reply. She was intensely curious. She was also developing a strong dislike for tea.

"Read them for me?" Lady Philippa asked, shoving the cup toward Aggy. It would keep the old woman occupied, and give Pippin time for some badly needed reflection. What was happening in Strachan, with, first, Katy dead and now, Valentine? And who had hurled that rock at her? "And for heaven's sake, try to find something encouraging this time!"

"That may be verra difficult, m'lady," Aggy said, but she sat down and inspected the cup. "But this is better. Here's scandal again, an owl." Pippin looked startled, but didn't speak. "A jug, a gathering of old acquaintances; and a hare, the return of an absent friend."

"This sounds promising," Lady Philippa remarked absently. Thought was proving very difficult; her mind clung molasseslike to the inexplicable Lord Afton.

"A tomahawk," Aggy continued, "gains by determination." The familiar scowl settled on her brow. " 'Tisn't all good, m'lady. Here's a coffin, and that's a sign of death."

Lady Philippa sighed and settled herself more comfortably on the hard sofa. Perhaps later she might make sense of all these queer events. Pondering Severin's concern with the dead women, Pippin fell asleep, only to dream that the charming Viscount plotted her demise.

Twenty-Three

~~~~~~

It was evening, and Lord Afton had brought Lady Cassandra, who insisted on seeing for herself that Pippin was unharmed, back with him to the inn. Pippin sat with the others in the taproom, and the pillow that Lady Cassandra had solicitously placed behind her back did nothing to ease the dull throbbing in her head.

Aggy withdrew into the kitchen to supervise the preparation of a light but substantial meal. She had little help; Janet Kirk's excitement at the startling news of Valentine Alversane's death, and the less startling news of the attack on Lady Philippa, had rendered her incompetent. Within fifteen minutes, the girl had managed to break an entire set of dishes and, by injudicious comments, antagonize Aggy beyond tolerance.

Janet had been a good barometer of the village's fluctuating opinions, but Aggy suspected she might retain a calmer outlook without that particular knowledge. True to her boast, Janet had been a good worker, but Aggy preferred to perform the extra chores herself and avoid further mischief. Then, too, there was Nabby, jealously eager to perform any task that concerned her mistress, and consequently of great assistance. Aggy glanced at that young miss, engaged in the freshening of a gown. If Nabby's frowning countenance was any indication, her thoughts were no more cheerful than Aggy's own.

Aggy still had sources of information open to her: primarily Gilly, who was only slightly less practiced than Andrew Macgregor in learning every relevant word spoken in the vil-

167

lage. It didn't improve Aggy's frame of mind to know that Gilly was seriously disturbed. She had known the lass from a bairn; Gilly was fanciful, but not unduly pessimistic. Gilly firmly believed that the incomers should immediately depart.

The village had been struck dumb by the news of Valentine Alversane's death, but that happy state didn't last. Rumor blamed Neville; he was alternately accused of driving his wife to suicide and of killing her himself. The contents of the cryptic note were known, and Katy's foreign gentleman was recalled. One contingent claimed that Neville was that gentleman and that Valentine, unable to bear this horrific discovery, destroyed herself.

An opposing viewpoint, voiced primarily by the minister, was that Valentine had died as the result of malicious witchcraft. He claimed Lady Philippa was to blame, not only for this disaster but for Katy's demise, the Macleans' slaughtered sheep, and the cows' undrinkable milk. The old man pointed out that Strachan's various trials had not commenced until after the lady's arrival.

The village also knew of her ladyship's verbal attack on the minister and was aghast; they knew of the rock that had struck her and were pleased. If anyone knew who had hurled that pellet, he was keeping his own counsel.

Janet Kirk's theft of Lady Philippa's belongings was also public knowledge. The cards were regarded with general awed horror, as were her ladyship's notes on Ailcie Ferguson, but the stained nightgown was considered definite proof. Of what, Aggy wasn't sure. She'd listened to Lord Afton's instructions carefully and had painstakingly carried them out, but she couldn't see that the tale of a fearsome nightmare that drove Lady Philippa to sleepwalk, and her subsequent tumble and rescue by the Earl, had achieved a happy result. It was not the sort of thing that the villagers, with their nasty minds and general contempt for foreigners, would believe; and Andrew Macgregor had twisted the story to suit his own incomprehensible purposes. He claimed that her ladyship had seduced the Earl, and having tired of him, had cast her eyes toward Neville, an act of unprincipled rashness that had resulted in Valentine's death.

Aggy wasted little time in ruminating on Andrew Macgregor, whom she would never have expected to act other than he did. His father had been another such one, and Aggy firmly believed in the awful powers of heredity, which was not to say that the present situation was anything but thoroughly absurd.

The story of Udolpho's capture and miraculous escape was also known. Aggy had her own ideas about that, having recalled Sandy Maclean's cherubic expression as he returned to the church, but Aggy intended to voice her suspicion to no one. Small Sandy was a lad such as she remembered her own Black Douglas to have been. Ah, he had teased and tormented her all their growing-up years. 'Twas no wonder she finally married him.

Aggy shook off these wistful thoughts. Black Douglas had gone to the worms, as had many a better man, as would she, and as would Andrew Macgregor, for all his pious ways. She derived great satisfaction from the latter thought.

Nabby gazed at an exquisite lace ruffle and sniffled. She felt Aggy's sharp eyes on her, but the old woman made no comment, and Nabby concentrated fiercely on her work. She knew she should never have agreed to accompany her mistress on the stroll that had resulted in her injury, but how was Nabby to refuse? Even had she drummed up sufficient resolution to say no, the impetuous Lady Philippa was quite likely to have set out alone. It was grossly unfair of Barnabas to accuse her of negligence, nor had it been necessary for him to hold out Katy and Valentine Alversane as examples of a fate that might yet stalk their mistress. Nabby brushed an angry hand across her cheek. She was only too aware that her beloved mistress was in danger! That very thought had kept her awake a good many nights.

Aggy was not unaware of Nabby's distress, but attributed it to yet another quarrel with the divine Barnabas. Having two sharp eyes in her head, Aggy didn't for a moment believe his apparent interest in Janet Kirk to be serious and thought that damsel fortunate for it. Young Barnabas might be dazzling to behold, but if Nabby's woebegone countenance was any indication, he possessed the devil's own temper. Aggy cast such trivialities from mind to concentrate on more serious matters.

Promptly upon her dismissal from the inn, Janet Kirk had begun to talk. Her exploits were generally admired and her bravery applauded. Aggy made a sour face and wished she'd exposed the girl to the full and devastating range of her temper, rather than just a mild taste of it. She cast a fond glance at the brindled cat sleeping on the kitchen table. Of all Janet's acts, her abduction of Udolpho was the one Aggy found hardest to forgive.

169

"Och, ye're a bonnie cuddie," she whispered and fetched a tempting morsel of fish. It pleased her to think of Janet's multitudinous scratches.

Udolpho purred, then suddenly abandoned the delicacy to march to the front door, demanding stridently that Aggy accompany him. Intrigued, Aggy did so.

The door was locked and bolted. Aggy did not underestimate the potential violence of the villagers, and she was prepared. Udolpho stood on his back legs and scratched on the wood. The old woman could not withstand his plaintive cries.

Aggy stared at the figure that stood on the threshold. "Ach, and who might *you* be?" she cried, then blinked and stared again. "If you're seeking lodging, we've no room at the inn."

The woman threw back her head and laughed huskily, revealing both a lovely throat and pearl-white teeth. Udolpho slipped past Aggy's ankles and rubbed against the stranger's skirts, uttering cries of greeting. Later, Aggy could not explain how it happened, but the woman set her aside as easily as she might a stick of furniture and walked unerringly down the hallway and into the taproom.

Lord Afton glanced up from his newspaper and smiled. "So you have joined us at last!" he said. "You behold us in the midst of siege. I suppose your luggage is outside?"

"It awaits your pleasure, my friend," the woman murmured, and cast an appraising look at the bandage on Lady Philippa's head. "I see I have arrived barely in the nick of time!"

Pippin, being engrossed in argument with Lady Cassandra, who remained determined to have her al fresco party, paid no heed to the newcomer. The Viscount, however, was more perceptive, and his eyes narrowed appreciatively. The stranger's gaze remained concentrated on the back of Lady Philippa's head, and Pippin suddenly spun around.

"Amanda!" She regarded Lady Viccars without overt delight. "I have a great deal to say to you!"

"I thought you might," murmured Lady Viccars. She was a raven-haired and amber-eyed lady, perhaps in her mid-forties, so fair of face and statuesque of figure as to make any gentleman's eye gleam. "I trust you can contain yourself until I am less fatigued." She yawned prettily. "I do apologize for my delay; there was a German princeling, you see."

"A princeling!" Lady Philippa repeated. Lady Cassandra blinked in amazement, and the Viscount's lips twitched.

"But of course!" Amanda opened wide her exquisitely dark-lashed eyes. "Surely you do not think I would have tarried for anyone less?" Despite her irritation with her friend, Pippin laughed. Lady Viccars was incorrigible.

"I've ordered your various paraphernalia taken to your room, Amanda," Lord Afton said, reclaiming his chair. "Do you always travel with such pomp?"

"One never knows," replied Amanda, seating herself gracefully near him, "when one may encounter an emergency. I am a creature of habit, and among those habits are both comfort and luxury! Did you release Archimedes?"

"Dear heaven!" Lady Philippa exclaimed. Various of Amanda's other habits, verging as they did on outright eccentricity, had long been the talk of the *ton*. But what in a lesser being might be considered downright bizarre was accorded in a Duke's daughter with a portion of several thousand pounds a year merely charming originality. "You didn't bring Archie!"

"My dear Pippin," replied Lady Viccars, with an hauteur that was nullified by the sparkling mischief in her amber eyes, "you know very well that Archimedes accompanies me everywhere."

"I left Archie," interjected the Earl, "inspecting the rafters. He will doubtless join us soon."

Lady Cassandra eyed the newcomer thoughtfully. If Lady Philippa could not be persuaded to take Bevis in hand, then perhaps Lady Viccars might. Wondering at the exact sum of Amanda's fortune, for wealth this lady obviously possessed, Lady Cassandra determined to invite her to the upcoming festivities. She eyed Amanda's ensemble—a cardinal mantle of black cloth, lined and trimmed with white fur; black gloves and half-boots of kid; a Prussian helmet; a deceptively simple black silk frock—and deduced that it had cost more than Duncan allowed her to spend for clothing in an entire year.

"I recall the occasion," Lady Philippa mused, not ill-pleased to set aside her own problems temporarily, "when Archie became offended with the hostess of a soiree."

"The woman was a boor," protested Amanda, raising perfect brows. "I thought Archimedes' behavior singularly apt. Do you know that terrible female dared ask me to replace her gown?"

Aggy appeared with her trays and stared again. If Andrew Macgregor thought Lady Philippa possessed of the devil,

171

what would he make of this one? That complexion was so fair that the woman must surely paint. She offered the tray to Lady Viccars and closely inspected her skin, but found neither a trace of cosmetics nor a flaw.

Amanda, aware of the scrutiny, a not unusual event, glanced up at Aggy and smiled with the effect of sudden sunlight on a cloudy day. Then Archimedes appeared, engaged in wavering and uncertain flight, and perched on the back of Amanda's chair. Aggy froze, her tray clutched in rigid hands, at sight of the creature, a vision of intermingled blackish-brown, grayish-white, and buff, with conspicuous ear-tufts. Archimedes was not small; his body was sixteen inches long, his wingspread all of forty inches wide. The owl and the old woman stared at each other. A few weeks ago Aggy's reaction would have been open-mouthed bewilderment, but exposure to the foreigners had vastly broadened her outlook. She leaned closer, and the owl turned his head to inspect her with lemon-yellow eyes.

Lady Cassandra introduced herself, patience at an end. "I am planning an al fresco party tomorrow night, Lady Viccars. I should be delighted if you will attend."

"Tomorrow . . ." mused Amanda, with what Lady Philippa immediately recognized as her scheming look. "Saint John's Eve. . . . It is kind of you to include me."

Pippin said nothing, wondering suddenly at Lady Viccars' interest in Strachan. Amanda was one of the few people who knew the old tale of Lady Philippa and Avery and the Earl; and she had learned it not from Pippin but from Severin, a long-time friend. Or, thought Pippin with an oddly sinking sensation, was he more? She tried to recall the various comments Amanda had let drop regarding Severin over the years. Few they were, but pointed, she recalled. But no conclusions could be drawn from Amanda's chance remarks. Lady Viccars was both unprincipled and devious, and in addition an accomplished, if charming, liar.

Saint John's Eve! Aggy gazed upon the incomers with consternation. Herbs attained their maximum virtue for good if gathered at the full moon, and Fires of Saint John, one of the shortest and most magical dates of the year, was extremely favorable for the picking of herbs. But if there was to be a moonlight picnic, Aggy, for one, had no intention of venturing out of doors.

"I have to be the one to interject a dissident note," the Viscount interrupted, moving proprietarily to Lady Philippa's side, "but don't you think it's a trifle ill-timed? Consider Valentine's unfortunate demise." He did not appear to notice that Lady Viccars eyed him thoughtfully.

"Piffle!" retorted Lady Cassandra, put out of patience with this persistent niggling. "It's exactly the diversion that we all need."

"It does not seem," commented Lady Viccars, with a curious look toward the impassive Earl, "that you have been precisely dull." She turned her gaze to Lady Philippa's bandaged head.

"You might consider," the Viscount added with a touch of impatience, "that Pippin has managed to endow the villagers with a very unfortunate opinion of her."

"You make it sound," Lady Philippa said indignantly, "as if I deliberately set them against me!" Archimedes dropped from the chair and waddled across the table to murmur soothingly in her ear.

"Did you not?" Lord Afton inquired. "Can you claim to have handled this situation with tact and discretion?" Lady Philippa glowered at him, but ventured no reply.

"Have you been up to your usual tricks?" inquired Lady Viccars, with an odd little smile. "Pippin, I despair of you." She awarded Lord Afton a comradely wink. "I ask you, what are we to do with a dab of a girl who is such a widgeon as to think she's up to snuff?"

"Dab of a girl?" Lady Philippa repeated, highly incensed by both her friend's words and the languid attention she bestowed upon the Earl. The Viscount laughed, and Amanda ignored them both.

"Consider," she continued sadly, "the inequities of my position. I am engaged in important undertakings—"

"Important?" interrupted Lady Philippa heatedly. Was it Amanda's purpose to make her look a brattish child? "Breaking half the hearts in Europe?"

"You misjudge me," Lady Viccars retorted, grief-stricken. "I fancy I've accounted for more than half! Important undertakings, in which I am constantly interrupted by an inconsiderate friend who thinks my main purpose in life is to extricate her from unfortunate situations."

"Unfair," Lady Philippa commented, amused despite her irritation. "I haven't seen you for two months."

"Ah, but consider the circumstances!" Lady Viccars said, afflicted by a realistic tremor. Lady Philippa did not care to

173

consider them, concerning as they had the luckless Marquis. "Dear Pippin, *how* can you be so lacking in prudence?"

The Earl smiled. "You go too far, Amanda," he said, "since prudence is hardly among the virtues you yourself can claim."

"It is true," grieved Amanda and touched his hand. "But virtue is so boring, is it not?"

Aggy had been both fascinated and dismayed by this conversation. "Pardon me, m'lady," she said to Amanda, at last setting down her tray. "But the lot of you would be best away from here before there's worse trouble than there already is."

Amanda reluctantly abandoned her game. "Indubitably," she replied, "but think how excessively dull!" She looked deceptively helpless. "Do you think someone might tell me just what this trouble is? I collect only that Pippin has started it."

"That is a gross exaggeration," Lady Philippa protested halfheartedly. So many people held her responsible that she almost did so herself. "I didn't start anything."

"But what about my picnic?" Lady Cassandra interrupted plaintively.

"Tomorrow night," Amanda mused. "To be sure, we must all attend."

Lord Afton's mouth twisted wryly. "Your logic astounds me, Amanda," he remarked. "I suppose you'll insist that Pippin be present?"

"Certainly not!" Lady Viccars was indignant. "I do not *insist* that my friends do anything except clean their teeth and bathe regularly." She regarded Lady Philippa critically. "Which I assume Pippin does. If she wishes to attend the picnic, she must certainly do so."

The Earl did not appear at all happy to have two reckless females on his hands. "It could be very dangerous for both of you."

"Pooh!" said Amanda, with an enchanting smile. "Dearest Severin, I like you not at all in this namby-pamby guise. Danger is one of the most stimulating emotions, as you should have learned by now."

Lady Philippa moved irritably and winced at the resultant pain. "Pippin," said Lady Viccars briskly, "you are not well! I suggest you go immediately to your room so that I may speak privately with Severin. Perhaps *he* will oblige me with an account of what's been happening here."

"I will escort you," murmured Avery, helping Lady Philippa to rise.

Pippin had no spirit left to rebel. In the hallway, she smiled at her companion. "You do not need to escort me, you know. I stand in no danger of being accosted, at least within these walls."

"One cannot take too many precautions," the Viscount replied, taking firm possession of her arm. "Danger may strike at any moment, even here. Have you already forgotten Valentine's suicide and young Katy's so-called accident? I cannot urge you strongly enough to take the utmost care."

Lady Philippa shivered, recognizing not only the truth of Avery's words but also remembering that his own loyalties were not without doubt. "Have I frightened you?" the Viscount inquired as he guided her up the stairs.

"Not at all," she retorted, wondering if such had been his intent. "I am no milk-and-water miss."

"Agreed." There was laughter in Avery's voice. "You are far too bold, my darling, although whether it stems from bravery or imprudence I cannot say."

"Avery!" Lady Philippa paused at the entrance to her chamber. Her heart was not in this idle banter, her mind engaged in heated speculation upon what Amanda might be saying privately to Severin. "These are hardly words designed to advance your suit with me."

The Viscount smiled and gently seized her shoulders. "It is good in you to remind me of my negligence," he murmured and drew her close.

"That was not," Lady Philippa protested, when she had regained her breath, "precisely what I had in mind."

"Such maidenly confusion!" the Viscount marveled. "I would not have thought it of you." His tone grew suddenly serious. "I do not mean to press you for an answer, Pippin, but I do ask you to believe that my heart and my person are yours to command. I believe I should be the happiest man on earth were you to consent to be my wife."

Lady Philippa stammered in confusion—what she scarcely knew, and escaped into her room.

Twenty-Four

Lady Philippa tossed and turned, seeking to reclaim her deep and dreamless sleep. Long experience had taught her that the effort would prove futile; at length she sat up and lit her candle. It was then that she remembered the small volume appropriated from Andrew Macgregor's church. She fished it out from beneath her matress, settled herself comfortably, and began to read. She frowned in concentration, her lower lip caught between her teeth, as she tried to decipher the cramped, crabbed handwriting.

Had Lady Philippa been observed by any but the faithful Udolpho, that audience would have been increasingly intrigued by her ladyship's facial expressions. Her eyebrows climbed by degrees up her smooth forehead, then abruptly lowered again, like a child's jumping-jack; her aristocratic nose twitched; her green eyes grew large as saucers, then narrowed to contemplative slits. At length she leaped to her feet with a satisfied exclamation, then strode purposefully from the room.

Lady Philippa had no doubt that Amanda was awake; Lady Viccars was as nocturnal as her owl, compensating for the lateness of the hours she kept by remaining in her darkened bedchamber till late afternoon. It was time, Pippin thought grimly, that Lady Viccars offered some explanations of her own conduct.

She paused on the threshold. Amanda's room bore little resemblance to the unexceptional chamber that had existed before her arrival. Crystal jars with diamond-studded lids were clustered on the dresser—the drawers of which hung open, granting the viewer a glimpse of the vast disarray within—and upon Lady Viccars' own dressing-table, rumored to have once belonged to Madame Pompadour. Exquisite gowns spilled out of the wardrobe and were even scattered on the floor. Lady Viccars' own linens, lavishly edged with exquisite French lace, were on the bed, as was the quilted satin coverlet that bore her family crest. The chamber looked like an exotic princess's boudoir, straight out of a fairy tale.

Amanda was curled up in the room's one chair, with a superb sable mantle draped across her lap. With her black hair hanging loose and curling almost to her waist, she appeared extremely youthful, an impression rendered somewhat incongruous by the extremely adult negligee that she wore.

"I certainly hope," Lady Philippa commented, with an unworthy touch of spite, "that I withstand the ravages of time as well as you have."

"Dear Pippin," Lady Viccars blinked her amber eyes, not at all piqued, "*I* do not age at all. Sit down." She observed Pippin's practical nightwear with apparent resignation and sighed. "Indeed, I do not comprehend how you do it, but it seems you have made another conquest. Do you mean to have Avery this time?"

Lady Philippa curled up on the hearth. So they were to parry? Very well! "I've not the slightest notion whether I shall or not. It is an odd thing to say, but I suspect the Viscount may act from ulterior motives, for all he professes to have formed a lasting passion for me."

"I doubt that he is playing fast and loose with you," Amanda retorted wryly. "One can tell at a glance that he is not that sort of man. And despite your shortcomings, you are not precisely an antidote." She wore a tiny, and entirely unprecedented, frown. "I do not at all care for Severin's account of your misdeeds. You have been busy, it seems! Dear Pippin, do you not think it high time you were settled in matrimony? With something to occupy your mind other than these harebrained escapades?"

"No," announced Lady Philippa baldly, rendered further short-tempered by the realization that it was not Avery she wished to wed. "Do you think you might close the window? It's cold."

"Resign yourself," Amanda advised callously. "The window remains open; owls must have access to the out-of-doors." She pulled the furs more securely about herself and, Buddhalike, smiled.

"Archimedes," snapped Pippin, "has forgotten that he's a bird! I've yet to see him do one owllike thing." The bird, perched on the windowsill, muttered indignantly. Lady Philippa tossed Andrew Macgregor's small book to her so-called friend. "Here! I've just finished it. It contains the answers to several of our little mysteries."

"Oh?" Lady Viccars picked up the volume gingerly. "Perhaps you might enlighten me."

"I might," Pippin retorted, "if I thought you'd return the favor! Tell me, Amanda, just *why* did you recommend this place? You must have known it belonged to Severin!"

"Oh?" Lady Viccars picked up the volume gingerly. "Perclosed it as quickly, horrified. "You cannot expect me to read this myself!"

"Why not?" Lady Philippa smiled benignly at her friend's annoyance. Amanda was, though she would never admit it, wretchedly near-sighted. "And why should I offer you explanations when you give me none?"

"Oh, very well, you wretched chit!" Recalling that such exercises led to early wrinkles, Lady Viccars smoothed away her frown. "But your tale first, since I suspect it is a great deal more to the purpose!"

What purpose? wondered Lady Philippa, but obeyed. "First, the perfume that I've smelled on a couple of occasions. Patchouli was Ailcie Ferguson's favorite scent."

"Ailcie Ferguson," mused Amanda. "Severin's witch? What a high-flyer *she* must have been! A lady, so to speak, after Severin's own heart. But surely you don't mean to tell me *she* haunts the inn?"

"Let us say, merely," murmured Lady Philippa, "that her influence lingers." An ignoble evasion, to be sure, but Amanda deserved a few nightmares of her own. "William Macgregor, on the other hand, is indisputably a ghost, as I can personally attest." Her shudder was not merely play-acting.

"So Severin told me." Lady Viccars licked her lips with a dainty tongue. "I might add that I don't believe either one of you."

Pippin shrugged. "To continue: Ailcie Ferguson was William Macgregor's *petite amie*."

Amanda stared. "His mistress? The pious minister? What on earth *is* this book!"

"The pious minister's diary," Lady Philippa replied smugly.

179

"And a most unsavory specimen he was. He also had a wife and children."

"I don't understand!" wailed Lady Viccars.

Neither did Lady Philippa, but she did not intend to admit that minor fact. "Ailcie didn't become his light-o'-love by choice," she said, "but once the thing was done she apparently thought it easier to continue as things were. William was in a position of power, and witches were not precisely popular in those days."

"So she really was a witch?" Amanda's amber eyes were wide. "Oh, nonsense! Why did William let her be tortured and killed? If she was his mistress?"

"You must remember his position," Pippin said, moving closer to the fire. "To intervene further than he did would have brought suspicion down upon him. Besides, William Macgregor had conflicting emotions regarding Ailcie. He hated her for the primitive emotion she aroused in him, but he lacked the moral strength to deny himself the pleasure of her company."

"Infamous!" Amanda was stunned. "So he let her die. It is no wonder that she cursed him."

"He kept her alive until the child was born—a girl, incidentally." Lady Philippa would very much have liked to utter a few curses of her own. "Dear William also supervised the tortures."

"Was it his?"

"The child? He believed so."

"Then why," inquired Amanda, rapt, "didn't she say so? Why countenance such abominable behavior? And why didn't she just admit she was a witch so they'd stop torturing her?"

"You are naive; the tortures wouldn't have stopped," Lady Philippa replied. Ah, but she had a superior imagination! So superior, in fact, that she could almost envision the events she described. They did not make pleasant viewing. "Her jailers would have persisted in their efforts until she named accomplices, and the thing would have spread. As for William Macgregor, I suspect Ailcie had her own plans for revenge."

Lady Viccars leaned forward in her excitement, displaying a shockingly immodest *décolletage*. "The patchouli! He smelled the patchouli, too. And heard the harp!"

Pippin nodded gloomily. Amanda was dressed in a manner that would inflame the most jaded gentleman. Had she expected a different visitor, then? And if so, who? "Frequently, and he also experienced severe cold. But Ailcie was stronger then: he also heard her voice."

"So he hanged himself." Lady Viccars shook her head. "What a fascinating tale! So William walks, his soul in torment, until his atonement is complete." She cocked her head on one side like an inquisitive bird and regarded Pippin. "When, I wonder, will that be?"

So much for inspiring Amanda with nightmares, thought Lady Philippa ruefully. Lady Viccars was of a decidedly ghoulish nature. "Who knows? Perhaps until the whole ugly story is brought to light. Now it's your turn, Amanda. I'll have some answers, if you please!"

But Pippin would have done well to remember that Amanda's promises were of no longer endurance than the breath with which she uttered them. "Dear Pippin," murmured that perfidious lady, "you have such an affinity for mysteries that I believe you must solve this one also. Indeed you should have already done so!" She appeared not to notice that Lady Philippa had risen to her feet, indignant and outraged. "Andrew Macgregor must have never read that book, else he would have destroyed it before it could fall into your hands. I do not believe I shall like that man!"

"I am sure you shall not!" Lady Philippa had reached the door. "Andrew Macgregor hardly ranks among Dukes and Earls and German princelings!"

"You forgot this." Her serenity unimpaired, Amanda held forth the book. "If you will heed my advice, dear Pippin, you will also forget whatever foolish fantasies you may entertain concerning my particular Earl."

Twenty-Five

Archimedes was disturbed. He raised himself to his full height, compressed his feathers close to his body, and elevated his ear-tufts.

"Sorry, old bird," said Lady Philippa, drawing the curtains. The day was dark and gloomy; little illumination filtered into the inn. Behind her, Lady Viccars paced idly, and with immeasurable grace, around the taproom. "So you believe you've pieced together the rest of the old tale?" Pippin asked, a trifle spitefully. "Tell me, then, why did William Macgregor hang himself in my room?"

Amanda turned away from her fascinated perusal of Ailcie Ferguson's portrait, which seemed eerily alive in the flickering firelight. "More of Ailcie's fascination," she replied. "I would imagine that your room is where they—"

"Trysted," supplied Lord Afton, as he passed through the room. The Viscount accompanied him.

"Exactly the word I'd intended to use!" Amanda awarded them a melting look. "Although I daresay Pippin has heard some of the more vulgar variations, no matter how unsuitable for her ears."

Pippin ignored this jibe and cast a curious glance at the Earl's outdoor attire. "Are you leaving us?"

"I am engaged at the castle," he replied. "There are arrangements to be made."

And why was it left to Lord Afton to make those arrangements rather than the laird? But Lady Philippa knew better than to inquire. "Will Macgregor preside over the obsequies?"

she asked instead. "I'm sure he would only be too delighted to oblige!"

The Earl's expression was even more sardonic than usual. "Perhaps," he retorted, "but that's one pleasure the old man will be denied. I trust that neither of you will experience an uncontrollable desire to venture forth during my absence."

Amanda, dressed in pale and shimmering green, spoke soothingly. "Set your mind at rest. We shall remain safely here." She glanced at Lady Philippa. "Naturally, Ailcie's influence would be strongest in the room where she spent the most time; in this instance, her bedroom."

Pippin stared after the gentlemen thoughtfully. The Viscount gave her a languishing glance. "Why didn't he just avoid it?" she asked absently. "In his place, I'd have never again set foot in this house."

Lady Viccars selected a lush apple from an overflowing fruit bowl. "Ah, but he was gloating. He'd vanquished the witch and her pernicious influence, or so he thought. Alas for William! Ailcie was not so easily escaped."

Enough of dead lovers! Lady Philippa was far more interested in Amanda's intentions toward Lord Afton, a matter which had kept her awake half the night. "The Earl," she said defiantly, "intrigues me."

"How can this be?" inquired Amanda, nibbling daintily on her apple. "You have told me repeatedly that you consider him a most exasperating man. I have often thought you would like him very well were you not forever at daggers drawn with him, for Severin is precisely the sort of rogue who would encourage one in every sort of excess." She smiled as might a cat presented with a bowl of especially rich cream.

So the wind *did* blow in that quarter! Amanda, reflected Lady Philippa, was remarkably conscienceless. Fortunate that she was also charming, for one could not remain angry with her long. "Severin might encourage *you*, but he is far more likely to read me a terrible scold," she replied with a rueful grimace. Lady Viccars looked faintly interested. "Why did he put me in that haunted room? Sometimes I wonder if he expected something like this to happen."

"Like what? Pray be more explicit, child!"

Lady Philippa shrugged. "The whole thing. Ghosts, murder, suicide. And that's another thing: what was Valentine to Severin? Neville was here yesterday, and his behavior was

184

most puzzling. Were it not so far-fetched a notion, I would believe he meant to apologize for his wife's death."

"One thing at a time, pray!" protested Amanda. She disposed of the apple core. "Severin's sense of humor inspired him to give you that room, nothing more. I doubt he intended you to be plagued by spirits or sleeplessness." She yawned daintily. "As for Valentine, I don't see why you shouldn't know; Severin himself would have told you if you'd asked him. She was his half-sister. Illegitimate, you understand."

"His sister!" A less well-bred lady might have been said to gape. "I thought he was the last of the line."

Amanda smiled kindly, as if upon a half-wit. "And so he is, except for a distant branch who may hope to inherit one day, since Severin shows no inclination to get himself an heir."

"And the old Earl was a rake?" Lady Philippa was startled.

"My dear Pippin," retorted Lady Viccars, "dispense with these missish airs! All the Earls of Afton are so inclined, although Severin is more circumspect than were his progenitors."

And Lady Viccars collected rakes and roués as other ladies collected teacups and used them far more carelessly. "He and Valentine were previously known to each other, then? Strange that he never mentioned her."

"Why should he, pray? Severin wastes little time in discussion of his relatives, from whom he has long been estranged. An ancient quarrel, I believe. He is unlike any of them; and they, I might add, consider him a blot upon the family escutcheon." Lady Viccars smiled at Pippin's expression. "They're a shockingly stuffy group of people, my pet; you wouldn't care for them at all. Or they for you."

"But Valentine? Is that why Severin came here?" Amanda, thought Pippin sourly, knew a damned lot about Lord Afton. Was she his confidante, or more? And why the *devil* had she brought about Pippin's reacquaintance with him?

Amanda nodded. "Partially. Severin hadn't seen her for years and I presume he was curious. They were raised together, and I believe he once held her in affection, although she apparently altered unbecomingly during their separation."

"I wondered why he never gave her a set-down," Pippin commented thoughtfully. "She was a dreadful shrew. Severin's family acknowledged her, then? How odd of them."

"Nothing of the sort," Amanda retorted in shocked tones. "Valentine was born to the housekeeper, a distressed gentle-

185

woman fallen upon hard times. Thus she grew up in Severin's shadow, which was not the best thing for a young girl. As I recall, he was periodically shipped off to Scotland whenever he was in disgrace, which was often, to stay with an aunt. An eccentric old lady, but charming."

"Heavens," said Pippin. So Amanda had known Severin since childhood. "How did Valentine meet Neville?"

Lady Viccars contemplated a peppermint stick. "The estates marched together. It was natural they should meet. There was quite a scandal when Neville took it in his head to run off with her; his father foamed at the mouth. But he eventually grew resigned; the St. George family claim to trace their line back to William the Conqueror."

Lady Philippa was briefly silent. Romance gone awry, as so often it did, she thought; a housekeeper's daughter had thrown her hat over the windmill for a feckless gentleman, and for all she'd been properly wed and welcomed into her husband's family, she'd ended in a suicide's grave. Men were untrustworthy creatures, at best! "Tell me, do you know anything about Bevis Alversane?" One of Lady Viccars' consuming passions was scandal, new and old; consequently, she was a veritable storehouse of information regarding even the least of the nobility.

"Good God!" cried Amanda, with unusual animation. "Pippin, you know I do not care to interfere, but that simply will not do!"

"What's this?" Pippin inquired, startled.

"My dear child, he's mad as a hatter! The whole world knows that the Alversanes are unhinged, in varying degrees. Bevis's mother had to be confined to a locked, barred room in her later years."

Lady Philippa stared with disbelief. "Lady Cassandra? And Neville?"

Amanda had no trouble understanding this disjointed speech. "Precisely," she murmured. "I believe Neville is by far the sanest of the lot, and even he is far from unexceptionable. Black rages, eternal womanizing, the constant desire for distraction; or so I hear. Hardly an acquaintance one would wish to pursue!"

"But Lady Cassandra appears harmless!"

"Cassandra," replied Amanda, waving her peppermint stick, "is not precisely dangerous, but crazed enough that she had no offers of marriage until your laird came to London in

186

search of funds to plump out his purse. Cassandra lives in a dream world, always has, and always will."

Lady Philippa looked skeptical, and Amanda surveyed her irritably. "Use your mind; I've been assured that it exists! A perfect example is before you: Lady Cassandra's reaction to Valentine's death was total absorption in her plans for the picnic. Believe me, there is no thought of poor Valentine in Cassandra's head."

"No," Pippin mused. "It's as if Valentine had never existed."

"As for Bevis," Lady Viccars continued with determination, "he's already been involved in several scandals, although the family has been fairly fortunate in squelching the rumors. I do not know the details, unfortunately, but he has not been seen in London for several years. I suppose Cassandra brought him here because it is so remote."

"The deuce!" said Lady Philippa, nicely tantalized. "No wonder he looks so grim."

"Oh, yes." Calmly, Amanda broke off a piece of peppermint. "It has always been the family's saving grace to know that they are mad."

And then Gilly appeared, so distrait that her pelisse was buttoned all awry, and had to be presented to Lady Viccars. Judging from Miss Graham's face, she did not consider her introduction to a duke's daughter any great privilege. She turned to Lady Philippa with an expression so ferocious that Pippin stared. "Lady Cassandra's wretched party! Isn't there anything I can do to stop this terrible thing?" cried Gilly with desperation. "Can't you understand what folly this is?"

"Well, no, I doubt there is," Lady Philippa said apologetically. Gilly looked ready to tear out her hair. "Lady Cassandra's heart is set on her picnic. Truly, I think you exaggerate the risk."

Archimedes disliked the sounds of strife; he inched closer to Amanda. Gilly stared at the owl. Archimedes, long accustomed to the rudeness of humans, returned the intent regard.

"Oh, heaven!" Gilly cried. "If there's anything that could make things worse, it's this. That creature is all Andrew Macgregor needs to see!"

"Why?" Pippin asked. Udolpho marched triumphantly into the room and deposited a dead mouse at the bird's feet. Archimedes murmured appreciation.

Gilly watched with fascinated revulsion as the bird dealt quickly with the mouse. "They're omens of evil and death," she faltered. "In the old days, an owl perched on a castle's battlements meant some member of the family was going to die." Indignant at such slander, Archimedes ruffled his feathers.

"Your knowledge of folklore is limited," objected Lady Viccars, with a scholarly air. "Some of the native inhabitants of America believe that at death the spirit passed into the body of an owl. If an owl was heard calling, it was thought to await the soul. The owl was also dedicated to Minerva, the goddess of wisdom."

"That's not all," Pippin added. "Circe was supposed to have turned her lovers into wildlife, including the owl." An excellent way to dispose of one's castoffs, she thought, and one that Lady Viccars had long wished to emulate.

"The barn owl," Amanda amended. "There's another legend concerning the snowy owl. The Golden Age, a time when men and beasts lived in perfect accord, ended when the animals began to quarrel. The reigning god became disturbed and departed, and ever since the snowy owl has uttered its lament."

"That's all very interesting," Gilly interrupted dolefully, "but please don't let old Macgregor see that bird. There's no telling what he'll take it into his head to do."

"I doubt if even your good minister is a match for Archimedes," Lady Viccars replied with amusement.

"Where will the picnic be held?" Gilly sighed.

"You hardly need ask," said Lady Philippa wryly. "Near the fairy mound."

"Och!" cried Gilly. "And how would you be knowing about that place? No one here will even mention it, let alone go near it. They prefer to pretend it doesn't exist."

"It's no good asking how Lady Cassandra learns of things!" Pippin replied. Gilly's fearfulness was setting her own nerves on edge. "She either claims communication with the spirit world or that she read it in her wretched cards."

Gilly was very disturbed. "Do you not know the things that are said?" she demanded. "Or that witches were often accused of having dealings with fairies? Each thing you do takes you further in! Why won't you just leave, before more people die?"

" 'An' see na ye that bonny road about the fernie brae?' " quoted Lady Philippa irrepressibly. In truth, she'd learned more about witches during these past few days than she'd ever wished to know! "'That wins back frae Elfland where you must wait to gae.'"

"You refuse to take me seriously," Gilly lamented.

"Lady Philippa," interrupted Amanda, "lacks sufficient prudence to take anything seriously. However, in this case, I anticipate no real danger."

"You're far too eldritch, the pair of you." Gilly's face had assumed its now habitual expression of gloom. "I can't think what will happen to the lot of us."

"Nothing irreparable." Lady Viccars wore an oracular air. "You may trust *me* for that!" She paused and Gilly eyed her with glum curiosity. "I fear you are not convinced."

"Nor will I be!" Absently, Gilly smoothed her gloves. "Nor will you be able to convince old Macgregor that the lot of you aren't in league with the devil."

"I see no reason," said Lady Viccars, at her most regal, "why I should even try. I would, in fact, be pleased to never set eyes on this foolish-sounding individual!"

"I wish you could be denied it," Gilly demurred. "But I greatly fear you'll encounter him. He's bound to have heard of Lady Cassandra's plans."

"How?" Pippin interrupted.

"How should I know?" Gilly shrugged. "It wouldn't surprise me if Lady Cassandra told him herself. She's sometimes extremely woolly-headed. And old Macgregor will be expecting some sort of diabolic ceremony, renunciation of God, allegiance to Lucifer, preparation of spells and ointments, that sort of thing."

"Evil is in the eye of the beholder?" Lady Viccars inquired, interested. "It must be, if your minister sees depravity in a rustic picnic that will doubtless prove as inconvenient as it is tedious! The gentleman appears to possess an exceptionally suspicious mind."

"Then why become involved?" asked Pippin, who was growing increasingly annoyed with her dearest friend. "If you think it's going to be so dull? Lady Cassandra will doubtless contrive to enjoy herself even without your illustrious presence."

"Doubtless," Lady Viccars repeated, with a mysterious little smile. "But, though you may fervently wish me elsewhere, dear Pippin, I shall still attend." Dark lashes fluttered to her cheeks, hiding the golden eyes. "For reasons of my own."

Twenty-Six

Nabby clenched her chattering teeth. Had she followed her own inclination, she would that very moment be lifting a mug of ale with Barnabas, and a great deal happier for it; but Nabby's devotion had been called into question, and she was determined that no one, particularly her short-tempered swain, should say that she had failed her mistress again. Barnabas seemed to feel that his own efforts in that direction, namely an assiduous courtship of Janet Kirk, were deserving only of the highest praise. Nabby's even features contorted ferociously, for she suspected that Barnabas was deriving a certain unscrupulous pleasure from his self-appointed task.

Be that as it may, she was disobeying both Barnabas and Lord Afton by her presence at the picnic. Nabby was fair exasperated at the both of them. First they impressed upon her the importance of keeping a close eye on her mistress, then they told her she must abandon that impetuous lady in her hour of greatest need. Nabby sniffled. It seemed to her that Strachan's inhabitants, visitors and residents alike, suffered a collective weakness in the head. She excepted Aggy, who had given warning that this night held countless dangers. Nabby pulled her dark cloak closer around her, and wished she'd remembered to arm herself with Aggy's wicked butcher knife.

A stream ran near the fairy mound; a bright bonfire was burning. Heavy mist obscured the scene. Dampness had made it necessary to build the fire in a recess in the mound, apparently in existence for that very purpose. Thirteen stones were placed around the flame.

Lady Viccars had already divorced herself from the festivi-

191

ties, professing a hearty disgust for such rustic amusements. She regarded the revelers somberly, from her perch on a time-pitted stone. "I suppose one should be grateful," she murmured, "that the weather makes nudity impractical."

Pippin laughingly agreed. Udolpho had refused to leave the inn, and Archimedes was engaged in some ghostly nocturnal pursuits of his own, so they were alone. "I wonder who all those other people are," Amanda mused. "Do you know them?"

"No, but Lady Cassandra was so enthusiastic about her revels that she probably solicited her guests from the streets of Inverness." She had also solicited a rudimentary band, and Lady Philippa wondered if it was the dampness that so adversely affected their instruments. Never had she heard such an unharmonious din. "This is a waste of time! I think we might leave. You'll find little to interest you here."

"What? And deny me of my only opportunity to regard the hayseeds at play?" Amanda's tone was ironic. "We might as well stay a while longer, since we're already here."

The merrymakers were more than mildly intoxicated, and their shouts of laughter sliced the air. There were conspicuous absences: the Earl, Lucius, Gilly, and Bevis Alversane had chosen not to attend.

"This entire thing," commented Lady Philippa sourly, as she scratched a mosquito bite, "has been even more absurd than I anticipated, beginning with Neville's inane theft of that poor sheep. Neville had some vague notion of sacrificing the animal, but reason, in the form of a horrified Lady Viccars, had prevailed. Neville was hardly one to deny a Duke's daughter and a lovely one at that. The sheep had been set free.

"The only thing you're going to observe from this display," Pippin continued, irritably attempting to avoid the insects that flew around her face, "is the infinite capacity of human beings to make asses of themselves." She watched with disgust as the Viscount embraced a dark-haired girl. "He won't even remember her name tomorrow."

"Does it matter?" murmured Amanda softly. "He will certainly remember yours. Dear Pippin, you are fast becoming a prude! You have only to beckon your Viscount, and he'll be at your feet—which is by far the most sensible thing you could do!" Her glance was quizzical. "Or can it be that you don't want him, having set your sights on more dangerous prey?"

An unfortunate choice of words, thought Lady Philippa, and shuddered. If her luck continued on its usual course, she had likely fallen in love with a murderer. "What is it?" asked Lady Viccars, all solicitude. "Have you caught a chill?"

Pippin shook her head. "It's nothing. Just someone walking on my grave."

Nabby, standing in the deep shadows of some venerable trees, was near enough to overhear this conversation. She, too, shivered. Nasty, this talk of graves.

Nabby was not the only watcher. "Acushla," whispered Lucius, crouched behind a large and leafy bush, "this is madness! I anticipate an early demise for both of us, from an inflammation of the lungs. If you won't let me return to my own snug bed, at least let's move closer to the fire and get warm."

"Fool!" retorted Gilly. "Any closer and we'd be seen."

"What of it?" Lucius demanded. Gilly hissed, and he lowered his voice. "We were both invited, and by the looks of them, they won't notice us anyway."

"It's not them I'm concerned with," Gilly replied. They were near enough to observe Lady Cassandra's disheveled condition and wide-eyed stare.

"The devil!" said Lucius. "The woman's been drugged."

"By her own hand," Gilly retorted. "Valentine's unhappy end has not deterred Lady Cassandra from the taking of laudanum."

Lucius peered into the haze. "Where's your carrot-headed friend?" he asked. "Or has she too by-passed the festivities?"

"Not she." Gilly pointed. "She's over there. Leaning against William Macgregor's headstone, blast her."

Lucius rubbed his eyes. "I'm seeing double," he protested, "and nary a glass I've had."

"You're seeing true," Gilly snapped. "The other is her friend and for sheer foolishness they're as like as two peas in a pod."

"The saints be praised," Lucius said fervently. "I was doubting my own senses. Just what is it you're expecting, by the way?"

"Old Macgregor," whispered Gilly. "And if I'm wrong, I'll go back to Edinburgh straightaway."

"Ah!" Lucius was ecstatic. "Then I shall pray passionately that you're misled."

But Gilly was not mistaken, nor had her misgivings been too severe. Andrew Macgregor moved stealthily toward the

193

sounds of revelry. With him were a group of villagers, armed and grim.

"Hecate," murmured Lady Viccars, who between trysting with German princelings and Oriental potentates had accumulated no small fund of exotic lore, used primarily to liven dull dinner parties. "The old Greek goddess of witchcraft. That locket of yours bears a crescent moon, doesn't it? With the two points upwards, and a third point in the middle between them?" As if chilled, she rubbed her arms.

Lady Philippa removed the item in question and stared at it. "Heavens!" she said. "Hecate?"

Amanda took the necklace in her hand. "Unquestionably," she replied. "It's a pity Severin could learn nothing of its history." Was nothing sacred? thought Lady Philippa ruefully. Was there nothing about Lord Afton that Amanda did not know?

The Viscount stumbled toward them and enveloped Pippin in a crushing embrace. He reeked of gin. "Come join in the festivities!" he cried. The words were slurred.

It was then that Archimedes, uttering hoarse cries, swooped down upon them. Lady Viccars leaped from her perch to the ground. Pippin, struggling to free herself from Avery's passionate grasp, was suddenly terrified. She saw Amanda stand in front of the fire, the locket dangling from one hand, her long cloak billowing, while Archimedes flew agitated circles around her head. When Pippin looked again, both Amanda and the owl were gone.

"Let go of me, you fool!" Lady Philippa cried, and with great effort shoved Avery away. He grinned and moved to recapture her, no whit deterred by this display of missishness.

For Nabby, the scene had assumed a nightmarish quality. Wraithlike figures stalked through the mist, and the fire cast a reddish tinge upon them all. It was like a macabre representation of hell.

Nabby was not fainthearted; she darted from her hiding-place to join in the fray. She grasped a heavy rock, with some vague notion of applying it to the Viscount's skull.

"Release me!" Pippin cried again, for Avery had gripped her firmly with every intention of stealing a kiss. She struggled, with no thought but to follow Amanda's example and disappear.

It was not Nabby's fault that her long skirts hampered her, causing her to trip over a root and thus spoiling her aim. The stone struck Avery's shoulder with a force that sent him tumbling to the ground. Nabby screamed, and Lady Philippa, infected with panic, struggled under the Viscount's weight. She did not see the villagers arrive.

Twenty-Seven

Andrew Macgregor was ecstatic. His parishioners had allowed themselves to be guided by his knowledge and wisdom, as he had foreseen they eventually would. It was ironic that the death of the detested Valentine Alversane, rather than that of their own Katy, had been the thing which had finally prompted them to action.

Even Andrew had been shocked by the lack of proper feeling that had allowed the incomers to indulge in gross revels so soon after the death of one of their numbers. The news had come to him only by chance; one of Lady Cassandra's foreign servants had let slip the information to an acquaintance in the village, and Moira Graham, Gilly's mother, whose illness had not affected her ears, had overheard her daughter make some strange and relevant remarks. A picnic, the Sassenachs called it! The minister was hardly a credulous fool; he knew they planned a witches' sabbat.

In truth, Andrew Macgregor had been somewhat disappointed at the mundane nature of the festivities. They had witnessed no children burned to ashes that would later be used in diabolic rites, no illicit relations with demons, no inverse parodies of the holy liturgy. He had expected at least to see rebaptisms by the devil, and the ritual of allegiance to Satan, the kiss of shame, obeisance paid the devil by saluting his hindquarters.

The villagers, at least, had found nothing remarkable in the relative dullness of the proceedings, and their resentment was easily enough sparked into wrath. Even now, the next morning, the entire town was in a state of tense anticipation. The silence of Strachan's streets was awesome, for not one person ventured out of doors. They waited safely in their own homes for further news.

Andrew Macgregor would have been dismayed to learn that many of his followers regretted their precipitate action of the night before, action that had been prompted by the discovery that one of the Macleans' rams had been stolen. It was the final indignity. Grasping whatever weapons came first to hand, the villagers had followed Andrew Macgregor to war against the heathens. It had disconcerted them somewhat to find the missing ram serving not as a bloody sacrifice, but calmly feasting on forest grass while regarding the revels, but the call of battle still rang in their ears.

It was less a battle than a rout, with none of their weapons used. The mist, and the villagers' stunned horror on viewing what they imagined to be satanic rites, had enabled many of the Sassenachs to escape. Viscount Rockingham had been forcibly subdued, but this was the only demonstration of might; and the means, the fists of two country-men. It was to their advantage that the gentleman was not in full possession of his facilities, due to the rock hurled at him, ironically, by Lady Philippa's serving-wench, for the Viscount's appearance was misleading. Even Andrew Macgregor had to admire his not inconsiderable strength.

The minister admitted to another disappointment: he'd envisioned hoards of prisoners, but had to content himself with only three. He had not, however, failed in the purpose of his mission. Lady Philippa was among the captives. If only he might also have in his possessions her hideous cat, the creature so willing to do her bidding! Andrew had not forgotten the occasion when the woman had entered into the animal's body and chased him from the inn. It was of no consequence, he mused. The life of the familiar was irrevocably bound up with that of the witch. Injury to one resulted in a corresponding injury to the other, including death.

He had expected Lady Philippa to be a more powerful adversary, but she'd accompanied her captors almost meekly. Perhaps she anticipated help from her fellow idolaters. If so, she would be disappointed! The villagers had returned to find the inn deserted. Not even the cat remained.

More likely the woman plotted some incredible escape, but Andrew Macgregor believed firmly in the invulnerability of his church. There were signs of activity at the castle, but he was content to let these pass, so long as the foreigners made no attempt to leave. There would be time enough to deal with them after the witch had confessed.

But before beginning the actual tortures, the minister had additional research to do. He opened the pulpit and drew forth its priceless treasures.

The only sure proof of the crime of witchcraft was the confession of the witch herself. There were ways to circumvent this: denunciation by one witness was sufficient evidence. Andrew Macgregor had seen the witch presiding over a devil's sabbat, as had any number of the villagers, but he still preferred to procure an actual confession. With such undeniable proof, no one could question his motives or the necessity of the measures he intended to take.

It would be illogical to assume that the witch would voluntarily confess. Torture would have to be applied.

Andrew Macgregor consulted the volume before him. There were various presumptions of guilt that justified the examination of a supposed witch. These included the existence of a devil's mark, testimony of a fellow witch, curses, and subsequent malicious acts against the victim of the curse. The old man nodded, satisfied. Lady Philippa qualified for examination on several counts.

The author also listed several rules for the acquisition of true evidence regarding witchcraft. If voluntary confession could not be procured, then the testimony of two witnesses was considered sufficient. The witnesses must confirm that the accused had entered into a pact with the Devil; that she had been involved in some known witchcraft, such as the entertaining of a familiar spirit; or that she had practiced divination. The minister thought of the evil cards currently in his possession, which Lady Philippa had spirited away from his church. Again, her guilt was overwhelmingly obvious.

Andrew Macgregor then turned his mind to the pleasant task of determining to what class of witch the woman belonged. The others were negligible in comparison to her, although he would also deal in time with them.

The variation of witches depended primarily on the imagination of the authority who discussed the matter, but the minister soon found a list that appeared both definitive and concise. It discussed seven categories ranging from the necromancer to the diviner or fortune-teller. Other classifications dealt with such topics as astrology, poison, exorcism, and magic. He paused to ponder which category best suited his present knowledge of Lady Philippa. More information would surely be revealed as her examination progressed.

Twenty-Eight

Lady Philippa had spent several uncomfortable hours on the cellar's cold stone floor. She managed to assume a sitting position and tried to wriggle her toes. They were numb, and her hands had not fared better. The ropes that bound her were cruelly tight.

Pippin was far too exhausted to experience a recurrence of despair, despite the cold and lonely gloom of her surroundings. No light entered her prison; it was impossible to distinguish anything in the total darkness. Her mind had achieved the acute clarity that sometimes is the aftermath of extreme fear.

The events preceding her capture still remained a jumbled blur. She'd been too engrossed in fending off Avery's advances to be aware of the villagers' arrival; she hadn't even understood the significance of their presence until three of them had hauled her roughly to her feet.

The triumphant march back to the village had given her much to contemplate, for various comments had made her probable fate unpleasantly clear. But it was the nineteenth century, Pippin reassured herself, and it was totally unimaginable that she should be burned at the stake. Then she recalled Andrew Macgregor's rabid fanaticism. What dim-witted fools they had all been to ignore Gilly's frantic warnings.

"Avery!" she whispered, into the gloom, hearing him groan. "Avery! Are you all right?"

"That is a thoroughly asinine question," he retorted, "and totally unworthy of you. I can't move, and my head is probably split in two. Where are we?"

Lady Philippa explained, tersely.

"Your girl is here, by me." The Viscount's voice grew faint. "She's breathing, so I assume she's alive."

"Avery, listen!" Pippin said, desperately. "Whatever they do, don't mention the others! I'm sure Severin will send us help, as soon as he knows of this." But how soon would that be? she wondered sinkingly. How was Severin to learn of their predicament? "There's no sense in putting them on guard."

"Very well."

"Tell Nabby the same, if you can."

"I don't think," Avery replied weakly, "that you need to worry about Nabby saying anything."

A noise at the door dispensed with further conversation. Lady Philippa tensed herself and waited grimly for any mischance that might give her an opportunity to flee.

Andrew Macgregor was not alone. He was accompanied by two stern villagers who took up positions on either side of the door. The minister lit candles and placed them at strategic points around the room.

The scene thus illuminated was not encouraging. Nabby lay on the floor where she'd been thrown, apparently senseless. Andrew Macgregor bent over her with a smothered exclamation, but the girl was alive. The witch had doubtless taken measures to silence her chattering tongue. It was a disappointment, but not one that couldn't be used to good advantage.

The Viscount had suffered damage, but the minister could summon up no compassion, despite the blood that still seeped slowly from the nasty wound on the man's head. Perhaps the pain of it would induce him to speak more freely. No half-measures would be taken in dealing with this one of the witch's paramours.

That the Viscount was her lover, Andrew Macgregor had no doubt. Again his suspicions had been proven correct, for all those who had beheld that hideously depraved scene had witnessed Avery and her ladyship writhing lustfully on the ground.

The minister thought complacently of how things had worked to his advantage. Even the inn's swarthy owner would provide no threat, now that his jade had abandoned him for another lover. And Aggy's magic was an old woman's sort, and no danger to a man of God. Even if they had been inclined to wish him harm, they were firmly barricaded within the castle, and would remain there until he otherwise decreed.

No one had actually seen them take refuge in the castle; there was an alternate possibility that they had fled the area. It was a pleasant thought; Andrew Macgregor hoped it was true, unfair as it would be if they escaped their just punishment.

He turned to survey the third prisoner, and startled an expression of extreme malevolence on Lady Philippa's face. It was uplifting to note that she was even more disheveled than the other two. Her long dark dress was torn in several places, and smeared with dirt and mud.

"You'd better loosen these damned ropes," she spat, "unless you plan to amputate my hands and feet."

Andrew Macgregor would have been disheartened if Lady Philippa's spirit had been broken for he considered it his duty to humble her, a task that would not be untinged with pleasure. Roughly, he pulled her to her feet.

Pippin swayed, her numbed feet could not support her, and one of the villagers left his post to force her upright. The minister ripped open the bodice of her dress; the villager averted his gaze.

"Where is it?" the old man demanded. "What have you done with the accursed charm?"

"I'll tell you nothing," Lady Philippa retorted, at a loss until she realized he referred to Severin's locket, "so long as I'm bound." She was determined to maintain her nonchalant pose as long as possible and met the minister's angry gaze with one of contempt.

The minister fell back a step under the force of that evil glare and gestured for the woman to be unbound. Escape was impossible; perhaps she would unwittingly betray herself if she thought that she might flee.

"Now," he said, "you will answer me. Where is the locket concealed?"

Pippin rubbed her nerveless hands and considered the situation. "It's safe from you and hidden where you'll never find it." Her rage was cold and logical. If the three of them were to be released from this horror, it would depend on her.

Instead of the blow that Pippin half-expected, the minister firmly grasped her arm. He meant to proceed according to protocol.

Lady Philippa was informed that she was being subjected to the traditional preliminary torture, in which the accused person was threatened and shown the various instruments to which he'd be exposed. Avery was not permitted to miss the minister's explicit explanation of each device; his face was harshly slapped each time he threatened to slip into unconsciousness. Nabby was largely ignored, although the old man did pause to nudge her urgently with the toe of his shoe.

It was all Nabby could do to restrain her temper. Who was this rubbishing upstart to treat her in such a way? But prudence won out over ruffled sensibilities. It would serve little purpose were her deception to become known. A senseless female posed little threat. Though Nabby would cheerfully have undergone torture herself to save her mistress from harm, she was too discerning a miss to believe that such noble self-sacrifice could but fail in its effect. That hell-born minister had no interest in a simple lady's maid. Nabby kept her eyes tightly closed and thought frantically.

Lady Philippa endured the lecture stoically, but Andrew Macgregor had seen her wince as he dealt with the Viscount, and he thought it likely that her confession would be hastened if she was forced to watch the suffering of her paramour. Accordingly, Avery was bound to the rack.

Pippin's composure deserted her; she was literally terrified, and not only for the Viscount. She had no illusions about her own ability to withstand pain.

"The Devil," commented Andrew Macgregor, as he gave the signal to rebind her hands, "is the personification of supreme evil, the foe of the Christian God." He glanced at his prisoners. "The three of you are charged with entering into pact with the Devil, the enemy of your salvation."

"Poppycock!" interrupted Lady Philippa recklessly. "The Devil is nothing but an invention of diseased minds like yours." Unnoticed, Nabby winced.

The pressure of Avery's bonds kept him in a state of semiconsciousness. He regarded the scene dispassionately.

"You have renounced your baptism," the minister raged. "You have given yourselves, bodies and souls, to the Devil!"

"I can't speak for the others," Lady Philippa said, attempting a desperate diversion, "but I was never baptized."

"You admit it!" The minister was elated; he never suspected the woman would prove so obliging.

"I admit nothing," Pippin retorted, and the old man turned on her with fury.

"You admit to being the Devil's servant! You admit to inti-

204

mate relations with the Devil, who appeared to you in human form, or that of an animal, or a bird."

"No!" Under different circumstances Lady Philippa might have laughed aloud at such absurdity, but not now when she was at the mercy of a village gone mad.

"Was it painful?" Andrew Macgregor inquired. "It is allegedly so."

"This is incredible," said Lady Philippa and turned her head away in disgust. The minister approached Avery, abandoning Pippin to his henchmen as he manipulated the ropes that bound the Viscount to the rack.

The proceedings seemed to Pippin to belong to some horrid dream from which she must surely soon awaken. It was a civilized age; such things as witch trials and tortures were no longer tolerated. At any moment the authorities would arrive, and Andrew Macgregor would be taken away to an institution catering to the criminally insane.

But this fine logic was of no practical assistance. Lady Philippa's senses told her that the things her mind refused to accept were definitely taking place. The Viscount's body was being slowly stretched upon the rack.

"Confess!" the minister demanded. "Confess that this woman came to you in the dead of night and corrupted you."

The villager forced Pippin's face toward Avery. She could not help but see his pain.

"Admit to your vile pact with Satan," the old man insisted. "Admit that this whore led you into sin!"

Pippin screamed as Avery moaned. "Stop it! You're hurting him."

"Bring the female closer," the minister ordered. Lady Philippa was dragged across the uneven floor.

"Look upon her," Andrew Macgregor said. "This woman caused the death of Valentine Alversane and an unfortunate young girl. She is guilty of divination and casting spells, and of countless other iniquities. Yet you do not renounce her! She has bewitched you, admit it!" The old man grasped the bodice of Pippin's dress and completed its destruction. "Look! She bears the mark of the Devil!"

"Charming," whispered the Viscount. Pippin thought that he must be delirious. "You realize, my darling, that should we survive this madness, you will have no choice but to marry me."

And under other circumstances, Nabby might have been elated at this speech, but she could not forgive the Viscount his part in their capture and had little sympathy to spare for his current plight. Gentlemen were subject to notoriously odd behavior when in their cups, but what might serve for any other lord of the realm would not do in Lady Philippa's chosen mate. Should they survive this fix with skins intact, an eventuality which seemed unlikely, Lady Philippa would find her maid unalterably opposed to such a match. Nabby wondered how much weight her opinion would carry.

"Still you refuse to renounce her?" the minister irately demanded. "Can you not see that she revels in your suffering? Admit that she is a witch and you will be spared!"

Avery opened pain-dulled eyes. He smiled weakly at Pippin. "This is a ridiculous moment to discover that I have scruples," he gasped and fainted dead away.

Andrew Macgregor was filled with disgust. There was no point to the torture of an insensible man, and he ordered the Viscount released.

Lady Philippa fought furiously to mask her growing apprehension. There would be no further respite for her and less hope of escape. She could not think what had prevented Severin from appearing to demand their release, but perhaps Severin too had been taken captive and was imprisoned elsewhere. Or perhaps Severin had abandoned her to work out her own fate.

"Consider your position," said Andrew Macgregor, "and confess. Admit to your vile sins and I will be merciful. You must burn, but you may be strangled first."

"Never," Pippin said wearily. "I've nothing to confess."

It was necessary that the woman be stripped, lest her clothing contain implements of witchcraft, and the minister performed this task with repugnance. The nude female form filled him at all times with revulsion, and this woman struggled so furiously, and so immodestly, that the two villagers had to be called on to subdue her.

This further indignity had the effect of recalling Lady Philippa's wandering wits. She swore fulsomely and wondered, looking at the slack faces of the men who restrained her, if she was going to be mishandled shamefully.

Such was not Andrew Macgregor's intention; he meant no more of his flock to fall prey to the witch's pervasive influence. Judging from his aides' nervous behavior, they appeared quite likely to do so, and he wrapped her ladyship in a filthy blanket. He refrained from judging the villagers' disgusting behavior; they lacked his sternly moralistic upbringing.

Nabby peered through slitted eyes, and wished that she were less securely bound. Screams would avail naught, for who would hear? She set herself fervently to prayers in which the Deity became inexplicably confused with Barnabas.

The minister paused to regard his captive, speculating on what manner of torture would be most efficacious. She suffered from the sin of vanity, as did all women; the threat of disfigurement might possibly induce her to confess. Andrew Macgregor preferred her to remain relatively unmarked for her execution, but she could not know that.

"How long have you been a witch?" the old man asked.

"I am *not* a witch," Pippin replied.

"Why did you become a witch?" Andrew Macgregor called upon his reservoirs of patience. "When did you become a witch? What transpired on that occasion?"

"I am not a witch." It was a tiresome litany.

"What was the name of your master among the evil demons?" The old man's eyes burned with a fanatic light. His evident enjoyment of the proceedings increased Lady Philippa's discomfort. She felt vaguely nauseated, and her head throbbed.

"What was the oath that you were forced to make to your demon? How did you make this oath?"

"For God's sake," Pippin murmured unwisely, and the minister pounced.

"Blasphemy!" he cried. "What spells have you cast? Has the Devil set a limit to the duration of your influence?"

"Rubbish," said Pippin, and wearily closed her eyes.

Andrew Macgregor's patience was at an end; the witch would not voluntarily confess. He nodded and one of his assistants brought forth the thumbscrews.

Twenty-Nine

Lady Philippa's scream turned quickly into a paroxysm of choking as acrid smoke billowed through the cellar. Andrew Macgregor and his faithful aides coughed and wiped their streaming eyes.

When the smoke began to clear, it was quickly discovered that Avery and Nabby were no longer in the room. Macgregor approached the open door with a furious oath.

"Shame, Andrew Macgregor!" came a mellow and unmistakably female voice. "And you call yourself a man of God."

The minister glanced at Lady Philippa, but she wore an almost imbecilic expression. The speech had obviously not come from her. The two villagers, terror-stricken, sidled toward the door. Andrew Macgregor turned around to discover the source of their distress.

A vision confronted him, and to the old man, who had often surreptitiously gazed upon Ailcie Ferguson's portrait, that vision was one of unparalleled horror. She wore a long and diaphanous silver-gray gown, medieval in appearance, with flowing sleeves and a plunging neckline. Andrew Macgregor dragged his fascinated eyes away from that creamy flesh. An ornate silver necklace hung round her throat, silver slippers adorned her feet. Rings bearing curious milky gray gems were on her fingers, and a thin silver band bearing a huge and perfect moonstone encircled her smooth forehead. An owl perched on her shoulder and the atrocious cat sat at her feet.

The minister clenched his jaw. Perhaps this was a vision and nothing more. But patchouli hung heavily in the stale air.

"You meddle in matters beyond you, Andrew Macgregor," the apparition said, "and you seek to blame others for your heinous misdeeds."

The old man swallowed and licked his dry lips. No mortal being could possess such knowledge.

"I am a man of God," he protested with dignity that was severely impaired by the wavering of his voice. "I have done His word."

"You have committed murder!" She was inexorable and so compelling that the minister did not even notice when Lord Afton, his dark features impassive, stepped into the cellar. "Has God named you His executioner?"

"I have done what must be done!" Andrew cried. "Corruption must be uncovered and destroyed!"

Lady Philippa, released from bondage, leaned against the Earl with relief. Never had she thought she'd be grateful for Amanda's passionate involvement in amateur theatrics! Lady Viccars made a very personable ghost. But this was a very dangerous role, and even more so if in truth the minister was responsible for the recent deaths. Pippin started forward, but Lord Afton pulled her back against his chest and held her immobile.

"Was Katy evil?" the vision inquired. Her pale eyes were cold as ice. "That you destroyed her? Was Valentine evil, that you connived at her death?" The old man goggled speechlessly. "Answer me!" Amanda thundered, obviously enjoying herself. "On what authority did you murder those women?"

"On my authority as a man of God!" Andrew Macgregor cried, trembling with combined fear and rage. "And I would do so again!"

"Valentine?" Lady Viccars prompted.

"Och, the woman was a fool. I told her that her husband murdered Katy, and she believed me." He squinted at his inquisitor through his myopic eyes. "It was necessary. The villagers were not convinced of the evil, but I knew, and I could not abandon them to suffering and eternal torment. They are like children, they must be led."

"You led them to corruption and depravity," Lady Viccars retorted. "You performed hideous acts in the name of God. You do not serve righteousness, you serve wickedness and perversion! You are a malignancy that must be destroyed."

Lady Philippa turned her face away, shocked. This was an aspect of Amanda that she had never before seen, and in it the Duke's daughter was herself dangerous. Pippin leaned weakly against the Earl, and his hands gripped her even more firmly, yet with a curious gentleness.

"I deny it!" the old man screamed. "I deny your foul accusations! I have spent my life following the paths of righteousness. I have obeyed the dictates of God!"

"Oh?" inquired Lady Viccars. "Can you deny that you have sinned?"

"I do deny it!" Andrew screamed. Udolpho, bored, sat back on his haunches and yawned.

"And I say you lie! You haven't tried to serve your God, you've tried to surpass your ancestor William, and everything you've done has been toward that end. You had no thought to save your people from evil: you knew no evil existed."

Outside, in the warm sunlight, Nabby glanced at her rescuer's stern visage and burst into tears. She was afraid. Barnabas moved from the Viscount's side to impatiently chafe her arms, where the tight ropes had cut mercilessly into her flesh.

Lady Viccars seemed unaware of danger, even as Andrew Macgregor's hand moved behind him to clutch a branding iron. Pippin cried out. "No," Amanda continued, "it was their adoration you wanted, their worship. You wanted them to revere you as they did William, you wanted to set yourself up as a little god!"

With an inhuman snarl, Andrew Macgregor lunged, the iron raised to strike. Archimedes forestalled him, heavy wings beating in the old man's face, talons poised to slash. Udolpho leaped straight up into the air, yowling, but the minister was aware of neither of them. He stared at the doorway, frozen with shock.

"And Katy?" Amanda said softly. She didn't stare, as did the others, at the fearful specter behind her, but at Andrew Macgregor. "Was it you that murdered Katy?"

" 'Twas not murder!" Andrew cried, staring at the hideous, contorted features of his revered ancestor. "She sinned! She was led astray by foolish promises!"

Was the Hanging Man truly a ghost, then? Severin held Pippin so tightly to him that her bones threatened to crumble, and she was grateful for the pain, else she might have thought herself caught fast in a nightmare. The ghost, if such he was, stepped forward; and Andrew Macgregor crumpled to the ground.

Thirty

Lady Viccars, clad in a most impractical but exquisitely becoming gown of Chinese silk, thrust her head through the carriage window to regard her friend. She frowned. "I wish you would accompany me, but you must know what is best. You will be deathly bored in Bath, my pet."

"That's as may be," Pippin replied. Recent events had taken their toll of her spirits, and the thought of dull idleness held no small allure. "We shall do well enough." In truth, time was unlikely to hang heavy on her hands. Nabby and Barnabas had temporarily patched up their differences, but Lady Philippa had no great hope that this blissful state would last. With an eye toward her own future comfort, she determined to see the troublesome pair safely and quickly wed before hostilities broke out anew.

"Well, I've done the best I can!" Lady Viccars' horses stirred restlessly.

"Wait!" Pippin swallowed her pride. "What did you mean when you told me to forget the Earl? And why the *devil* did you send me here in the first place?"

Lady Viccars gave voice to her husky laughter. "I had an excellent plan, or so I thought, but you very neatly tossed a spanner in the works! Ah well, it is for the best, I daresay." The elegant carriage lurched forward, and Amanda's fashionable bonnet was knocked askew. "But if you take my advice, which I don't for an instant think you will, you'll have the Viscount!"

Perplexed, Lady Philippa watched the carriage move into the distance, then turned and walked slowly into the inn.

Strachan's most illustrious inhabitants waited to make their farewells.

"Is it true," Lady Cassandra inquired, "what Avery tells us? Valentine actually believed Neville to be the father of Katy's child?"

"Apparently so," Pippin replied.

"But how absurd!" The older woman's indignation seemed sincere. "We all knew that Bevis was to blame. He's always suffered this unfortunate attraction for females of the lower classes. Can you imagine, he actually wanted to *marry* the girl!"

"Perhaps it's as well that he didn't have the chance!" the laird commented. "It's bad enough he must become an actor without adding any more scandal to your name."

"Nonsense!" said Lady Cassandra, with unusual firmness. "If not for Bevis pretending to be William Macgregor, there's no telling what that mad old man might have done!" She glanced at Pippin. "Wasn't he *convincing*, my dear? I almost believed him a ghost myself! And he did such an exquisite job on Lady Viccars with theatrical makeup and one of my wigs!"

"And the patchouli?" asked Lady Philippa, still thunderstruck to learn that Bevis's particular mania was only for the stage. "How did you explain that?"

"A clever stroke, was it not?" Lady Cassandra preened. "It was my small contribution to the farce. And of course it was Bevis who played the harp."

"Very convincing," agreed Pippin. "You knew your brother was the inn's ghost, then, all along?"

"Of course!" Lady Cassandra's faded eyes were opened wide. "But one doesn't discuss such things, you know." She winked. "Now we shall go to London, where we shall witness Bevis's theatrical debut. Dear boy, he's earned his right to tread the boards."

"Under," said the laird sourly, "an assumed name."

Lady Philippa murmured politely and followed her visitors outside. She applauded the prudence that prompted them to allow the villagers time to recover from the recent events. Soon all the detested Sassenachs would be gone, for Lord Afton had decided to turn the inn over to his agent, who would dispose advantageously of the property. The Earl remained in Strachan only long enough to relinquish the keys. Pippin sighed; if only her own situation could be so easily resolved.

She cast a reproachful glance at the Viscount, whose sardonic expression might have done justice to Lord Afton himself, and who was so little inclined to conversation that he appeared taciturn. She knew Avery waited for a private word with her, but callously abandoned him in favor of a last walk down Strachan's rustic streets. Udolpho followed at her heels. There was no danger, now, in such a pursuit. Should Avery grow tired of waiting for her, he could pass the time in conversation with Lord Afton, engaged in a last-minute inspection of the inn. Nabby and Barnabas were also within those walls, completing preparations for their imminent journey, but Pippin doubted if even the sociable Viscount would enjoy their company, for the love-stricken pair displayed a rather tiresome tendency to bill and coo.

Pippin kicked an inoffensive pebble. Amanda had gone, to continue the misadventures that so thrilled and titillated high society; Gilly and Lucius had departed for Edinburgh, leaving Moira Graham, whose illness had been discovered to stem from nothing more alarming than a desire to keep her daughter safely at home, comfortably installed with an obliging relative. What of herself, wondered Lady Philippa? She'd doubtless resume her position in the marriage mart until her advanced years made even her considerable fortune unpalatable to those who sought her hand.

Strachan's natives were safely within their homes; even Aggy, who'd declared that these mad goings-on entitled her to at least a week's idleness. The old woman could be idle the rest of her life, unlikely as that was, thought Lady Philippa with a smile. Lord Afton had awarded his housekeeper a handsome pension indeed. Glancing about her, Pippin saw an occasional curtain move, but no one accosted her. The villagers waited patiently for the incomers to depart.

Strachan could no longer escape change. With the departure of the Earl, the Viscount, and herself, the last of those involved in their debacle, the villagers would be able to sigh with relief, but never could they return to their old ways. Already the new minister had arrived, bringing with him the winds of change.

Pippin made her way to the churchyard and paused by the fresh grave. She was saddened by the senseless tragedy of the old man who had taken the exorcism of evil into his own hands, and who had in the end been stricken dead by fear. Udolpho perched on the tombstone and began to wash himself.

But there was one resident of the village who could not let

215

the Sassenachs depart without bidding them farewell. Small Sandy Maclean once again escaped Janet Kirk's watchful eye.

He found them in the cemetery, the fiery-haired lady and her mottled cat. He honored Lady Philippa with an enchanting grin, yanked Udolpho's tail, and then scampered away. Finding no more excuses to delay the inevitable confrontations, Lady Philippa turned back to the inn.

The Viscount was in the taproom, looking remarkably at home among the claymores, the Highland swords, and the Lochaber axes that adorned the walls. "My darling," he inquired, "have you been avoiding me? I had not thought you a coward! Do you mean to shatter my hopes, to tell me you'll have none of me?" He smiled ruefully.

Lady Philippa sighed as she absently twisted an errant curl and recalled Amanda's cryptic advice. "I have hesitated in forming my decision, Avery, for I like you very well, and I thought that we might suit."

"And you thought also that I was more than I should have been to young Katy." The Viscount's tone was wry. "No, don't protest! Let us talk without roundaboutation, pray. I trust I have been absolved of guilt, on that score at least. It is my open countenance, I fear; the girl took to confiding in me."

"I did not seriously doubt you," Pippin replied. Avery's peccadillos were not hers to judge. "Can you forgive me?"

"You need not ask." The Viscount had suffered no irreparable damage during his sojourn in Andrew Macgregor's torture chamber, due entirely to a magnificent constitution, but he now suspected that Lady Philippa meant to deal him a more severe blow. "I must have an answer, Pippin; tell me yes or no."

"It must be no, Avery." Lady Philippa's voice was low. "I do not love you well enough to become your wife, but you shall always be the dearest of my friends."

"I must count myself honored," the Viscount replied with great sincerity. Then he grinned. "The truth be known, my darling, I had begun to wonder if I possess the strength and stamina necessary for a longer and more intimate relationship with you!"

"Wretch!" retorted Pippin, greatly cheered. "It is not gentlemanly to admit to such vast relief."

"You will wish to make your good-byes to Severin," the Viscount remarked. "He is in the garden."

"I do, indeed." There was a sparkle in Lady Philippa's eye that suggested the interview would not be a peaceful one. The

216

Viscount toasted her retreating figure with a glass of the Earl's excellent brandy, then removed himself discreetly from hearing range.

The fifth Earl of Afton surveyed his surroundings with a benign air, as if no unfortunate mishaps had ever occurred to disturb his impassivity. "And now," Pippin said, placing herself firmly in his line of vision and glowering at his serene countenance, "you may explain!"

The Earl glanced down at her. "Why so indignant, infant? Surely you cannot be desolated to leave Strachan behind?"

"Faith no!" her ladyship replied, so startled she forgot her rage.

"Your sojourn here cannot be considered a success," Severin murmured, amused. "Ghosts, hauntings, murder, suicide, and a mangled thumb. I should have demanded that you leave."

Pippin surveyed the bandaged appendage ruefully. "It could have been much worse," she replied. "Thank God you intervened when you did. Which reminds me, how *did* you get out of the castle? Lady Cassandra said it was surrounded by villagers."

"The secret passageways, of course; many of them are still usable. Bevis utilized them to good effect when impersonating our William." He paused. "We actually arrived earlier, but Amanda was waiting to make a dramatic entrance."

Lady Philippa snorted. "She would."

"I confess I found the suspense almost unbearable," Lord Afton added. "I wanted to rush indignantly in when the old man, uh, divested you of your clothing, but Amanda insisted we await a better cue."

"I daresay I have learned a lesson," Pippin sighed. "No more interference in things that don't concern me."

"I find that difficult to believe. You'll be in trouble again before the month is out."

Lady Philippa sought to restrain her increasing wrath, lest Lord Afton become involved in yet another murder—this time his own. "You knew all the time, didn't you?" she demanded. "That the old man was behind it all? Why didn't you tell me?"

"I had no proof," the Earl protested. "The authorities would have been useless and probably inclined to disbelief. You must admit it made a rather farfetched tale, although I did know the old man had seen Valentine the night she died." He raised an eyebrow at Pippin's startled face. "Ah, I see

217

you've underestimated me once again. Macgregor also slit the sheep's throat, and threw that rock at you."

"But why didn't you stop the picnic, then? Surely you realized there'd be trouble."

"Naturally," Lord Afton retorted scathingly. "*I* am not addlepated. I hoped that we might persuade the ambitious minister to incriminate himself. As is obvious, we succeeded."

"My Lord!" Lady Philippa whispered. "Do you mean you *knew* what was going to happen? That you *let* that man drag me off?"

Severin winced. "Would you prefer that a demented murderer be let go free?" He frowned at her white face. "My dear child, surely you don't think that either Amanda or I ever intended you to be harmed! If so, disabuse yourself of the notion immediately, for it's thoroughly absurd. We didn't tell you of our plans simply because you're so odiously transparent. Macgregor would have known instantly if your terror was merely assumed."

"Only a pawn," Pippin murmured. The Earl smiled.

"Consider my own discomfort, skulking about at night like a lowly burglar. I would have much rather been in your place."

"Yes," said Lady Philippa, "I imagine so." She cast him a discerning look. "It was because of Valentine, wasn't it? Sometimes you frighten me."

"Ah, Valentine," murmured Lord Afton. "Amanda enlightened you, I presume? I suspect your notions of my association with Valentine were both disillusioning and depraved."

"Oh?" inquired Lady Philippa frigidly.

"Avery is your culprit there," said the Earl gently, "if culprit there was. As to the other, there we are even, for at times you have also roused a horrified emotion in me."

"I?" Pippin was astounded. "You jest!"

"Not at all," the Earl replied. "Granted, I once thought you totally unsuited to Avery, and sought to interfere before the two of you condemned yourselves to a lifetime of marital misery, but believe me, Pippin, I was well paid for my interference! My good girl, I cannot blame you in the least for hating me. I bungled the thing from first to last."

"Oh," said Lady Philippa weakly, her emotions turning dizzying somersaults.

"Yes," agreed the Earl. "Having saved you from Avery's sort of life, I could hardly have invited you to share mine."

218

"But I thought you disliked me!" Pippin cried. "You made it obvious."

"I know what you thought, and it was what I intended." Almost absently, he tucked back an escaping curl. "There is very little that I do not know about you, Mrs. Watson-Wentworth!" Lady Philippa gasped. "You have a very pretty knack for biting parody. I confess I am always apprehensive lest I find myself skillfully dissected in one of your volumes."

"That pleasure," snapped Lady Philippa, "is one that I reserve." Curse the man, did he mean to amuse himself at her expense once again?

"Never fear: your secret is safe with me." Lord Afton was remote. "But we digress. Having quite skillfully turned you against me, I successfully avoided you for years, and might have continued to do so had not Amanda taken a hand. The results were, I fear, not precisely what she anticipated."

"Dear, dear Amanda," said her ladyship. "Do you mind telling me to what end she directed me here? And before you refuse, I might add that it is the price you must pay for allowing me to be so abused!"

Lord Afton looked extremely uncomfortable. "I believe," he murmured, "that she wished to see you happily settled in matrimony, and thought it an admirable opportunity for your reunion with Avery, whom she knew to be visiting me."

"Odd," mused Lady Philippa. "It is unlike Amanda to so exert herself." She eyed the Earl narrowly. "At least on anyone's behalf but her own. Which brings me to another question, Severin. Just what is Amanda to you?"

He might have scathingly rebuked her for impertinence, but instead he fixed his blue-eyed gaze on a distant tree. "What a shocking mind you have, Lady Philippa! Have you always held so reprehensible an opinion of me?" She said nothing. "Very well, if you must know! Amanda and I have been friends for a very long time, but as I have at various times informed her, I cherish no desire to become a part of her tame menagerie. She refuses to be convinced, however. This is not the first time I have had to send her away."

"You sent her away." It was Lady Philippa's turn to regard the distant treetops. "Has it occurred to you, Severin, that your scruples need no longer apply? I am no longer a green girl to be saved at any price from temptation. My reputation, as you yourself pointed out, is almost as reprehensible as your own."

"There is that, of course." The Earl wore an arrested expression. "Pippin, have you played fast-and-loose with poor Avery *again?*"

"Shocking, is it not?" murmured Lady Philippa demurely. "I fear I am positively steeped in vice. It will take a strong man indeed to induce me to reform my way of life."

"A strong man?" mused the Earl, his blue eyes alight as he cupped her face in his hands. "Such as myself, perhaps?" He bent his dark head. "Are you trying to tell me, in your own incomparable way, that you would like to marry me?"

Lady Philippa gazed up at his lean and swarthy face with those high cheekbones and that sensuous mouth, those discerning eyes that surveyed her with such intensity, and found herself speechless. "If so, my dear torment," Lord Afton added, "we find ourselves for once in perfect accord." He drew her into his arms, thus demonstrating both a remarkable aptitude and unmistakable enthusiasm; then, with a small frown, set her away from him. "You have not answered me, Pippin! Do you not mean to become my wife?"

Lady Philippa raised her fingers to his lips and blinked at him mistily. "Well, yes, I rather think I would," she whispered breathlessly. "But you have not said you love me, Severin!"

"Baggage!" said the Earl and enfolded her once more in his strong embrace, there to repair the omission speedily. A most satisfactory conclusion, mused Lady Philippa muzzily, and then Lord Afton's intoxicating ardor sent the last of such logical reflections flying over the hilltops and away.

Romantic Fiction

If you like novels of passion and daring adventure that take you to the very heart of human drama, these are the books for you.

☐ AFTER—Anderson	Q2279	1.50
☐ THE DANCE OF LOVE—Dodson	23110-0	1.75
☐ A GIFT OF ONYX—Kettle	23206-9	1.50
☐ TARA'S HEALING—Giles	23012-0	1.50
☐ THE TROIKA BELLE—Morris	23013-9	1.75
☐ THE DEFIANT DESIRE—Klem	13741-4	1.75
☐ LOVE'S TRIUMPHANT HEART—Ashton	13771-6	1.75
☐ MAJORCA—Dodson	13740-6	1.75

Buy them at your local bookstores or use this handy coupon for ordering:

FAWCETT PUBLICATIONS, P.O. Box 1014, Greenwich Conn. 06830

Please send me the books I have checked above. Orders for less than 5 books must include 60c for the first book and 25c for each additional book to cover mailing and handling. Orders of 5 or more books postage is Free. I enclose $_____in check or money order.

Name_____

Address_____

City_____ State/Zip_____

Please allow 4 to 5 weeks for delivery. This offer expires 6/78.

A-20

Historical Romance

☐ THE ADMIRAL'S LADY—Gibbs	P2658	1.25
☐ AFTER THE STORM—Williams	23081-3	1.50
☐ AN AFFAIR OF THE HEART—Smith	23092-9	1.50
☐ AS THE SPARKS FLY—Eastvale	P2569	1.25
☐ A BANBURY TALE—MacKeever	23174-7	1.50
☐ CLARISSA—Arnett	22893-2	1.50
☐ DEVIL'S BRIDE—Edwards	23176-3	1.50
☐ A FAMILY AFFAIR—Mellows	22967-X	1.50
☐ FIRE OPALS—Danton	23112-7	1.50
☐ THE FORTUNATE MARRIAGE—Trevor	23137-2	1.50
☐ FRIENDS AT KNOLL HOUSE—Mellows	P2530	1.25
☐ THE GLASS PALACE—Gibbs	23063-5	1.50
☐ GRANBOROUGH'S FILLY—Blanshard	23210-7	1.50
☐ HARRIET—Mellows	23209-3	1.50
☐ HORATIA—Gibbs	23175-5	1.50
☐ LEONORA—Fellows	22897-5	1.50
☐ LORD FAIRCHILD'S DAUGHTER— MacKeever	P2695	1.25
☐ MARRIAGE ALLIANCE—Stables	23142-9	1.50
☐ MELINDA—Arnett	P2547	1.25
☐ THE PHANTOM GARDEN—Bishop	23113-5	1.50
☐ THE PRICE OF VENGEANCE— Michel	23211-5	1.50
☐ THE RADIANT DOVE—Jones	P2753	1.25
☐ THE ROMANTIC FRENCHMAN—Gibbs	P2869	1.25
☐ SPRING GAMBIT—Williams	23025-2	1.50

Buy them at your local bookstores or use this handy coupon for ordering:

Jean Plaidy

"Miss Plaidy is also, of course, Victoria Holt." —PUBLISHERS WEEKLY

☐ BEYOND THE BLUE MOUNTAINS	22773-1	1.95
☐ CAPTIVE QUEEN OF SCOTS	23287-5	1.75
☐ THE CAPTIVE OF KENSINGTON PALACE	23413-4	1.75
☐ THE GOLDSMITH'S WIFE	22891-6	1.75
☐ HERE LIES OUR SOVEREIGN LORD	23256-5	1.75
☐ LIGHT ON LUCREZIA	23108-9	1.75
☐ MADONNA OF THE SEVEN HILLS	23026-0	1.75

Phyllis A. Whitney

Ms. Whitney's novels constantly appear on all the bestseller lists throughout the country and have won many awards including the coveted "Edgar". Here are some of her finest romantic novels of suspense that you may order by mail.